Something kicked over in Lyman's heart.

It might have been his own adrenaline or how vulnerable she looked, the disheveled bride who was clearly not having a dream wedding.

While he struggled for words, she peeled off her gloves and shoved them into a pocket of her gown. Wedding gowns had pockets? Lyman's brain searched for anything logical to say as he watched his high school sweetheart tug off her veil and shake out her long blond hair.

After years in the Coast Guard, he reverted to his rescuer training. "Are you all right?" he asked.

Abigail let her arms fall to her sides, and the veil dragged on the ground. "Do I look all right?"

"You look—"

She held up a hand. "You don't need to answer that."

With relief, Lyman watched her turn and walk into the arms of several women who were running toward her, sparing him from telling her she looked like a beautiful but disappointed bride.

Dear Reader,

When I was growing up, my parents took me and my three sisters on lots of trips within driving distance of our Ohio home. With four kids, it was economical to stay in campgrounds, and we never complained about campfires, fresh air and the freedom of riding our bikes. One such campground was near Niagara Falls, New York, and we went back year after year. I've always loved Niagara Falls, and I still go back every summer—although I stay in the beautiful hotels now.

Have you ever stood next to Niagara Falls on either the American or Canadian side? If you have, you've experienced the misty air, the rush of falling water and the rainbows. That exhilarating feeling—and the fact that it's the honeymoon capital of the world—inspired me to write a series of romances featuring weddings at Niagara Falls. I hope you love *Falling for Her Fake Fiancé* and you'll come back for the rest of the series.

Happy travels,

Amie

FALLING FOR HER FAKE FIANCÉ

AMIE DENMAN

Harlequin

HEARTWARMING

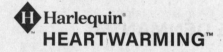

H Harlequin®
HEARTWARMING™

ISBN-13: 978-1-335-05120-2

Falling for Her Fake Fiancé

Harlequin Enterprises ULC
22 Adelaide St. West, 41st Floor
Toronto, Ontario M5H 4E3, Canada
www.Harlequin.com

Printed in Lithuania

Recycling programs for this product may not exist in your area.

MIX
Paper | Supporting responsible forestry
FSC® C021394

Amie Denman is the author of over fifty contemporary romances full of humor and heart. A devoted traveler whose parents always kept a suitcase packed, she loves reading and writing books you could take on vacation. Amie believes everything is fun, especially wedding cake, roller coasters and falling in love.

Books by Amie Denman

Harlequin Heartwarming

Return to Christmas Island

I'll Be Home for Christmas
Home for the Holidays
A Merry Little Christmas
Last Summer on Christmas Island
Under the Mistletoe

Cape Pursuit Firefighters

In Love with the Firefighter
The Firefighter's Vow
A Home for the Firefighter

Starlight Point Stories

Under the Boardwalk
Carousel Nights
Meet Me on the Midway
Until the Ride Stops
Back to the Lake Breeze Hotel

Visit the Author Profile page at Harlequin.com for more titles.

To my parents, who took me to Niagara Falls for the first time and gave me a love of going places.

CHAPTER ONE

#RainbowsAndHoneymoons

THE WEDDING OFFICIANT walked a few steps away and sat on a park bench, and the photographer put down his camera and unwrapped a chocolate bar. Abigail Warren considered asking for half of it, dangerous though it was eating chocolate on a summer day in a white gown. She glanced down at her wedding dress, hemmed to stop just above her shoes, three-inch heels with an ankle strap, white satin to match her gown.

Her veil caught the breeze coming off the nearby waterfalls and brushed across her face. It picked up a hint of red lipstick, and Abigail brushed the veil back so she could watch the steps coming down to the platform at the top of the Bridal Veil Falls—the most appropriate location imaginable for her wedding. Her best friend, Minerva, Minnie for short, produced a tissue and blotted the red lipstick from the veil. Minnie was a wedding planner and also her maid of honor.

"A picture-perfect Niagara Falls wedding, the best one I've arranged," Abigail's mother, Ginny, said. And that was saying something. Ginny and Minnie owned Falling for You, a custom wedding business.

The wedding photographer angled in for shots of Abigail with the falls in the background. Abigail heard the thunder of the cascading water and smelled the clean, moist air.

"Any word from Josh?" she asked her mother between shots. She glanced over to the large group of her own friends and family watching the shoot and taking in the scenery. None of Josh's guests were here yet.

"I bet they got one of those party buses and they're going to roll up any minute," Ginny said. "That must be why none of Josh's friends are here. They're all coming with him in the bus."

"Do you think he couldn't find a parking spot?" Abigail asked Minerva. "Or they're lost?"

Minerva motioned the wedding photographer away. "Don't worry, it's only ten after one. And it's tourist season. I'm sure that's what's causing the delay. Josh selected this location himself, didn't he?"

Abigail nodded. She'd driven all around the American side of the falls with Josh and given him the options for ceremony locations. After helping her mom and Minerva set up countless outdoor weddings, Abigail had been ready with a list of pros and cons. Josh had chosen Bridal Veil Falls. He'd even made a little joke about the name suiting the affair.

Maybe he hadn't said *affair*. Occasion? Blessed event? Happiest day of his life?

No, Abigail thought, head cocked to the side. He'd said *affair*.

But he had chosen the location for their wedding. Her big day, the one she'd dreamed of all her life as she'd helped her mother and then her best friend pull off wedding after wedding. Some weddings were creative, some intimate and sweet, some loud and joyful, but the hope embodied by choosing another person for life always made Abigail feel a bit teary-eyed, even if she never let anyone see her discreetly dab at her eyes. She hadn't chosen to join Ginny and Minerva in their business, opting instead for tours and history, but she'd been conscripted into being a witness, DJ and even cake cutter in a pinch.

In fact, she'd met Josh at a wedding three months ago, and it had been so romantic. She'd been slicing and serving cake, and he'd asked her to take off her apron and dance. And from there, they'd seen each other almost every day. There was clearly some magic in the way their hands touched and how he held doors and pulled out chairs for her. He was the one. Was it any wonder that she'd asked him three weeks ago to marry her? She couldn't take a chance on letting *the one* get away, not when he'd swept into her life and swept her off her feet.

He'd been surprised, of course, but sometimes love came over a person like that. And he'd said yes after only the tiniest hesitation. Finally, she would get her own happy ending instead of smiling from the sidelines for other brides.

Abigail glanced at her wrist, where she usually wore a smartwatch, but only the lace edge of her gloves greeted her. "One fifteen," Minerva said, reading her mind. "I'll call the best man to check in. There's always an explanation."

"I'll run up to the parking lot and check," Abigail's dad, Blake, said. "I'll text any updates." He gave Abigail's hand a quick squeeze and dashed off.

Abigail gave up watching for Josh and shifted her glance to the railing right over Bridal Veil Falls. Tourists usually lined that railing all summer long to enjoy the rush of standing on the precipice, where it seemed as if the world fell away under their feet. A group of men and women wearing uniforms, the dark navy blue crisp against their white shirts, stood posing for a photographer. Were they military? Police? There was something familiar about those uniforms. Abigail watched them as the group dissolved and, one by one, the uniformed people got their pictures taken alone with the falls right below them.

She heard a man clear his throat behind her and turned to find Garrett, Josh's best friend. Finally!

"Uh, Abigail," Garrett said. He pulled at the collar of his T-shirt. He was wearing a T-shirt and shorts for his best friend's wedding? Something wasn't right. "Abigail, I'm supposed to tell you…" His words trailed off, and Abigail felt her mother on one side and Minerva on her other side, as if they were offering support for whatever the groom's casually dressed friend was about to say.

"Josh isn't coming," Garrett blurted out.

"What?" Abigail asked. "Is he sick?"

"Stuck in traffic?" Minerva asked.

"Dead?" her mother inquired in a hushed whisper.

Abigail clutched her bouquet as if it were a lifeline for a drowning swimmer. She noticed the photographer holding up his camera, as if he wanted to document this unexpected wedding moment just as he might capture cutting the cake or a first kiss as man and wife.

"He's not dead," Garrett said. "He's gone. He left this morning for Denver. He's got a buddy with a place in the mountains where he can clear his head and—"

"Denver?" Abigail said, interrupting Garrett's story of her groom's preferred destination. "Why on earth did he… Oh."

She tried sucking in a breath and couldn't.

"He asked me to tell you he was sorry. Everything moved so fast and he just… Well, he thought he was ready, but…"

"He said he was ready," Abigail whispered. "He said yes." She swallowed despite the heavy lump in her throat. The lovely pearls at her neck felt as if they were choking her, and every click of the photographer's camera felt like a slap.

"Jilted," her mother whispered in much the same tone she'd used to inquire if the groom had met his demise.

"Oh, goodness," Minerva said, putting an arm around her shoulders. "Oh, Abigail. I did not see this coming. He loves you. I see it when he looks at you."

Abigail released a long, slow breath and stared hard at her summer bouquet of roses and daisies. The rush of water over the falls drummed in her ears along with her own heartbeat. Josh hadn't shown up to their wedding. He didn't want to marry her after all. And he was going somewhere far away, where he could clear his head.

She couldn't look at her mother and her best friend. Their sympathy and kindness would make her cry, and she didn't want to cry. Not right here where dozens of tourists were looking on curiously. She'd been attracting their attention all afternoon. Some stranger had even snapped a picture of her earlier. *Niagara Falls, land of honeymoons and rainbows.* It would be a nice addition to their vacation photos.

It would be an even better snapshot if the groom had shown up.

How could he do this to her? He'd said yes, and they'd bought rings—albeit very simple gold ones at a local souvenir shop—and booked one of the nice hotels on the Canadian side overlooking the falls for their honeymoon. And then he'd sent his friend to tell her he was backing out? He hadn't even told her in person after all she'd shared with him. All the hope that he was the one and she'd finally be the bride after watching countless weddings—that hope rushed out of her.

Today wasn't the day for her happy ending.

Anger replaced the hope with a cold rush of reality. Adrenaline coursed through her veins, giving her a fight-or-flight response that had her trembling. She wouldn't be tossing that beautiful bouquet of roses and daisies in the Falls Inn conference room later as the sound system blasted out the playlist she and Minerva had made. No one would line up to catch the bouquet and linger at the cake table hoping for a corner piece with lots of icing. She wouldn't be dancing a father-daughter dance.

The flowers shook in her hands as her family and friends stood by silently, shocked and waiting for her reaction. Abigail turned and faced the falls, where majestic whirls of mist rose into the blue sky. That natural wonder had seen plenty of triumphs and heartbreaks. It had stood the test of time—unlike her relationship. The falls gave her solace and hope and peace.

She started walking, bouquet clutched in one hand and a fold of her skirt in the other. No one would catch that bouquet at the reception, but she could give it one big final fling anyway. Her steps became rapid despite her gown and high heels. She felt her veil tug on the back of her hair as the wind off the falls caught it, making it billow out behind her.

Abigail began running, racing toward the brink. No one could stop her from tossing the bouquet, even a groom who'd left her standing there like a fool. She ran faster and faster until she was almost at the railing. She raised the bouquet over her head, prepared to send it sailing out over the falls.

And then the hem of her gown caught her shoe and she was flying, flailing, soaring through the air. Her leg bumped the top of the railing and she let go of the flowers at the moment she knew it was too late to stop the forward momentum sending her over the precipice.

LYMAN ROBERTS LOVED the water. Rivers, lakes, ponds, oceans. All of them. But did he love being home in Niagara Falls? After six years of serving in the United States Coast Guard, he was back where he'd started, wearing a boat captain's uniform. Not a service vessel, not a rescue ship or an ice cutter. Nope. He wore the colors of the Maid of the Mist, a tourist boat giving visitors a thrilling up-close view of the magnificent Niagara Falls from below, every half hour on the hour, weather permitting.

This was his life—at least for now. He tried to smile for the pictures with the other boat captains. They were all reliable, experienced, sincere captains who knew the waters below the falls and kept thousands of people safe and happy all season long. He liked and respected them, but he'd never thought he'd be one of them, even temporarily. The group photo with three other men and two women went fine. Being the tallest, he was happy with his position in the back of the picture, which would be used on the website and brochures.

But he'd rather be out in a storm at sea than posing for the individual shot the company required. Still, he'd checked his collar, made certain his buttons lined up and brushed dust off his shoes. And then he'd stood near the railing and waited for the photographer to adjust her camera and take a phone call. His boss, Tom, had high expectations for these publicity pictures, and Lyman was in no position to be a curmudgeon about it. Whether people in his hometown believed it or not, he wasn't the same restless kid who'd left town at eighteen.

He was now a twenty-four-year-old who needed to figure out his future.

He resisted fidgeting but wondered how long the

photographer was going to take. Tourists paused and snapped pictures of him. The massive waterfall behind him thundered away as always, the same sound and smell he'd grown up with as the background of his life. Nothing changed around Niagara Falls. The view was the same. The tourists came in a never-ending stream. And, always, there were honeymoons and rainbows, just as the billboards promised.

"Ready?" the photographer asked. She put away her phone and raised her camera.

Finally. He would cooperate and smile, place a hand just as directed on the railing, and then he could slip out of public view. Lyman composed an appropriately cheerful expression, squared his shoulders to invoke confidence and counted to ten in his head in the hope it would all be over soon.

A blur of something white caught his peripheral vision. The white blur grew closer and seemed to be moving faster. Lyman had excellent vision and quick reactions, skills he'd honed in the military. It took all his effort to stay posed for the photo and not turn toward the white object moving at an alarming speed.

"Perfect," the photographer said. She continued to hold her camera in front of her and appeared to be on the verge of suggesting something, perhaps another pose. But Lyman's resolve finally broke. He turned to go just in time to watch the white streak resolve into a bride, who raised a bouquet over her head and then tripped over the hem of her long white dress.

Without a second's hesitation, Lyman half ran, half dived toward her and caught her just as she went airborne and nearly cleared the railing. His arms were full of slippery white fabric and a warm, thrashing woman, and he watched her bunch of red and white flowers fly over the falls, a ribbon following them like the tail of a kite.

Stunned, he gazed down at the blonde in his arms. Their eyes met, and they both breathed heavily. Her cheeks were pink, and he felt the heat in his own face, too. Lyman held Abigail Warren in his arms.

He stared into her blue eyes as her veil flew out on the breeze, and he felt the wild sense of disbelief he saw reflected in her expression.

"This is amazing," he heard someone say. He heard a camera clicking and glanced up to see a crowd of tourists, phones aimed right at him and the bride in his arms.

"You," Abigail said. "Of all the rotten days for me to run into you after all these years." She pushed at his chest and fought to get down. Still shocked by the events of the last thirty-five seconds, Lyman lowered the bride to her feet but kept his hands on her shoulders, steadying her. She'd lost a shoe in her near flight over the railing and stood lopsided. Something kicked over in Lyman's heart. It might have been his own adrenaline or how vulnerable she looked, the disheveled bride who was clearly not having a dream wedding.

While he struggled for words, she peeled off her gloves and shoved them in a pocket of her gown. Wedding gowns had pockets? Lyman's brain searched for anything logical to say as he watched his high school sweetheart tug off her veil and shake out her long blond hair.

After years in the Coast Guard, he reverted to his rescuer training. "Are you all right?" he asked.

Abigail let her arms fall to her sides, and the veil dragged on the ground. "Do I look all right?"

"You look—"

She held up a hand. "You don't need to answer that."

With relief, Lyman watched her turn and walk into the arms of several women who were running toward her, sparing him from telling her she looked like a beautiful but disappointed bride.

CHAPTER TWO

#CatchTheBride

"SPECTACULAR," KIRSTEN SAID. "Never seen anything quite like it, and I've been a captain on the Maid for ten years." She hurried to keep up beside him. The other Maid of the Mist captains were fifteen paces behind as Lyman stalked toward the van being used to chauffeur the captains around for their publicity shots.

"I've seen weddings and marriage proposals and one time a woman went into labor on the boat, but this takes the cake. You caught the bride instead of the bouquet," Kirsten finished, laughing.

Lyman heaved a sigh and held open the van door for his colleague. "I'm sure it will be a blip on the tourist radar. Not nearly as exciting as a double rainbow over Horseshoe Falls."

Jackson and Jasper, twin brothers with deep wrinkles and gray temples, exchanged a look as the rest of the captains caught up.

"Kirsten is right. That was something we've

never seen, and we've been working here since before you were born," Jackson said. "I can't wait to show my wife the picture I took." He took a bench seat and held up his phone. "Do you want to see it?"

Lyman got in the van and slid the door shut. He took the seat in front of the twin captains, but he swiveled around to take a polite look at the offered phone. The picture was blurry and too far away. *Thank goodness.*

"That's no good," Murphy said. He was the youngest boat captain next to Lyman. "I got a way better one." He tilted his phone toward Lyman and used two fingers to zoom in.

Oh, man. Lyman saw himself on the screen clear as day. He cleared his throat. "Much better. But you should still delete it and…uh…save space on your phone."

Murphy laughed. "I have cloud storage. Even if I'd taken video like other people were, I'd still have room."

Other people. Lyman remembered that wall of tourists with phones held high.

"That poor bride," Kirsten said. "It was pretty obvious her wedding got called off, but she does have a heck of an overhand throw. That bouquet went way out there."

"She played softball in high school," Lyman said without thinking. The van began moving, but all his coworkers swung their attention to him.

"This is too good," Jasper said. "You know her." He slapped his leg.

"I know she's a good runner and pitcher, and I'm guessing she was having a bad day and we should respect her privacy," Lyman said.

Kirsten gave him a raised eyebrow and then scrolled through something on her phone. "There's already a hashtag," she said. She gave Lyman a sheepish look. "Hashtag 'catch the bride.'"

Lyman pinched the bridge of his nose.

"You do look heroic and handsome, and she's beautiful," Kirsten continued. "Look at how her veil floats out on the breeze and your gazes are locked together, her white gown against your dark uniform. You make a pretty picture."

He highly doubted Abigail Warren would view a hashtag and a pretty picture as any consolation for whatever had gone wrong with her special day. Whatever they'd shared that one summer was history, and he hadn't been in touch with her since. Since then, she'd apparently found someone and planned a wedding in the beloved hometown she'd sworn she'd never leave. She'd gotten up that morning expecting to say her vows to someone and had gotten a hashtag instead. Lyman had no doubt a picture with him wasn't the keepsake she'd expected.

The van reached the parking area that overlooked Horseshoe Falls. "One more picture here and we're done," the photographer said as she looked back from the front seat. "Although I doubt these pictures will compare to the other ones."

Lyman heard his fellow captains chuckle as they climbed out of the van. Jackson had told him it had been at least five years since they'd bothered to take a group shot of the captains and do promotional pictures, and Lyman wasn't entirely certain he should be in the team picture, considering that this was a temporary gig for him. He'd be long gone before another five months rolled around. Probably.

After smiling pleasantly for the pictures and willing the photographer to get it over with quickly, Lyman went down to the Maid of the Mist dock below the observation tower and took over from the part-timer captaining the three o'clock boat. Back behind the wheel of a boat, he took a moment to process what had happened. Of course he'd known there was a chance of running into the girl he'd dated the summer before he left for the Coast Guard.

The girl he'd made no promises to and then thoroughly ghosted.

Abigail had always been clear that Niagara Falls was her home forever, and he'd made it clear he wanted more out of life.

There'd been no exchange of pleasantries after he caught her today. Once he'd stood her on her feet, she'd been swept up by her mother—Ginny Warren had hardly aged in six years—and Minnie, who he guessed was still her best friend. Abigail hadn't changed. Her long blond hair still curled and her blue eyes flashed—not with humor or excitement as he'd seen in the past, but with anger. Hurt. Betrayal.

What kind of a man would leave Abigail Warren at the altar?

Lyman passed a hand over his eyes and focused on the swirling water ahead and the rocks to his right. There were 281 people onboard his boat, all wanting a taste of danger under the falls but counting on him to deliver them safely back to the dock with their company-issued blue raincoats intact.

He'd left Abigail. Walked away from her six summers ago even though she'd said she'd wait for him. He'd made her no promises, though. They'd just been kids, not even close to a proposal and a ring. But someone else had gotten there with her. And it wasn't any of his business who the guy was or what had happened. Lyman had prevented Abigail from following her bouquet over the railing, and that was the end of the story.

"YOU WERE THE most beautiful bride I've ever seen," Ginny Warren said as she cut two pieces of toast into triangles, dusted them with cinnamon and set them in front of her daughter.

It was the morning after the wedding flop, and Abigail's eyes were as tender as her feelings. The triangle toast was a childhood treat, usually reserved for sick days home from school.

"What happened was not your fault," her mother added. "Although it could have ended in tragedy, but thank goodness it didn't. I'll always be grateful to Lyman Roberts for catching you. Even though he's a louse, of course."

Abigail loved her mother, but there were times when Ginny's propensity for filling dead air space with conversation wasn't her most endearing habit. Still, Abigail forgave her for mentioning the name *Lyman Roberts* before coffee.

"Lyman hasn't changed much, has he?" her mother continued. She poured coffee into Abigail's favorite vintage Niagara Falls mug, which had a picture of a man going over the falls in a barrel. "And that was a Maid of the Mist uniform he was wearing. It looked like all the boat captains were there for a big picture. Imagine the irony of that."

"I don't think that's irony, Mom."

"Coincidence then? Luck?" Her mother put the sugar bowl in front of Abigail.

Abigail put two spoonfuls in her mug, watched the sugar dissolve and then added a third. Her mother took the sugar bowl and put it on a high shelf.

"I was supposed to be on my honeymoon today," Abigail said. "We were going to do all the fun tourist things on the Canadian side, but Josh is clearing his head in Colorado." She paused and sipped her coffee. "Instead," she added matter-of-factly, as if he'd chosen to wear a blue jacket instead of a black one. Someday, she'd think about what had happened, but first she had to breathe through every minute of a day that was supposed to be her first day as Josh's wife.

Her mother sat across from her and squeezed her hand. "I'm here for you, honey. Your dad's busy getting ready to go back on the road, but I'm free. Tell you what—I could go do those tourist things with you today."

Abigail forced a smile. "You'd hate going up in the falls overlook tower."

Her mother swallowed. "I could close my eyes."

Fresh tears forced their way into Abigail's eyes at that brave offer.

"I think I'll get back to work on my notes for the museum," Abigail said. "I've neglected it a lot in the past three months while I was…" She trailed off, not wanting to remember how she'd thrown herself into her relationship with Josh. Had it been a mistake right from the start? Had she misread the signs so terribly?

"That sounds nice," her mother said.

"I suppose," Abigail said. She sighed. "But it's that wedding project."

"Oh."

In addition to leading two walking tours five days a week, Abigail researched and developed exhibits for the Niagara Falls History Museum. Her current research project was on a mass wedding with fifty couples that took place in 1950. She had identified thirty-seven of the couples and found information about their romances. How they fell in love, where they were from, what happened to them after the wedding. It had taken a lot of digging to track down their happy endings.

She was still investigating the final thirteen couples, a complicated task of following paper trails of birth and death records, land transfers, divorce records. Not all the fifty marriages had ended happily, even though Abigail wanted them to. It would make a much better story when the exhibition opened in the fall.

"I'm sure people will love the exhibit," her mother said. "And you can use the stories when you give your tours. I don't think there's anyone who knows the history of Niagara Falls better than you do."

Abigail appreciated the compliment. Her goal was to make the past come alive through stories and imagination. Her job as a local tour guide specializing in history walks through the town of Niagara Falls and the state park—the oldest one in the United States—overlooking the falls gave her the chance to connect with tourists and history lovers. Her life in her hometown with her family, her friends and her dream job was almost perfect, but it had been missing something. She'd thought Josh filled in that missing part.

Maybe she'd been looking too hard. She'd gotten caught up in wedding fever and allowed Minnie's zest for matchmaking to go to her head. Was that how she'd managed to blunder her way to a wedding that wasn't, fooling herself into thinking that Josh's heart was in it?

Her phone pinged, and she glanced at it. Had it been anyone other than Minerva, she would have ignored the text. Instead, she swiped the screen and read the message.

I'd rather you hear this from me than stumble on it yourself.

What?

The picture. It's...gone viral.

Abigail sank back in her chair. *Viral* could mean a lot of things. Her friend could be exaggerating. Who cared about one silly picture of a bride and a man in uniform?

#CatchTheBride

With trembling hands, Abigail opened a social media app and began typing the hashtag her friend had texted. She gasped. The picture of her in Lyman's arms, her beautiful gown draping elegantly and her veil drifting on the wind, mist from the falls rising behind them into the clear blue sky, was everywhere.

"What's the matter?" her mother asked. "Is it Josh? Does he have the nerve to try to text you after what he did? He should be sorry. He should be begging you—"

"It's not that," Abigail said. She slid her phone into the middle of the kitchen table and showed her mother the picture.

"It looks like a postcard," her mother said. "You look so beautiful."

"Mom," Abigail said, a touch of exasperation in her tone. "That's not the point. This picture is everywhere." She swiped the screen and scrolled past dozens of pictures, most of them almost exactly the same, although a few were from a slightly different angle. "There's even a video," she said. She tapped the play icon on the video and, to her horror, watched herself running toward the falls, tripping and falling headlong toward the railing. At the last moment, a tall, handsome man in a dark uniform raced into the frame and caught her as her bouquet flew over the falls.

"Like a movie," her mother said, her words quiet and almost reverent.

Abigail sighed, shoved her toast plate aside and put her head on the kitchen table.

CHAPTER THREE

#AnythingForNiagaraFalls

It was a perfect June day. Lyman descended to the dock where the Maid of the Mist awaited tourists with a taste for adventure. When he'd started a month earlier, he'd wondered where all those tourists came from. Day after day, by the hundreds, clad in souvenir blue raincoats, people trooped onto one of the two boats owned by the company. Hadn't everyone within a three-state region already taken the daring ride to the base of the falls?

But they hadn't stopped coming. And his conflicted feelings about coming home to help with his father's recovery from heart surgery had begun to dull with each trip he captained. Had his senses dulled, too? The roar of the falls was just as loud, the sun shining through the water droplets just as bright. And the rainbows that appeared without fail all day long were brilliantly colored.

It was nothing like the unpredictable life in the Coast Guard, where they trained for anything and everything and still managed to find themselves facing the unexpected. Every moment of the thirty-minute boat ride he now captained was completely scripted.

Lyman stood by the gangplank as passengers boarded, smiling and nodding at the tourists and exuding warmth and competence—two things his boss considered nonnegotiable. He was happy to comply. Life at sea with the Coast Guard was sometimes lonely and monotonous. He got tired of seeing the same shipmates every day. Working the Maid of the Mist at Niagara Falls was anything but lonely, as he was lost in a sea of new faces every hour.

"Welcome aboard," he said to a family of five with two boys and a girl, each with a hand held firmly by a parent. The kids had knots tied in their plastic raincoats to customize the fit, and they all wore waterproof sandals. They'd clearly heeded online advice about enjoying the ride in comfort. "The first trip of the day is always the best," Lyman said. "I'm glad you're here."

Honestly, every trip was the same, but he'd found that tourists liked being reassured they'd made a good choice. Who didn't? Every morning when he left his parents' brick ranch house outside the city of Niagara Falls, he knew he'd made the only choice he could. His mother needed help, and his father's worsening heart disease meant it was time for Lyman to come home before it was too late. At least for the tourist season. When cold weather rolled around in November, where would he be? He had two years of reserve service left to fulfill, but it would only be one weekend a month. Where would he spend the rest of his time?

A set of grandparents, their silver hair secured under sun visors, towed two kids who were about seven or eight years old. The kids' raincoats dragged on the ground, and they had a hard time keeping up.

"Can I give you some help with those raincoats?" he asked, smiling at the kids.

"Are you the captain?" the little girl asked.

"Yes, I am. And I get to stay nice and dry in the pilothouse while you're out having fun and getting soaked. But I can share the secret sailor knot that will keep you from tripping over your coat."

"Really?" the little boy asked.

Lyman glanced up at the grandparents, and they nodded and smiled. He swiftly tied a knot in the side of the boy's raincoat to take up the girth and length. "There you go."

"I'm next," the girl said. She stood still as a statue while Lyman tied a knot in her plastic raincoat.

"Stay close to your grandparents and have fun," he said.

He straightened and shaded his eyes to see how long the line for boarding stretched back, and to his surprise he saw one of the other boat captains threading his way through the crowd. When he got closer, Lyman could see it was Jackson.

"I'm supposed to relieve you and take this one," Jackson said.

Lyman frowned. "It's the first trip of the day. I don't need relief."

"Boss wants to talk to you."

Lyman felt a chill. He needed this job for the summer. Was the company unhappy with him? He tried to show a good attitude at work, followed all safety protocols and had—he thought—settled in and begun building decent relationships with his coworkers, some of whom had known him when he was a teenager who wanted to be anywhere but Niagara Falls.

Jackson leaned in and whispered. "It's about the bride."

"Abigail?"

"Is that her name?" Jackson asked.

Lyman hadn't told his coworkers how well he knew Abigail. He'd dated her at the end of senior year in high school. Gone to the prom with her. Driven her home after a graduation party. And spent a glorious summer stealing time away from a job as a deckhand on the Maid of the Mist to enjoy takeout food with her by the falls and walks under the stars.

"What about the bride?" Lyman asked, avoiding the question.

"You'll have to ask Tom. But I'll say this—that picture of you two is all over the internet."

"Still? That picture was taken three days ago. You'd think people would have forgotten about it by now."

Lyman swallowed. He'd faced down fear and danger, storms and high seas plenty of times, but he'd been able to see the enemy in those cases. There was nothing he could do about people circulating an intriguing picture of a captain and a bride. Poor Abigail. She couldn't be happy about it, either.

"I guess not," Jackson said. "The boss is waiting for you at the tourist center. He said to use the golf cart, and he's promising coffee."

It took only ten minutes for Lyman to make his way through the grounds of the state park that encompassed the American side of the falls with spectacular views, winding paths, trees and bridges. He followed the aroma of coffee when he arrived at the tourist center located near the entrance of the park. At an outdoor table, he saw his boss, two people he didn't know and Abigail Warren and her friend Minnie.

"Before you ask," Abigail said, no hint of a welcoming smile, "I don't want to be here, either."

Lyman took the only empty chair at the table. "I didn't say I didn't want to be here." He smiled at the two strangers and his boss. "Good morning. I hope this coffee is for me."

Tom pushed a cardboard tray filled with packets of creamer and sugar toward him. "Glad you're here, Roberts," he said.

Lyman had gotten accustomed to being referred to by his last name in the military. Tom had also served, Navy for him, and Lyman respected his boss's discipline, which hadn't faded in the thirty years he'd been a civilian. There was no doubt the brotherhood of the military was the reason Lyman had a job—at least for the summer.

He poured one sugar into his coffee, stirred it and then looked up at Abigail. She wore an ocean-blue shirt that matched her eyes, and her long blond hair was pulled back from her face. She was every bit as pretty as he remembered, but she looked tired. How had a called-off wedding affected her? Was her heart broken? Had she lain awake the last several nights crying for the groom who hadn't shown up? He didn't dare wonder what she thought of him or that summer when they were eighteen—if she thought of him at all. It was a long time ago.

"I'm Macey Daniels," the woman said. Lyman didn't know her, but he guessed she was a few years older than he was. He half rose and reached across the table to shake her hand. "I'm the head of tourism for the city, and this is our freelance photographer Sam." She indicated the man next to her. Sam briefly shook hands with Lyman and then put both hands around his camera as if were his comfort zone.

Lyman sat down and nodded to Minerva Lark. "Nice to see you again, Minnie."

She gave him a measured smile and glanced at Abigail.

"We went to high school together," Lyman explained to the others at the table.

"Interesting," Macey said. "All three of you?"

Lyman's and Abigail's eyes met for a moment. "Yes," he said.

Macey clasped her hands together and leaned forward. "Please tell me there was more."

ABIGAIL HELD HER BREATH. Was Lyman going to reveal that they'd dated? A long pause ensued, and she decided to take control.

"We went on a few dates after graduation," she said. "It was nothing."

"Ha," Macey said. "That's definitely something. Oh, this is great. I can see the whole story unfolding."

Abigail felt Minerva's reassuring hand on her knee under the table as she watched Lyman across the table. He was in the same uniform he'd worn three days ago when she'd accidentally launched herself into midair, only to end up in his arms. She knew what that uniform fabric felt like. Knew that, close up—very close up—Lyman was just as handsome as he'd been six years earlier.

And strong. She'd felt as if she weighed no more than a paper clip the way he held her. In the days since, as she'd tried to come to terms with Josh's desertion, her mother's fussing and the realization that a long summer stretched before her, she'd tried to forget the way being in Lyman's arms had made her feel.

Feelings were dangerous. They were responsible for perfectly sensible historians sprinting into a hasty wedding and nearly being dashed on the rocks at the foot of one of the natural wonders of the world. Feelings could not be trusted, which was why she had every intention of suppressing hers as she suffered through a business meeting.

Whatever the tourist board asked of her, she would normally agree to, and quite happily. But if this had anything to do with that picture—and it had to, or else Lyman wouldn't be seated across from her—then it was a hard no from her. No matter what Minnie might say. Her best friend had persuaded her to show up by suggesting the tourism board might want to help suppress the photo or retell the story in a way that made her seem less pathetic. But the moment she saw Lyman, she gave up on looking like anything better than what she was—a jilted bride.

"As we all know," Macey began, "that photo of the two of you has absolutely lit up the internet. It's everywhere. I even got a call from one of the morning shows wanting to know if I knew who was in the picture."

Abigail froze. "Did you give them our names?" she asked. Her voice was a whisper, fear gripping her throat at the thought of being on television as a humiliated bride in the arms of a man who'd left her years ago. Would everyone see it? Would *Josh* see it out in Colorado? Was there no mercy for jilted brides?

"Of course not," Macey said. "I wanted to, but I said we needed your permission for that, and we were not going to violate your privacy."

"Too late for that," Tom said. Abigail had known Tom for years. Niagara Falls wasn't a huge town, and people involved in local history or tours tended to stumble across each other pretty often. She knew the owners of the restaurants, the drivers of the shuttle buses and staff at all the local hotels.

"I'm not going on a morning show," Lyman said.

That was one thing she and Lyman could agree on.

"Let's get down to business," Macey said. "Niagara Falls has always been a magnet for weddings, honeymoons and romantics of all kinds. That's why we have hotels and restaurants and wonderful wedding businesses like yours," she said, nodding to Minerva.

Abigail glanced at Minnie and hoped her friend wouldn't fall for the flattery. Minnie loved her wedding business and her co-owner, Abigail's mom. The two women worked tirelessly to ensure every detail was perfect for brides and grooms, and they'd only had one failure to date—hers. Not that it was their fault. The officiant, photographer, flowers and cake had all been perfect. Even the weather had been perfect. It should have been one more lovely photograph or video on the website.

She stopped herself from sighing, something she'd done a lot during the past few days at home. Abigail sat up straighter and took a deep breath. She avoided looking at Lyman's face, instead focusing on the third button of his uniform jacket.

"Which is why we need to capitalize on this image of the two of you," Macey continued. She held up both hands to point to Lyman and Abigail simultaneously. Being included in that gesture with Lyman felt oddly personal. "But we want to reshape the story for our use, of course. And get rid of the 'jilted bride' hashtag so it's more romantic and benefits us."

"It's already everywhere on social media," Minerva said. "How can you control it now?"

"Billboards," Macey said, leaning forward. "Brochures. The official Niagara Falls tourist website." Her voice took on a reverent tone. "Picture it. A jilted bride runs into the arms of her former sweetheart, and sparks fly. All with the beautiful falls in the background." Macey waved a hand in the hair as if she saw the whole story on a giant sign.

"They'll quickly forget about the jilting part and focus on the reunited lovers part if we do this right."

Abigail didn't even need to take her attention from the third button to notice Lyman was shaking his head. She had to agree with him. The last thing on earth she wanted was to be on the billboard out on the interstate directing people to *exit here for the fastest route to the falls.*

"You didn't get rid of the dress, did you?" Macey asked.

Abigail blinked.

She did not like the sound of that.

"She has the dress," Minerva said. Abigail elbowed her. "Sorry," her friend whispered. "But I was thinking of asking if I could add it to my emergency closet."

Abigail was quite familiar with the emergency closet, which contained extra shoes, veils, hair accessories, makeup, painkillers and tissues. There were five wedding gowns in various sizes that her friend had purchased at thrift shops, and Abigail knew that at least four of them had been worn by a bride who either needed a backup or made a spur-of-the-moment decision.

"Of course," Abigail told her. "Anything for you." It wasn't as if she would ever need the dress again, and it had remained mercifully unharmed in her running bouquet toss.

"That's the spirit," Macey said. "Abigail, I know you're a champion for Niagara Falls. A girl who loves this town and will do anything to keep it going. We have to compete with those gorgeous hotels on the Canadian side, and it's not easy keeping up. We need a secret weapon, and that photograph of you two," she said, pointing at them both again, "is our chance."

Lyman stood up. "I'm sorry, but no."

"But this is your hometown, too, isn't it?" Macey asked.

"It was."

It was. Lyman had moved on. She bitterly remembered he couldn't wait to leave Niagara Falls and go *do something with his life,* as he'd put it. It had bothered her, the implication that staying in town was the opposite of *doing something* with her life, but she'd tried to forget about him and chalk it up to teenage bravado. Until now.

She allowed herself to look at his face instead of button number three.

Tom cleared his throat. "The photographer I hired to do publicity photos of my captains said it was hands down the best picture she's ever taken."

Abigail watched Lyman's reaction. Would his boss have any sway with Lyman?

"Luckily for us, Sam here was also there, since he was supposed to be the photographer for Abigail's wedding," Macey said. "We have no shortage of high-quality photos of that moment."

Abigail turned to Sam. "You wouldn't."

He gave a shy shrug. "It's a great picture, and

Macey has offered me the job of documenting what comes next."

"What does come next?" Lyman asked, his expression dark.

"You know how it was in the service, Roberts," Tom said. "You put yourself aside and do what's needed for the greater good. Mission first."

"This is hardly a military maneuver," Lyman said.

Abigail felt a breath of relief for the first time in several days. She wasn't going to have to argue her way out of this or defend her privacy. Lyman would take care of that. She relaxed a bit, confident he would say no and that would be that, problem solved.

Lyman gave her a tight-lipped glance.

"The greater good," his boss reminded him. "It wouldn't hurt us all to have some good publicity."

Lyman's grim expression relaxed. Was he seriously considering saying yes?

"And it's out there anyway," his boss continued. "Everyone is talking about it, including your lovely mother."

Lyman's eyebrows rose. "My mother called you about this mess?"

"I ran into her at the pharmacy. How's your dad's recovery, by the way?"

Abigail noticed Lyman's shoulders hunching. What had happened with his father? She tried to remember the last time she'd seen his dad around town. It hadn't been that long ago, had it?

"He's fine. Look, I'll do whatever Abigail wants," Lyman said, and it sounded like he was trying to move the subject away from his family. Interesting. He sat back in his chair as if he'd just agreed to a restaurant that wasn't his favorite, but he could eat there anyway. As if whatever happened didn't really matter to him and he didn't feel like arguing.

So did this mean he was empowering her to decide or dumping the decision on her?

"It's up to you, Abigail," Macey said. "Have I told you how gorgeous you look in that picture?"

"I look furious in that picture," she said.

"Fiercely beautiful," Sam said. "As if nothing could stop you."

"Josh didn't show up for our wedding. That definitely stopped me."

Even saying his name brought a fresh wave of misery, and she felt her face heat. This was not the time to be emotional. She tried thinking about her history books, where she'd learned to put things into historical perspective and assign reasons for whatever had happened.

"This is your chance to triumph over circumstances. Make lemonade," Macey said, leaning toward her and nodding enthusiastically.

Abigail turned to Minnie. "Do you think this is making lemonade?" Her best friend had never let her down in the two decades they'd shared hopes, dreams, secrets and heartaches. She would be truthful.

"I think it's your way of thumbing your nose at Josh," Minnie said. "There's a good chance he'll see the pictures of you and a handsome man, and he'll know he missed out."

Did she care what Josh thought? If he was concerned about missing out, he'd have shown up for their wedding.

"This isn't about him," Abigail whispered as she stared at a ripped-open packet of sugar. He'd forfeited the right to be part of her decision.

"You could be the face of Niagara Falls, New York," Macey said.

She had felt powerless when she'd realized her wedding wasn't happening. She'd tried to regain that power by racing toward the falls and flinging the bouquet in the face of the fates that had denied her.

Maybe this was also an empowering step. If she could take control of that picture and the story, she could take back ownership of that moment. And suddenly, that felt very appealing. Yes, she'd be helping the wedding business in her hometown, but could she help herself, too?

"Okay," she said. "But I want a deciding vote, some control, in however that photo is used."

Lyman's head came up, and he shot her a glance full of surprise and shock. He'd been certain she'd say no, she could tell from his expression.

Macey nodded. "You and Lyman. We'll include you both in planning the promotional campaign, and you're not going to regret this."

Abigail's eyes met Lyman's across the table. The falls thundered away beyond the trees, just as they always had, and the comforting sound dulled her belief that there was a very good chance she was going to regret it.

CHAPTER FOUR

#FallInLoveAtTheFalls

LYMAN TRIED NOT looking at the billboard, but it was no use.

"I don't understand," his mother said from the passenger seat. "You said you hadn't seen Abigail since high school—"

"Since the end of the summer after senior year," Lyman corrected patiently.

"And yet, she ran straight to you when she realized her fiancé wasn't showing up to the wedding?"

"She was running straight at the *falls*. I happened to…intercede."

"Why was she running at the falls?" his mother asked.

Lyman wanted to tell his mother about all the foolish things he'd seen people do on or around the water in his time in the Coast Guard, but he doubted she needed a lecture. She had enough on her plate.

"I believe her intent was to throw her bouquet over the falls."

"Why?"

Lyman sighed. "Do you want to go in to the drugstore or use the drive-through?"

"Can we go in? I want to get a case of bottled water, and it's heavy. With you along to help this summer, everything seems a bit lighter."

He pulled into a spot close to the door. "I'm happy to help." And he was. Happy he was easing his mom's burden a bit and being an extra person to take his dad to appointments, someone to be an extra set of ears at the cardiologist.

His mother got out of the car, and he followed her into the drugstore. She got a cart and steered toward the pantry items. Lyman picked up a twenty-four-pack of bottled water and put it in the cart, and his mom added items on top of it. Some over-the-counter painkillers, sunscreen for his dad, whose medicine made him susceptible to burns, a family-size package of cookies.

"I guess she wanted to toss the bouquet even though her wedding fell apart," his mother continued as she browsed the hair-care aisle. "I can't blame her. Sometimes, even when things are a mess, you just latch on to one thing. A tradition, a plan, something you can control." She paused and used her shirt collar to wipe her eye. Lyman wanted to reach out and hug his mom right there next to the hair spray, but he was afraid she'd fall apart. She'd been stoic through his dad's heart surgery and recovery, but it was a lot to handle.

"It'll never work, though," she said, straightening up and continuing her march down the aisle.

"What won't work?"

"The ad campaign they want to do. No one will believe it."

She turned the corner and picked up a huge package of bath tissue.

Lyman helped her stuff the package in the cart. "Why won't they believe it?"

"Because it's just one picture. You two need a backstory."

"We…have one."

"But no one is going to know about it from just one picture of you looking handsome in your uniform and her looking surprised in a wedding dress. How is that a story that will sell Niagara Falls? Does the tourism board think people will want to come here on the off chance they'll catch a mate before they tumble to their death over a natural wonder?"

Lyman gave up trying to stuff the package of bathroom tissue in the cart and shouldered it. "None of this was my idea."

"But you're in it now. I have to tell you, your dad is really excited that you're showing an interest in Niagara Falls and promoting it. Even though I know coming home wasn't your choice, it makes him happy."

Lyman stood in the paper products aisle with a twelve-pack of bathroom tissue on his shoulder and felt about fifteen inches tall because of all the internal grumbling he'd done about coming home and now being the "face" of Niagara Falls. He hadn't said a word aloud, and he just hoped his efforts were going to help.

"I always thought it would be nice if you and Abigail got back together," his mother continued.

"We're not getting back together."

"You see, that's why no one's going to believe the ad campaign. It needs substance."

Lyman eyed the painkillers and cookies in the cart.

"I see that look," his mom said. "But if your face is going to be ten feet tall all over town, you want to be part of a success story."

"When you say substance…" he began as he waited for her to select a magazine from the rack at the register.

"People should believe in the idea of romance. That's what they want. The romance and mystique of the falls." She put a glossy magazine on the conveyor belt and stacked her smaller items on top. The clerk scanned the purchases and then pointed to the bathroom tissue balanced on Lyman's shoulder.

"Those are buy one, get one free this week. You should go get another one." The clerk paused. "You look like that guy with the bride on the new sign."

"Thanks," he said. He turned to go pick up another toilet tissue package before the clerk asked him anything about the picture or suggested anything involving romance.

"He is," he heard his mother tell the clerk.

"So are they, like, together?" the clerk asked.

Lyman didn't wait for his mother's answer as he made his way back through the aisles, but he had the nagging feeling that she was right.

ABIGAIL STOOD STILL, fighting a sense of déjà vu, while Minerva zipped her into her wedding gown.

"It's a good idea," Minnie said.

"I don't know," Abigail said. "I'm starting to think I haven't had a good idea in quite a while. Just a series of things that seemed right…or inevitable…and I got swept along by my own current."

Minerva took Abigail by the shoulders and turned her. "You don't mean that."

"You saw what happened with Josh, the man I thought was the jelly to my peanut butter. I, well, I thought he swept me off my feet —which he sort of did—but my mistake was that I thought that was a good thing. That rush of excitement and feeling breathless and giddy. I thought that meant I was in love."

"It can," Minerva said.

"For other people. Maybe. I thought it was the speedway to my happily-ever-after, but it was obviously not my time."

"Your time will come."

Abigail's mom popped into the dressing room. "The photographer is ready." She paused, and a sentimental expression came over her face as she gazed at Abigail in her white dress. Abigail willed Ginny not to say anything about how she looked. It was bad enough going through with this farce. And she wouldn't be if it didn't directly assist her mother and her best friend's wedding business.

"Red lipstick," her mother said. "You were wearing red on your... In the original photograph."

Minerva pulled a tube of lipstick out of her pocket. "We'll be right out."

Abigail's mother left, and Minnie held a mirror for Abigail to apply her lipstick.

"Just don't let anyone get in your head today," Minnie said. "You're a team player, and the job on the team you've been assigned is chief smiler while wearing a costume. Think of this dress as a costume."

"With red lipstick," Abigail added.

"Which is very flattering," Minerva said.

Abigail led the way through the hotel where her mother and Minerva housed their wedding business. Their partnership with the hotel, which sat on a bluff near the American Falls, was profitable for both parties—Minerva and Ginny got to use the banquet room for receptions and sometimes ceremonies if the weather didn't cooperate, and the hotel got to fill rooms with bridal parties and guests.

A green screen was set up in the corner of the empty banquet room, and Macey from the tourist board was standing in front of it talking with the photographer and Lyman. Lyman wore his dark blue captain's uniform. He had his hands clasped behind him as if he was standing at parade rest awaiting orders. The photographer, Sam, leaned in behind his tripod and used a remote control to adjust the lighting.

Macey turned, and when she saw Abigail, she gave her a once-over. Then she nodded her head in approval. "You got all the details right, with the pearl necklace and the lace gloves. Your hair looks the same, too, except for—"

"On it," Minerva said. She stepped in front of Abigail and attached her veil, fluffing it out so it caught the breeze from a fan on the floor.

"Perfect," Macey said. "I already gave Lyman some instructions, but just so we're all clear, we're going to take a series of shots of you two in front of the green screen, and then we can edit the photos to add backgrounds from all around the area."

"You're not going to use that cheesy background where it looks like they're in a barrel about to go over, are you?" Minerva asked.

"I'm ruling nothing out. The internet is already loving the original picture, and we're going to grab this opportunity. I didn't want to drag you both all over the region, so the green screen is our friend," Macey added.

"I'm a better friend," Minerva whispered to Abigail, who flashed her a smile in return.

"That's the smile I want to see," Macey said. "But aimed at this handsome guy instead."

"Here we go," Sam said. "First, let's do some standard bridal poses."

Having helped her mom and friend with their business dozens of times, Abigail knew the standard poses. Hands held, gazing into each other's eyes. The bride's hands clasped behind the groom's neck. Cheeks pressed together as they looked down at the bouquet or the rings. A foreheads-together picture. A kiss picture.

Lyman cleared his throat. "Just tell me what to do."

"I believe we both want to get this over with as fast as possible," Abigail agreed.

"Try to look romantic," Macey said.

Abigail smiled through a series of poses and— she had to hand it to him—Lyman managed a convincing smile, too. Maybe the military had accustomed the guy to following orders.

Macey circled behind the photographer, cheering them on and nodding with approval. At first. After the first three poses, her enthusiasm seemed to flag. By the sixth pose, she wasn't circling, and she was no longer smiling.

"Something's not right," Macey said at last.

"What?" Ginny asked. "Everything is perfect.

His uniform, her dress. She's a picture-perfect bride."

"It's not what they're wearing," Macey said.

"They look good together," Ginny insisted.

Abigail took a step away from Lyman and waited.

"There's something missing," Macey said. "We're trying to sell the whole concept of romance and finding love at Niagara Falls."

Lyman stood attentively, hands clasped behind his back. Abigail looked over at Minerva, whose eyebrows were up.

"Romance doesn't start at the wedding," Macey said.

"Are you saying it ends at the wedding?" Abigail asked.

"I hope not," Lyman said.

Everyone turned to look at him.

"We need to sell the romance," Macey said, brushing past his quip. "Which means we need a series of photos of you two doing different things in different clothes."

Abigail and Lyman groaned at the same time and then stepped farther apart.

"I already planted the story that you were 'caught' by Lyman when you saw him across the falls and ditched the guy you were about to marry because you happened to see the true love of your life—the one that got away."

Abigail sucked in a breath. "You what?"

Minerva's mouth hung open, and so did Abigail's mom's.

"You told people that?" Lyman asked.

Macey shrugged. "It's plausible, and you have to admit it's a great story that explains the look you're giving each other in the picture. Thunderstruck. I might even give it a hashtag."

"Hashtag thunderstruck," Ginny whispered.

"People will think I'm a jerk," Abigail said. "A fickle, silly fool."

"Did…you want them to think you were jilted instead?" Macey asked. "They're not using the jilted hashtag anymore. You can check that for yourself."

Abigail shook with rage—outrage, actually—and pulled off her wedding veil with trembling hands. She dropped the white tulle on the ground. Lyman retrieved it and draped it over a banquet chair nearby, leaving Abigail alone in front of the green screen.

She knew she looked downtrodden. Defeated. The photographer leaned toward his camera tripod and put his finger on the trigger button.

Abigail held up a hand. "No. Do not."

"Have a heart," Lyman said to the photographer. "This isn't anyone's best moment."

"It's just a suggestion," Macey said, "but there is a way to fix this so everyone wins."

Macey steepled her hands in front of her and tapped her fingers together as if she were an evil villain plotting world domination. Abigail considered suggesting the barrel backdrop. They could tell everyone the happy couple went over the falls and were never seen again.

"You fall in love for real," Macey said.

CHAPTER FIVE

#TrueLoveNiagara

LYMAN HEARD GINNY WARREN GASP. He looked over and saw her hand fly up to her mouth, the other covering her heart. His own heart was racing. How had he gotten himself into this situation? Instinct had made him rush toward the falls and catch Abigail, but instinct wasn't giving him any directions right now. He didn't want to run away, exactly, but he'd be happy if he could blend in to the banquet room walls.

Fall in love *for real*? What the heck did that even mean? You couldn't make someone fall in love, even in the land of rainbows and honeymoons. Lyman risked a glance at Abigail. He might not be having the summer of his dreams, but he suspected things were even worse for her, and she'd been at the point of crumbling just a moment ago when she'd torn off her veil.

Framed by the green screen behind her, Abigail's reaction was not what he expected. She appeared to go through a transformation. She stood straighter and pulled her shoulders back. She raised her chin and met his gaze, and her expression could only be described as fierce determination, much like the moment she'd rushed the falls. Oh, goodness. Was she determined to slay him right there in front of the camera, giving that photographer an epic shot at a photo-of-the-year prize? Was she determined to find a way out of this mess? His heart took a frightening pause in its rapid racing. Did she—oh, man—did she think this was a good idea?

"I have had entirely enough of this nonsense," Abigail said. She raised her hand and pointed at Macey. "I'm out. I rescind my permission to use my image in your campaign. I will not be used, reduced to a red lipstick–wearing woman in a gown that is a mere costume prop." She turned to her mother and her friend. "I'm sorry, but I'm not the bride who'll bring in more business, no matter how much I love you. I'm not that bride." Her voice lowered. "I'm not any bride."

Lyman held his breath. He'd witnessed tough times in the military. Colleagues getting bad news from home. Boaters losing their lives at sea. His own heartache when he'd gotten the call from his mom that his dad's previous heart attacks had weakened him and she needed help getting him through a difficult surgery.

He'd seen his share of sorrow, and he knew that

bravery and bravado were effective covers. For a limited time. And then they vanished and left the painful truth exposed. He'd just watched Abigail go from bravado to agony in less than a minute. He wanted to reach out and hug her, smooth away that deep line between her eyebrows—

"And you," she said, pointing to him. "You got us into this by agreeing in the first place."

So much for a soothing hug.

"You agreed, too," he said.

"But you said yes first and then I felt obligated and now we're supposed to escalate this charade and fall in love just to make the pictures look good."

"If I may interrupt," Macey said. "I want to point out that it's not entirely ridiculous. You were in love before—"

"We dated," Lyman and Abigail said at the same time.

"Which, I've heard," Macey continued with a hint of a grin, "can sometimes lead to falling in love. So you have a head start."

"No," Lyman and Abigail said, again speaking in unison.

Lyman took his eyes off Abigail long enough to see that Ginny and Minnie were exchanging a humorous glance, as if they didn't see this as the disaster it was. Abigail was backing out. His boss would be disappointed in him. And he'd have to admit to his mother that she'd been right. No one was going to buy the happy billboards without some substance and follow-through backing them up. He could see that now.

"I feel like there's chemistry between you two," Macey continued. "What do you think?" she asked, turning to the photographer. "You see a lot of couples. Chemistry?"

Sam stepped back from his camera and held up both hands. "I prefer to remain neutral."

Not helpful but probably smart, Lyman thought.

"But," the photographer continued, "I would point out that chemistry can be either very productive or explosive, which means a situation can appear—"

"Okay," Abigail said. "I've already told you I'm out. And now I want to get out of this ridiculous dress."

"You loved that dress," Ginny said.

"I loved the idea of this dress. And it's now a bad idea." Abigail began to work the buttons on her gloves, but then she paused and reached into her gown's pocket. She produced her glasses and put them on. Her glasses had red rims that matched her lipstick, and the effect was intriguing. She hadn't worn glasses when they'd dated, or at least she hadn't around him. They suited her. She was nice to look at, especially when she wasn't on the verge of tears or preparing to put a shot across his bow.

Was that what the photographer meant about chemistry having two distinct effects?

Lyman heard the camera click at least ten times in rapid succession before Abigail had a chance to respond.

"Perfect," the photographer said. "The brainy bride, local history guru, puts on the finishing touches."

"I do like that look," Minnie said.

"Think about it, Abigail," Macey said. "We orchestrate a campaign. Lay out the whole thing with specific dates. The tourism board will pay your expenses, of course. You don't even have to plan anything. I'll tell you and Lyman where to show up and when, what to wear, and I'll arrange all the social media so there will be continual posts and this—" she waved her hands between Abigail and Lyman "—thing between you two won't just be a one and done. It will have legs and…heart."

Lyman already had legs—although they felt like stone posts—and a heart, despite its inability to keep a steady rhythm. He couldn't imagine the upheaval of drifting from date to date and having pictures and posts following his every move with Abigail.

"And it'll be a nice distraction," Macey continued, "especially after getting jilted. You've got to get back on the horse."

Lyman wished he had a horse at that moment

so he could saddle up and gallop away. The whole situation felt as if it was a runaway horse, and he suddenly realized he had the power to stop it. It was the only safe thing to do, and he was trained to handle emergencies, especially dangerous ones. Everyone was staring at Abigail, waiting for her response, but he had the power to rescue her.

"Let me make this easy for everyone," he said. "I'm backing out. Everything happened too fast. I never planned to reunite with Abigail like that, and I sure didn't want all this attention. I have plenty to worry about this summer, and I'm sure Abigail would rather do anything but get back on the horse, especially after getting her heart broken."

Silence fell, and the tenseness in the room told Lyman he'd blundered. What had he said?

Finally, Abigail pulled off her gloves and tucked them and her glasses back in the pockets hidden somewhere in the fluffy white gown.

"My heart is not broken, and, even if it were, it's none of your business," she said. "You do not speak for me."

OF ALL THE things Lyman might have said, bringing her heart into the discussion was the catalyst for her. He had no right to discuss her heart or her feelings. He'd trampled on them himself years ago in pursuit of whatever he'd thought he wanted—a life that didn't include her. No matter how handsome he looked or his good-citizen effort to save her from going over the falls, he was not going to navigate anywhere in the vicinity of her heart.

"Well, that could be good," Macey said. "No danger of actually falling in love for real. You can approach this objectively. Free dinners and entertainment and you're doing a good deed for your hometown. It's a win-win."

The photographer's lights were hot. Taking off the veil and gloves had helped, but Abigail still felt encumbered by her clothing and everything else. She reached down and pulled off her shoes and then held them by the straps with one hand. She could make a quicker exit that way without risking a trip or a flying leap like the one that had gotten her into this situation.

"I already said no. You'll have to find someone else for your campaign. I respectfully ask that you take down the billboards or at least allow my friend Minerva to help me spray-paint over my face so I can stop being a pathetic laughingstock who got jilted and started this whole freak-show chain of events."

"But—" her mother began.

"No buts," Abigail said.

"But I don't see the harm," Macey said. "You said yourself that you're not emotionally involved. The jilting didn't break your heart, and Lyman seems to have no claim over it. So why not?"

"I already told you I'm not doing it."

"Oh," Macey said, nodding and glancing over at Lyman. "I see."

Abigail considered throwing her white satin pumps at Macey. Perhaps it was the smug expression that suggested Macey thought she knew something Abigail didn't. Maybe it was the silence from her best friend and the confusion on her mom's face. Perhaps it was Lyman standing in the shadows just outside the photo zone, his hand on the chair where he'd carefully draped her veil.

How dare all of them insinuate that they knew what was in her heart and what was best for her? Why wasn't anyone saying anything?

"What do you think you see?" Abigail asked, even though she knew it would be wiser and safer to make a graceful exit.

"I see that there is some unresolved business between you two, and I don't want to put you through an emotional wringer," Macey said. "I'm sorry I suggested fake dating. I didn't realize that would be such a problem for you."

"It's not a problem," Lyman said.

What was he doing? Of course it was a problem. Fake dating anyone was a recipe for disaster. Deceiving people was wrong. Lying to herself was wrong. Was that what happened with relationships that didn't work out? When Josh said yes to her proposal but no to showing up at the wedding…was that because there had been a lingering lie in their whirlwind romance? Maybe not a lie, she thought, maybe something that she'd wanted to believe…or he did…that wasn't quite true.

"What do you mean, it's not a problem?" she asked Lyman.

"I mean it's not a problem to pretend to fall in love with you, because there's nothing unresolved between us. There's nothing between us at all."

It was the right answer. The one that would absolve her of worrying about his feelings or hers or anyone else's. There was nothing between them. And that should make it risk-free to pretend.

Everyone was waiting for her answer to that whopper of a statement. Ex-boyfriend making a cool claim that he felt as much emotion toward her as he would a pair of shoes that he'd outgrown in high school. Gosh, wasn't that a relief. It should have set her free, but something about that statement made her want to reclaim some of her dignity. If she backed out now, her mother and her best friend would believe she had feelings for Lyman. Worse yet, Lyman might think so.

People in Niagara Falls would think their pretend romance verified the rumors. But she didn't care what those people thought. The only opinions that had power over her heart were the ones in the room.

"Fine. I'll do it. I'll read your script and put on a winning performance with this guy." Abigail heard her mother gasp for the second time in the last ten minutes. The poor woman wore her heart on her sleeve, where it could be easily bruised. Abigail would not make that mistake. Her heart was locked up tight behind a wall of practical determination. "Bring on the social media and the hashtags and the pictures. It's not a problem."

She threw Lyman's words right back at him and waited for his reaction. He would certainly back out. Why would he want to tie his summer evenings and free time to her and an advertising campaign for a city he'd escaped from years ago without a backward glance? From context, she'd picked up that he was in town to help out with his father's recovery. Which meant Lyman probably wouldn't stick around for long. He had a lot less to lose than she did, and the thought was unsettling.

Niagara Falls was her home, but Lyman was just passing through.

Lyman plucked her veil off the chair and walked over to where she stood before the green screen in the glare of the lights. He held the veil by its comb and carefully inserted it into her hair exactly where it had been. Abigail didn't move. She didn't have to duck down like she did when her mom or Minerva had helped her put on the veil. Lyman was easily a foot taller than she was, especially because she was barefoot. He turned her so she was shielded from the lights and the other people in the room.

Standing in his shadow with his hands gently arranging the bridal veil around her head and shoulders, Abigail had a flash of memory from that six-years-gone summer. They'd been eating lunch outdoors. She remembered the July heat on her fair skin, a hint of headache from the intense sun. Lyman had stood over her and removed his hat. He'd kissed her and then placed the hat on her head, leaving his own exposed.

"We're going to need more pictures if we're going to make this work," he said now.

"Do that again, but turn so we can see," Sam said. "I love that bit with you putting her veil on. Romantic."

Lyman moved so they were both in profile for the photographer and repeated the action of adjusting Abigail's veil, but, for her, it didn't have the same impact or dredge up a memory like it had the first time. It was only for the camera.

CHAPTER SIX

#NiagaraDateNight

LYMAN HAD SPENT four days regretting his conduct at the photography session, and he knew this was only the beginning. Maybe it was his Coast Guard training, but he couldn't resist trying to swoop in and rescue Abigail when it appeared she was in distress. It was a way for him to turn off his own feelings and focus on the struggle at hand, a simple matter of putting the mission before himself. Allowing emotion to use up any of his oxygen or brain space was dangerous and something he'd overcome in countless rescue drills.

"The official Niagara Falls tourist feed is teasing something big tonight and using the hashtag from the bride thing," Kirsten said as she met Lyman at the dock to relieve him. "I came in a little early because I had the feeling you might have someplace to be."

It had been a peaceful morning of piloting the Maid of the Mist and giving hundreds of tourists a thrill under the thundering falls. Although Mother Nature could be a tough mistress, Lyman had been firmly in control of every movement of the boat. No surprises, nothing to elevate his own heart rate.

Standing on the dock, he felt a spike of adrenaline—his response to the unknown and his body's preparation to face it, just as he had at sea with his fellow rescuers. But tonight he would be alone at the dinner table with Abigail.

Kirsten cocked her head. "Are you going to make me tune in to the live stream after my shift tonight or are you going to give me a hint?"

"It's just dinner."

"With…"

Lyman loosened the top button of his white dress shirt. "Abigail Warren."

Kirsten smiled. "Interesting."

"It's not interesting. If you must know, the tourism board doesn't want our infamous picture to be a one and done, so there will be a series of date nights all summer to build up some kind of romance campaign they're selling."

Tourists stood in a long line at the dock, most of them already wearing their blue plastic raincoats. A little boy waved to Lyman, and he waved back. Kirsten also turned and waved to the people waiting to board. Several tourists took pictures of the two captains, and Lyman stood up straight and smiled. It was all part of the show.

Kirsten turned her back to the waiting tourists and looked up at Lyman. "You're dating your ex-girlfriend, who happens to be on the rebound."

"It sounds terrible when you put it that way," he said, keeping a pleasant expression for the vacation photos possibly being snapped.

Kirsten patted him on the shoulder as she stepped around him. "Not at all. This is going to be great entertainment."

Lyman swallowed and changed the subject. "When you take the boat in tonight, have maintenance look at the oil-pressure gauge on the dashboard. It's working fine, but there's some condensation under the glass."

"Will do. You watch out for yourself tonight, too," Kirsten said.

An hour later, Lyman was showered, dressed and hovering at the kitchen door of his parents' house. "Do you need anything before I go?" he asked his dad, who had his elbows on the kitchen table as he did the daily crossword on his phone.

"I'm fine. Your mother is picking up dinner. Going to have those Cobb salads from that place by the bridge. You have fun this evening with your girlfriend."

Lyman sighed. "Not my girlfriend. Abigail got roped into this just like I did, by being in the wrong place at the wrong time."

His father laughed, and his cheeks brightened.

He already looked better than he had two months ago, just before his bypass surgery.

"I saw all kinds of things driving that tourist shuttle all these years. It's going to be fun hearing your stories while I'm stuck here waiting to get better and get back to work."

At fifty-seven, his dad was too young to retire, but Lyman doubted he'd pass a physical to get a commercial driver's license again. Lyman's mother worked full-time as a dental hygienist, which would pay the bills, but that was part of why he was home. Between the two of them, they could care for his dad.

"Are you sure you don't want me to wait until Mom gets home before I go?"

His father flashed a grin. "Do you think I'm going to get too excited over this crossword puzzle and keel over at the kitchen table?"

Lyman considered using his father's health as an excuse to cancel his date with Abigail, but then he remembered her face after she'd been left at the altar. It wasn't the same, of course, but he was a man of honor who kept his word. He'd said he'd be there at seven.

"I'll see you later, Dad," Lyman said.

"I'll be waiting to hear all about the new restaurant. It's about time they added something nice right by the visitors' center."

When Lyman pulled his used pickup into the lot by the new Falls Fare Restaurant, a wave of nausea rolled through him. He had a strong sailor's stomach, but it was currently empty. He was running on fumes from working all day and then making a quick turnaround. But it wasn't the emptiness that had him taking a deep breath before unbuckling his seat belt. It was the photographer standing at the entrance.

Abigail stood there, too, waiting for him. She wore a white top with a knee-length white skirt. Something sparkled at her neck, and her long blond hair was up with only a few curls loose around her face. She noticed him first, and then the photographer followed her gaze and locked in on him. He had to do it. He had to get out of the truck and walk up to Abigail, knowing his every move would be recorded and posted online, where it would forever have a life of its own.

Why had he agreed to this?

If it hadn't been for Abigail standing there looking as if she were lost at sea, he would have squealed the tires leaving the parking lot.

FINALLY. OF COURSE they'd agreed on seven o'clock, but Abigail had arrived fifteen minutes early. That way she could control the field. She wouldn't be taken by surprise. Minerva had offered to come along as moral support, but Abigail had assured her she didn't need it.

Seeing Lyman pull up in an older-model truck and hesitate before getting out made her wish she'd taken her friend up on the offer. Was he just going to sit there?

When he opened the door and swung his long legs out, Abigail released a long breath. He wore a collared shirt neatly tucked into dark pants, and he strode confidently toward her as if he didn't see the photographer from the local tourism board standing off to the side.

She held out a hand, not knowing what he would do as a greeting. They hadn't been given instructions by Macey. It was a date. How had she and Lyman greeted each other during that summer they'd dated? In a flash, she remembered. Lyman was a temple kisser. He said he loved the scent of her hair.

Abigail took a step back as he approached. He couldn't kiss her right over her ear. It was too personal. She kept the hand extended in front of her with her elbow stiff, holding him at a distance.

He took her hand and reached out a long arm to touch her on the shoulder. "Abigail. You look nice," he said, leaning his head toward her. She leaned backward but smiled, aware of the camera.

"I hope you're hungry," she said. "I had a sneak preview of the menu, and it looks wonderful."

"I am," Lyman said. "I got off work an hour ago. Did you work today?"

So he was going to start in on the pleasant conversation before they even entered the restaurant?

The photographer would fall asleep from boredom at this rate.

"Let's go inside," Abigail said.

Macey had assured her there would be a table with a romantic view reserved for them. She'd also said the photographer would only stay for the first half hour to get pictures as they were seated and had glasses of champagne. Dinner itself would be private—at least as private as any restaurant.

As they walked in, Abigail had an anxious moment wondering whose name the reservation was under, but the man at the host stand recognized them right away. Lyman held Abigail's hand as they walked to a table by the window with a view of the falls. The table had an elegant white cloth, gleaming silverware, champagne flutes and a vase of red roses.

Lyman pulled out Abigail's chair and held it for her, and Abigail took her time being seated so Sam could snap pictures. Was this what the summer would be like? Moving in slow, exaggerated motions for the benefits of social media?

A waiter appeared and served champagne five seconds after Lyman took his seat across from her, and then Abigail lifted her flute.

"I believe we're expected to toast something," she said.

Lyman picked up his flute and held it an inch from hers. His hand didn't tremble. He appeared calm and in control, as if the date was nothing more than an assignment to him. Good. She felt exactly the same way.

"You decide," he said.

She smiled for the benefit of the camera. "To our successful campaign to bring more tourists to Niagara Falls."

Lyman touched his glass to hers and then waited for her to sip first before taking a drink himself. "How will we know if it's successful?"

The champagne was good, and Abigail let the tiny bubbles tickle the back of her throat while she considered Lyman's question.

"I believe that's someone else's concern."

"But we should know what metrics are being used to decide if this…thing…is even working," Lyman said. "You have to know the end goal of the mission."

"Is that what they taught you in the Coast Guard?"

"I learned a lot of things in the military."

"Like following orders?" she asked.

"Of course."

"Well, then, maybe we should just follow orders and not overthink anything," Abigail said.

Lyman took a long sip of his champagne instead of answering, and then he opened his menu. Abigail took her glasses—white-framed ones—from her purse and put them on. Lyman glanced up and stared at her for a moment.

"What?"

"Your glasses were red the last time I saw you."

He'd noticed?

"I have five different pairs. They're inexpensive, just for reading up close, not prescription."

"So you match them to your outfits," he said.

She gave a little shrug. "It's a harmless indulgence. I wear my green ones when I'm giving tours because they match my official lanyard."

Lyman smiled at her, and for a moment he felt like an old friend.

"Nice," the photographer said as he leaned in to take a picture. "That was a good look between you two."

Abigail was torn between hoping Sam would stick around as a third wheel and wishing he would leave. She cleared her throat and gave her attention back to the menu. "Dinner is covered, of course, so you should order whatever you want. Seafood is their specialty."

"I was thinking of having the prime rib," he said.

"Are you tired of seafood after being out on boats all the time?"

Lyman laughed. "Do you think they fed us the fresh catch of the day in the Coast Guard?"

"I have no idea," she said. "Perhaps you can tell me all about life on the high seas while we eat. That should pass the time."

"Do you really want to hear about that?"

"We need to talk about something," Abigail said.

"Okay, but then you have to tell me all about your work as a tour guide."

"A history guide," she corrected.

Lyman nodded.

"And we can save that for the next date so we'll have something to talk about," Abigail added. After that date, she'd have to think of something else to discuss to fill the time. Perhaps favorite podcasts or television shows. Nothing too personal.

"After we order, I'll tell you about some of our missions, but don't expect anything like you see in movies. Mostly what we did was a group effort, carefully following our training."

"But you have rescued people, haven't you? Or saved sinking boats?"

"As part of a team, yes," Lyman said.

She hadn't expected him to brag about his heroics, but the way his chest had filled out, his strong arms and hands, and the maturity she saw in his eyes told her that he'd seen a lot of things in the past six years. Had those things made him stronger? Had they made him rethink his vow to get out of Niagara Falls and "do something important" with his life?

"And now you're on the Maid of the Mist team," Abigail said.

Lyman closed his menu and folded his hands on top of it. "For the summer."

That was exactly why Abigail was not going to

get invested in Lyman Roberts again. The camera clicking away and the social media posts wouldn't convey that their relationship was a complete sham with a ticking clock, but she would be wise to remember it.

CHAPTER SEVEN

#PicnicAtTheFalls

"I FOLLOWED THE POSTS," Abigail's mother said to her the next morning as Abigail helped Ginny and Minerva decorate the banquet hall at the hotel for an afternoon wedding reception. "At least until you ordered dinner, and then there was nothing after that."

"There *was* nothing after that. We talked. I had the bruschetta chicken."

"Uh-huh," Ginny said, clearly waiting for more details.

"And a salad with berries and walnuts. Very good." Abigail unpacked and smoothed out the tails of a white satin bow they used for table decorations. "What color candles for the hurricane lamps?"

"Pink," her mother said. "This bride wants pink, pink, pink."

Abigail shrugged. "It's her wedding." It had been thirteen days since Abigail's attempted wedding. She'd chosen sky blue accents for the reception that would have taken place in this very room. Perhaps a future bride could use her unlit candles. It would be a shame to waste them.

Minerva came through the double doors of the banquet hall and called out, "I met the bride and groom at city hall and helped them find the office to get a marriage license. They're from California. Can you believe that? They decided on a quickie trip to Niagara Falls to get married when they could have more easily chosen Las Vegas." Minerva came over and high-fived Ginny. "Chalk one up for Niagara Falls weddings."

"That makes me feel better," Ginny said. "After the cancellation last week from the couple who decided to fly to Jamaica instead and the couple who picked Gatlinburg over us, I was starting to wonder if the falls were losing some magic."

"Not at all," Minnie said. "Especially with Abigail here taking one for the team. Nice pictures from the restaurant, and hopefully good PR for them, too," she said, giving Abigail a one-armed hug as she juggled a bouquet of fresh flowers in her other hand.

Abigail's phone buzzed with a message, and she glanced at the screen. It was a group text from Macey that included her and Lyman. *Oh, yay.* She was on a group text now.

Good job, you two.

Good job wasn't exactly a glowing accolade. If she was going to go through with this charade, she wanted to do an excellent job. She had some pride, despite her very public failure at getting married. She could have been home last evening working on the text to go with the photographs she was researching, but instead she'd heard stories about boats and personal flotation devices and stormy weather and helicopters. Lyman had stuck with facts, not glorifying his role in any of the incidents at sea. Was he being evasive or just purposely humble?

Another text followed.

But we have work to do. #CatchTheBride didn't get as many views as I'd hoped, so we have to build on this right away to gain momentum.

"What is it?" Minerva asked. "You look like someone stole your car and ran over puppies with it."

Abigail showed Minerva the screen.

"So you need another date soon. Free food, right?"

"Maybe this is a terrible idea. If I'm going to suffer and make a fool of myself, I at least want it to be successful."

"I'm fact-checking," Minerva said. She pulled out her own phone and scrolled.

"Well?" Abigail asked. "How many views?"

Minerva pressed her lips together. "A lot of people followed the lead-up and the hype, but only about half of them liked or commented on the actual date. Maybe they were…respecting your privacy."

"Maybe this is a stupid flop," Abigail said.

Her phone pinged. It was a response from Lyman to the group text that simply said, Awaiting orders.

Abigail sighed. "Ugh. 'Awaiting orders.' Like this is some kind of mission."

Minerva shrugged. "It could be worse. He could claim he's busy or, worse yet, give up on the whole thing."

"We just started. He can't give up." Even though Abigail had considered it fifteen seconds ago. If anyone was stepping aside, it would be her. She wouldn't have him quitting on her.

Minerva smiled. "I was hoping you'd say that. This city has a lot to offer, but every year we have to compete harder with other attractions. Every little bit helps." Minerva put a hand on Abigail's upper arm. "Thank you."

"Yes!" Ginny yelled from across the room. "Look at that disco ball. I had them take it down and clean it yesterday, and woo-hoo, does it sparkle now!"

Abigail and Minerva exchanged a smile. "Mom loves weddings."

"We all do."

Abigail didn't point out that Minerva was in her midtwenties, just like Abigail, but she'd hardly dated anyone despite having a reputation as a matchmaker as well as a wedding planner. Not counting tourists who came and went, the number of eligible bachelors in the city of Niagara Falls was finite. Minerva claimed to be talking to someone she'd met online, but Abigail hadn't heard any gushing from her friend about it.

Another text from Macey hit the group conversation.

I'll be in touch soon.

I'll be waiting, Abigail typed. She thought about it a moment and then added, for my orders.

THIS WAS STUPID, Lyman thought. Mixing business with…nonbusiness. Sure, he was a boat captain for tourists, but he wanted to be taken seriously.

"I agreed to this photo shoot because it's good advertising for us, too," Tom was saying.

"It's not even realistic," Lyman said. "We don't take lunch breaks on the boat between runs, and we sure as heck don't have picnic hampers delivered by—"

He'd been about to say *pretty women*, but he stopped himself. Abigail's appearance wasn't any of his business or part of his argument.

Tom put a hand on his shoulder, and Lyman felt

as if he was being advised by a superior officer, just like back in the service. "Relax, Roberts. It's a quick lunch, some pictures, and you can send her back down the gangplank and get to work."

Lyman stood on the deck of the Maid of the Mist just before noon on a sunny day. A rainbow appeared upriver from the dock. He glanced way up at the observation deck hovering over the gorge, which was crowded with tourists on this beautiful summer day, all taking photos of the falls and the rainbow. He waited, and then he saw her.

Abigail wore a white sundress and a wide-brimmed hat and carried a wicker basket. Just like a movie. Behind her, Sam captured the scene—probably taking video he'd edit and upload to the various social accounts.

"Smile," Tom said. "You could have it a lot worse."

Abigail strode up the gangplank and paused. It had been awkward like this outside the restaurant three nights ago. How did they greet each other? He wondered if her hair still smelled like fruit and flowers.

He reached for the basket and gave her a broad smile.

"Open the top and peek in and then act like you're surprised," Macey said from behind the photographer.

He was starting to get accustomed to surprises.

He lifted the lid and found foil-wrapped sandwiches and cans of his favorite brand of root beer. Had Abigail remembered?

"Good, nice look of wonder and surprise," Macey said. "Now take her arm and lead her to the table on the deck."

Lyman took the basket by its handle and offered Abigail his free arm. His boss had conveniently disappeared, leaving them alone on the docked boat. He had only thirty minutes until it would be time to start boarding the next group of passengers, which was usually enough time for a hastily eaten packed lunch.

He put the basket on the table, which was draped with a white cloth, and waited for Abigail to take her seat. She opened the basket and laid out the food while the photographer snapped pictures with the falls in the background.

"Thank you," Lyman said. "This is lunch and dinner for me today."

"Working late?"

He nodded as they both unwrapped a sandwich. "Covering the evening shift for one of the other captains."

"Do you work a lot of overtime?"

Lyman took a big bite and shook his head. "I try not to. My main job this summer is helping out at home."

Abigail's head tilted, and her eyes searched his. He hadn't meant to reveal anything personal about his father's health or his reason for coming home for the summer, but facts were facts. Abigail was likely to find out anyway.

"I've heard your father is having some health problems."

Of course she already knew. Niagara Falls was, basically, a small town that happened to have a giant tourist attraction. Lyman cracked open the can of root beer. "I love this kind."

"I know," Abigail said.

Lyman sucked in a breath and then took a long drink. He might as well tell her. "My dad has had two heart attacks in the last five years, and he finally had a quintuple bypass. The big question now is if and when he'll go back to work."

Laying out the facts like that was the safest way to go—nothing personal, clear of emotion.

"Driving the trolley?"

"If that's what he wants."

"I always thought that would be such a fun job. Sometimes I arrange to use the trolley for my tour groups." She paused and seemed to be considering her next words. "I've ridden with your dad quite a few times."

Of course she knew his dad. Had been over to the house for dinner the summer they dated. Had gone with him as his date to a family wedding. And it seemed that while he'd been far across the globe, she was spending time with his dad.

Should he have been here, too? Growing up,

Lyman had seen nothing fun or interesting about his dad's job, driving the same route in an endless loop every day with tourists getting on and off, giving the same facts and details about how much water went over the falls every minute and old stories about people surviving going over the falls. He'd wanted something much more important for his life, but all his dad wanted now was to get back to that job.

"He loves that job," he said at last, reflecting on the fact that there were definite parallels with his captain's job on the Maid. "It's all he's ever done and…well, I hope his heart doesn't stand in his way."

Abigail looked up from her sandwich with a curious expression. Maybe it was the idea of a person's heart standing in the way. Was her heart healing after being tossed aside by her intended groom?

"How are you doing?" he asked.

Her gaze sharpened. "I'm fine."

"I mean…"

"Like I said. Fine."

"Can you finish those sandwiches?" Macey asked. "I'd like to get some action shots, and I know we're on a tight time schedule."

Lyman glanced over and saw tourists lining up, their blue raincoats flapping in the breeze that always swept down the Niagara River gorge. Despite the breeze, it was a hot summer day. He wanted to warn those tourists to take off their plastic coats until they actually boarded and got underway so they wouldn't overheat.

"What kind of action shots?" Abigail asked. She wrapped foil around her sandwich and shoved it back, half-eaten, into the basket. She dusted off her hands and turned to Macey.

"First, how about one from behind where we can see his arm around you as you both look up-river toward the falls?"

Lyman finished his sandwich in one big bite, knowing he wouldn't have the luxury of coming back to it later. He stood and went to the railing, and when Abigail joined him, he put an arm lightly around her shoulders, leaving a nice safe gap between them. He thought about how he'd ended things with her six years ago. She'd been lovely and friendly and made his summer fly. But, he had to admit to himself, she hadn't been enough. He wanted more, and Abigail, with her deep local roots and her love of the city, was part of the problem, part of the anchor he felt dragging him down if he stayed here and accepted a life like his father's.

"Get closer," Macey instructed.

Lyman made a slight move, and Abigail moved at the same time, so their sides touched with an unexpected bump. He didn't flinch. He was following orders. But Abigail moved enough to allow a sliver of daylight between them.

"That's better."

Lyman heard the camera clicking. Was his shirt tucked in neatly? Had he missed a belt loop? He thought about what his commanding officer would say if he appeared sloppy in photos on the internet. What would all his former colleagues think of him being the lovestruck poster boy for a town he'd been anxious to leave?

"It'll be over soon," Abigail said quietly, and he wondered if she was talking to him or herself.

"And now, just take a step back so we can get a side angle with you showing her something, pointing at something upriver."

"I'm the local guide," Abigail protested.

"We'll get to that," Macey said. "I have plans for Lyman to tag along on one of your tours. Really promote as many aspects of life in Niagara Falls as possible."

Lyman stepped back and swept out an arm, pointing to an imaginary point upriver toward the falls. He glanced down at Abigail's stormy expression. She was turned toward him with the camera behind her so only he could see her feelings reflected in the thin set of her lips and the line between her eyebrows. He found himself frowning, too.

"You're supposed to look happy, Lyman," Macey called out. "You're falling in love, remember?"

Falling in love. Getting swept away. It all made a great connection to the rushing waters of the falls. But whatever feelings he and Abigail had shared that summer—he didn't want to think about the day he'd left—were behind them. You couldn't just jump right back into a river you'd let run dry.

"Yes," Macey said. "That captivated and confused expression. Nice."

Captivated and confused. Great. What had started with good intentions, rescue instincts and a desire to be a team player and follow orders now had him looking like a fool.

"Are we done here?" Abigail asked. "I have to change out of this silly dress and get ready for an afternoon tour."

Her dress didn't look silly to Lyman. But he certainly felt silly posing like this. How much longer could they both pretend for the camera?

"Good enough," Macey said. "We just want to give people one little taste at a time. Not overwhelm them, but tease them with hints and hopes about what's coming."

Abigail gathered up the picnic basket, and Lyman thought she was going to walk off the boat without another word, but she turned at the top of the gangplank. Macey and the photographer were ahead of her, so they couldn't see or photograph her when she turned to him and said, "I hope your father gets better soon and gets back on the trolley. It's a good thing when a person knows just what he wants in life."

Although her words were kind, Lyman felt the edge of a blade of criticism in there, too. Did he know what he wanted from life? He watched Abigail walk away and then turned his attention to the waiting tourists. Figuring out what he wanted in life wasn't a good summer project. He had plenty of other things to do.

CHAPTER EIGHT

#TrendingNiagara

THE PHOTOGRAPHS WERE the problem. Abigail was sure of it. If she hadn't spent the previous six months studying the mass wedding at Terrapin Point, she might not have had weddings on the brain. Maybe she wouldn't have jumped to marriage so quickly with Josh. *Josh.* She hadn't heard a word from him in the almost three weeks since their June 1 wedding date. No text. No email. No phone call. Nothing since the message sent via a friend that he was going to go away and "clear his head."

She hadn't found any clarity herself since that fateful day. In fact, each day contributed to the clouds obscuring her summer skies.

So, yes, it was the large panoramic photograph and the dozens of pictures of individual couples that had invited chaos into her usually ordered life. Those fifty weddings from 1950 had befuddled her. Finding out the couples' stories and researching what became of them had occupied her since January, but it was time to let it go.

"Almost done," Minerva said, her elbows on the wide desk Abigail used in the history museum. "I never thought you'd uncover all fifty happy endings."

"Almost," Abigail corrected. "In the past few weeks, I've gotten the number up to forty-eight, but I still can't find out anything about two of these couples. Plus, a few of the others didn't have what I'd call a happy ending."

Minnie cocked her head. "And what would you call a happy ending?"

Abigail snorted. "The usual. Anyway, I'm almost ready to do the final write-up on this and hand it over to the company that makes our permanent displays," Abigail said. "People can ooh and ahh all they want in about six weeks, when this goes up for public viewing."

"I thought you'd be sad when you finished this project," Minerva said. "You usually get wrapped up in whoever you're researching. Remember that time you did the research on that daredevil family? I think you would have joined them if they were still around—and hadn't met such a gruesome ending."

"I'm ready to move on," Abigail said.

"What's your next project?"

Abigail sighed. "Anything except weddings."

Minerva sat down and picked up a copy of a

large historic photograph, which was kept safely in a preservation folder. Abigail knew that photo right down to the pinstripes on the men's trousers and the bouquets in the brides' hands. She'd studied that copy relentlessly, searching for any detail that might identify some of the couples or tell their stories more completely than a typed summary in a newspaper or a passed-down recollection from a family member.

"I was just talking with Macey about the social media stats from the campaign," Minerva said. Since she did all the marketing and social media for Falling for You, she'd stepped in as Abigail's unofficial liaison with the tourism board.

Great. She didn't want to know how much she and Lyman were a source of amusement to others.

"Trending...down, I'm afraid," Minerva added.

"Oh." Despite not wanting to do the campaign in the first place and definitely not wanting the humiliation of being left at the altar to become known far and wide, Abigail's pride stiffened her back. "We're not getting likes and shares?"

"You're getting them. Quite a few. And the metrics from the hotels, shops and the park district are ticking up."

"Good."

"Just not as much as they should. After the initial picture, the dates have been popular, but—"

"Not as popular as Macey thought," Abigail

said, finishing her friend's statement so Minerva wouldn't have to strike the blow.

"But I have an idea that—I hope you won't hate me—I already ran past Macey, and she's over the moon about it."

"I'm not kissing him for the camera," Abigail said. "Or going over the falls in any kind of boat."

"Of course not," Minerva said. "At least not the boat part."

Abigail felt her face heat. Was her friend really suggesting she should kiss Lyman for the benefit of social media watchers and—perhaps slightly more compelling—to aid local tourism, which directly helped people she loved and cared about?

"See this?" Minerva said, holding up the copied photograph of the fifty couples.

"I see it in my sleep," Abigail said. "Every veil and necktie."

The door to Abigail's office opened, and her mother walked in, her step light and her face filled with expectation. "Well?" Ginny asked.

"I haven't quite gotten to it," Minerva said.

A wave of suspicion washed over Abigail. Her friend occasionally dropped by her office. Her mother sometimes did, too, to bring her something to eat or just to say hello. But this unusual tandem visit suddenly felt like an ambush.

"It'll be amazing. Just like the original event but twice the size," Ginny said. She clasped her hands together and stared in admiration at the photograph Minerva was holding up.

"What in the world are you two talking about?" Abigail said.

"We want to boost tourism, especially weddings, and since that picture of you and Lyman accidentally started things off, it seems like a sign, especially with you completing this project, and—"

"No," Abigail said. "No way are you two cooking up a plan for another mass wedding."

They both sucked in their lips and glanced at each other, guilt hanging in the air between them.

"That was 1950," Abigail said. "Not long after the war. Mass weddings were more of…a thing. A celebration of life getting back to normal. The start of the baby boom. This is not the same time period. Not everyone dreams of a big wedding." She flinched at the twin deflated expressions that greeted her, but she was the historian. She understood how times had changed, how cultural expectations weren't the same as they'd been when the panoramic photo now hanging from Minerva's hand had been taken.

"Think about the possibilities," her mother said. "We put together a contest, like a big invitation, for one hundred couples to come here and get married in the most romantic place in the country, among the thunder of the falls and the rainbows and…" Her voice faded as Abigail shook her head, and Abigail felt as if she'd trampled on hallowed ground with muddy boots.

Minerva cleared her throat. "The ad campaign. It…needs some excitement, needs a hook and a goal. If the whole thing leads up to a major event, it'll have purpose and impact."

Abigail crossed her arms and shook her head. "This will never work."

"Think about it. After almost seventy-five years, people are still talking about the mass wedding in 1950."

Abigail scoffed. "We'll see if anyone is interested. I'm interested as a historian. Everyone else might walk right past the display when it opens."

"Unless a big local event drums up interest first," her mother said, scoring a direct hit. Of course Abigail wanted the historical exhibit to be a success. And, yes, a lead-up event would help ensure that…but…

"I thought you'd love this idea," her mother said. "It combines history and weddings, which are two things you love. Isn't that why you proposed this display in the first place?"

"It was your idea," Abigail protested.

"Because your grandparents are in that picture," her mother said. "Think of how wonderful it would be to repeat it two generations later." Her tone was reverent, as if a sacred torch was being passed.

"It's not repeating it," Abigail said. "It's not

like another generation of our family is getting married."

"It's still nice. You're participating by promoting the event, and it gives you and Lyman something to do. Since you don't seem to have any chemistry on your dates, this could be a practical thing for you to do. Join forces, something like that."

Her mother meant well. She did. Ginny Warren probably thought she was letting Abigail off the hook by declaring that there was no chemistry on her dates with Lyman. She should be glad there was no apparent chemistry.

"Wait a minute," Abigail said. "You said you ran this past Macey."

Her mother and her best friend nodded, guilty expressions on their faces.

"She loved it," Ginny said. "She's talking to Lyman, and we volunteered to talk to you. That Macey is so clever. I could just see her wheels turning, and she started churning out great ideas for exactly how this would look. Of course, she promised that our business could be one of the main sponsors."

Abigail sank down in her chair and mentally recounted all the mistakes that had led her to this moment. Falling hard and fast for Josh. Getting jilted and attempting a wild bouquet toss that landed her in the arms of an ex who was now her internet boyfriend. If she gave up now, though, it wouldn't just disappoint Macey and the tourist board, it would ultimately be a setback for Niagara Falls—and especially wedding businesses like Falling for You.

Minerva's phone rang, and she looked at the screen. "It's Macey."

"She said she'd call with Lyman's answer," Ginny said.

"Should I answer it?"

Abigail sighed. "Why not. I can guess what he's going to say."

Minerva answered and listened a moment, and then she covered the mouthpiece and whispered, "Lyman says he'll do it if you want to. It's up to you."

Of course he did. Once again she wondered if he was hoping she'd be the one to say no so he didn't have to be the bad guy. Then another thought occurred to her. What if he thought this was her idea, like she was trying to exploit the situation for her own professional gain? She'd told him about her project on their first "date."

"I need details before I decide," Abigail said. "And a few days to think about it."

Minerva relayed the information to Macey and listened, nodding. "Macey wants to know what date the 1950 wedding happened?"

Abigail knew the date, the time and everything that existed in the historical record about that event. She also knew what Macey would want to do when she heard the date.

"August 15," Abigail said, her words coming out on a sigh.

Ginny did a little dance. "That gives us just under six weeks to recruit one hundred couples who want to get married together in a whirlwind wedding weekend."

She hadn't said yes, but Abigail had the impression that "yes" was what everyone else had heard.

"She wants to meet with all of us tomorrow morning," Minerva reported, the cell phone still pressed to her ear. "Lyman is available at eight before he has to go to work. Should I say yes?"

Say yes. Two words closely connected to the magic of proposals and weddings and happily-ever-afters. Josh had said yes to Abigail and hadn't had the courage to tell her his answer had turned to a no. He'd let her down.

Abigail didn't let people down. "Yes," she said, nodding at Minerva.

CHAPTER NINE

#100WeddingsAtTheFalls

LYMAN GRABBED A chocolate chip cookie from the kitchen counter.

"Don't get that on your shirt," his mother said. She carried a tray with her dinner and his father's. Lyman stuffed the cookie in his mouth and held open the kitchen door that led onto the patio, where his dad was already sitting at a table in the early-evening sun. His mother smiled her thanks. "Chocolate is impossible to get out of white cotton."

"Thanks, Mom," Lyman said with an indulgent grin. "And I doubt there will be cookies at this event—certainly none as good as yours."

"It's being catered by the Falltown Chic, which I heard someone at work say was bougie, whatever that means."

"I think it means it's too nice for someone like me, who would rather be on a boat than sitting at a table with name cards, candles and napkins you can't wad up and throw away."

"I raised you with good manners, and I'm not responsible for the military taking them away."

Lyman followed her out to the table and put a hand on his dad's shoulder. "You're not going to stay up late following this on social media, are you?"

"What else do I have to do?" his dad said. "This business of recovering is so dull. You're both probably going to die of boredom watching me."

"No chance," Lyman said. "I'm having a ridiculous summer. Not at all the geriatric-companion job I was promised."

His father laughed, and the sound was like the fresh breeze off the ocean. He'd missed his father's laugh, but would he miss the ocean? Sometimes you didn't realize what you missed until you were missing it, Lyman thought.

"You spent the last six years rescuing people with the Coast Guard, and now you're trying to help revive tourism here," his mother said. "You must get tired of doing things for other people."

"It keeps me out of trouble," he said, smiling at his mother. She wasn't smiling back, and he had a feeling she'd sit him down for the big talk one of these days, just as she had when he'd announced he was leaving for the service right after high school. He hadn't been paying close attention back then, too focused on being eighteen and thinking he had the world by the tail. But he did remember something about her advice to figure out what he wanted for himself. Abigail had said a similar thing after the boat picnic.

"You'd better get going." His mother made a shooing motion with her hand. "And I want to hear all about it tomorrow morning."

It was Saturday night, and Lyman knew there would be no avoiding questions over Sunday breakfast. Even in the privacy of his childhood home, he couldn't escape the public role he'd stumbled into.

He got in his truck and started toward the event venue—the lobby of a large hotel not far from the casino—when he passed the post office that marked the turn onto the street where Abigail lived. She'd mentioned that she still lived with her parents, and he guessed she'd been planning to move out when she got married. What had happened to that plan and all her plans for a life with a man Lyman had never laid eyes on?

The post office was on the corner of Oak Street. He'd made that turn dozens of times when they were younger and had what he'd come to consider just a summer romance. If it had meant more than that, he'd let it slide beneath the waves of his ambition—getting out of Niagara Falls, escaping the tourist cycle, the rainbows and the endless churning of the water.

Lyman turned right at the next street and then made another turn to bring him back to Oak Street. It wasn't the worst idea, dropping by her house to see if she wanted to ride with him. She'd be free to have a few drinks at the party, and he'd make sure she got home safely. Maybe it was good press for them to show up together.

Abigail's brake lights flashed red as she paused at the end of her driveway, waiting to pull out. He'd gotten there just in time. Lyman parked right behind her on the street and rolled down his window. Abigail leaned out her window. "You're blocking my driveway."

"I'm offering you a ride."

"Do I look like I need one?"

The obvious answer was no.

"We could make a nice entrance together," Lyman said.

"You could have called."

Lyman put on his four-way flashers and got out of his truck. There was no traffic on the quiet street. He walked up to Abigail's open window. "If I'd called and offered you a ride, you would have said no."

"How do you know?"

"Because you insisted on meeting me at the restaurant on our first date."

"Our first *pretend* date," Abigail corrected. She paused and seemed to take in Lyman's black suit. "You look nice, by the way."

"I'm sure you do, too."

"How do you know?" Abigail repeated her question, but this time with a hint of a smile. Maybe there was a way to get through this summer on a friendly note, working together as allies and not adversaries tossed into the same campaign.

"Can I get your door for you?" Lyman asked.

Abigail put the car in Park, rolled up the window and turned off the ignition. Lyman took that as consent and opened the door. When Abigail stepped out of the car, he took a swift breath. She wore a fitted white gown that stopped just below her knees. It didn't have any lace or puffy sleeves. White, but not like a wedding dress. Even with her high heels—pink ones—she only came up to his shoulder, but her long blond hair was piled up, leaving her elegant neck bare except for a small heart on a chain.

He wondered who had given her that heart.

He cleared his throat. "You *do* look nice," he said, repeating her assessment of him, and was rewarded with a smile.

"Let's get this over with," she said. She tossed her car keys into her small white purse and strode toward his truck, leaving a faint floral scent behind her. She got in his truck, and he turned off the flashers and began the short drive to the hotel. "Do you want to talk about the plan or rehearse or anything?" she asked.

"I read the speech Macey emailed me. She said there would be a copy at the podium, too."

"Yes," Abigail agreed.

"I'm betting your speech is longer, since you're

the expert on local mass weddings and your project basically inspired this whole thing—at least, that's what it says in my speech."

Abigail sighed. "I never imagined any of this when I started the project."

He hadn't imagined a summer like this, either. "What inspired you to start it?"

There was a long pause from the passenger seat.

"I'm a historian," Abigail said.

"How did you get to be a historian?"

"What kind of a question is that?"

"An honest one. I'm a boat captain because I took the course and got in the required hours and passed the test."

"I went to college and got a degree in history, specializing in American history with an emphasis on this region."

"Did you always want to do that?" Lyman knew he was treading in dangerous waters, bringing up the past. Had she talked about history when they'd been in high school? He'd known she was staying local and going to college, but had she ever told him what major she intended to study?

"I always liked stories about the past. People's stories and pictures, learning about what happened to them."

What did she remember about their story? Did she recall nights under the stars and watching fireworks over the falls? Did she have any pictures of them from that summer?

They were approaching the hotel's portico, where cars were lined up and uniformed parking attendants were circulating.

"Macey said we'd have free valet since we're the guests of honor," Abigail said.

"That will be a first for me and for my truck."

Abigail gave a quick chuckle. "Don't get too used to it. This whole thing is on an accelerated time schedule now, ending August 15, so we'll get to the finish line and then we disappear right back into whatever we were doing."

"Back to history tours and helping your mom's business?"

Lyman risked a glance at Abigail. She nodded. He waited for her to ask him what he'd be doing at the end of the summer, but she didn't. It was a relief.

He pulled up, unrolled his window and gave the valet his name. He almost slipped and gave his rank and title, but he caught himself. Here in Niagara Falls, he was just Lyman Roberts, with a title only when he was piloting tourists for an up-close view of the falls.

ABIGAIL STOOD UP from her red velvet–covered chair when the announcer called her name and then Lyman's. She was surprised by the applause from the other tables. People online didn't know their full names, but locals did, and their applause suggested they appreciated the campaign's efforts so far.

Lyman took her arm, steadying her as they navigated through tables to reach the podium while Macey made a short speech acknowledging the tourism board and the work of the man she called the best photographer in town. Abigail noticed Sam's shy smile when he looked at Macey. His smile lingered on Macey, perhaps because she was a familiar face in the crowded room and he wasn't accustomed to being the center of attention. Next, Macey introduced them, and Abigail had time to scan the room while Lyman made his brief remarks and Sam took pictures. She already knew what he was going to say. She'd read both of the speeches Macey had emailed.

He stuck to the script. Paused at the right moments for applause, did a nice job with self-effacing humor about being in the right place at the right time instead of being any kind of a hero. Did an equally nice job with his line about the real heroes being the locals who made Niagara Falls a welcoming and exciting vacation spot for people from around the world. Would the Lyman she'd known at eighteen have been able to pull off such a speech?

Probably not. Six years had a way of adding experience and depth. She'd certainly changed. The more she'd seen of life, the more she'd dug in her heels, believing that if she just looked hard enough at photographs and journals from the past, it would reassure her that there was a happy ending for everyone. Someday.

She'd thought she'd found hers. Abigail felt her throat tighten and shoved thoughts of Josh away. Maybe she hadn't been fair to him. Had she roped him into her desire to see something that wasn't there, at least not yet? History would look back on her behavior and be the judge. Unfortunately, the photograph that would go down in the historical record from the day wouldn't be her wedding photo. It would be Lyman catching her as her bouquet flew.

"Abigail," Lyman said, giving her a tiny nudge. He leaned close, and she smelled the crisp vanilla scent of his aftershave. The aroma reminded her of Christmas cookies. "You're up," he said.

Abigail lifted her chin. "Of course." She put on a pair of glasses with white frames to match her dress. Lyman noticed and smiled.

She took the podium and nodded to the person controlling the large screen behind her. She knew that as soon as the panoramic photograph went up on the screen and fifty couples in their wedding attire were enlarged for the audience to see, the attention would be off her. She'd planned to save it for a moment partway through her speech, but she went straight to it to begin. It felt better having all eyes in the room on the screen, not on her.

"They say a picture is worth a thousand words,"

Abigail said. Throughout the audience, men in suits and women in colorful summer dresses gave their attention to the photograph. Abigail had seen this image hundreds of times and had analyzed it under magnification. But for many people in the room, this was their first glance.

"We're here tonight to celebrate love," Abigail said, reading from Macey's script. She'd practiced it several times at home. "Niagara Falls is, of course, a town and a national wonder we all love. But it's also a place for people to celebrate their weddings, honeymoons and anniversaries. Perhaps it's even a place to fall in love."

She knew she should look over at Lyman at this moment and give the audience a little tease about their relationship. Macey had added a cue for her to do so in the script.

But she couldn't. She needed instead to focus on the story of these fifty couples. Most of whom had found their happy endings. People in the audience could assume whatever they wanted about her and Lyman.

"In this photograph taken August 15, 1950, you see fifty couples standing at Terrapin Point, their backs to the magnificence of the falls but their shining faces showing their hopes for a bright future. Not long after World War II, these couples were taking the ultimate leap and claiming their own happiness."

Abigail paused and looked at the photograph.

She used a laser pointer to draw the audience's attention to certain details. "For those history buffs among you, you may notice a few things that look different, such as the railing or the signage, perhaps a tree that's no longer there. But for the most part, it looks the same as it did then. The happy couples in the picture might be dressed differently and have different hairstyles than us, but fundamentally, they could be any one of us in this room. Because everyone wants to find love and happiness."

A lady at a table near the front applauded loudly, and a few others joined in.

"That's what this campaign is all about," Abigail continued. "We want to remind people to come to Niagara Falls and fall in love." She did risk a glance toward Lyman and noticed a very slight raise of his eyebrows. He'd come back to his hometown, but clearly not with the goal of falling in love. She knew he was there to help care for his father and then he would leave again.

She swallowed and traced a finger down the page to find where she'd left off. "We're very excited to announce that…we're going to recreate the photo! We have only six weeks, but with everyone's help, on August 15, there will be another mass wedding at Terrapin Point." She paused for applause and then added, "But we're not just going to copy what was done in 1950. We're going to double it."

The applause grew louder as the idea had a moment to sink in, and Abigail's heart thundered along with the clapping.

"Is it ambitious to persuade one hundred couples to come to the falls for their wedding? Sure. But that's why you're all here. As generous sponsors of this event, you'll help spread the word and offer enticements and package deals to couples who are willing to travel here and take part in this spectacular testament to love. Already, you've pledged hotel rooms, a giant dinner event, sightseeing packages and even a group trip on the Maid of the Mist, perhaps piloted by a special captain we all know."

This time, Abigail did glance at Lyman as instructed in the script. He smiled and acknowledged the applause, but only Abigail was close enough to see his ears grow pink.

"Perhaps someone in this room knows a couple planning to get married. Reach out to them and invite them. Use your outreach, your newsletters, your connections, and help us find the people who will be immortalized in a photograph much like this one."

Abigail paused. This next line was going to be interesting, and she was probably the only person in the room who knew how it was going to go. "Look closely at this photo," she said. She counted to ten to give people time to follow her instructions and also to build a moment of suspense. "And now, I'm going to ask you to stand up if you know someone in this picture."

She waited for a breathless moment. How closely did people know their own family history? She knew there were descendants in the room, but did they know it, too? The owner of the hotel they were in stood up, and Abigail smiled. She'd already discussed this with him and given him a heads-up so he could play along. It was part of the reason he'd agreed to host the event. He pointed to the far right in the photograph, and Abigail circled a couple with her laser pointer.

"My great-aunt and-uncle," the man said.

Abigail nodded and gave their names, including details about how they'd settled in nearby Lewiston and had been well-known for giving big Christmas parties at their home. She knew this photograph and all its local connections. "Anyone else?"

A woman Abigail knew who managed a family restaurant in town stood up. "I don't know which couple it is, but I've heard my grandparents or maybe great-grandparents were in a mass wedding here."

Abigail smiled. She used her laser pointer again. "Right there. Same last name as your family restaurant. They are one of the more mature couples in the picture, and my research tells me that they are your great-grandparents."

The woman left her seat and came closer to the

screen with an expression of wonder on her face. "I wish I had that dress," the woman said. "But I do have the wristwatch that she's wearing in this picture. Wow."

Abigail went off script. "It's magic like this that will make this an event no one will ever forget," she said. "I don't have a complete guest list for tonight, but if I did, I'd bet I could cross-reference it with my research and find quite a few more connections to local families. Although a number of the couples pictured here were from other states, too. Why were they drawn to participate? How did they hear about the event? Most importantly, did they plan to get married when they came to Niagara Falls, or did lightning strike when they got here?"

She had the attention of the room, and she gave herself goose bumps just thinking about that long-ago event. "Through my research, I know some of these answers and quite a few of their stories, but some are lost to time. As we invite couples to join us here and celebrate their love, we want to be sure to capture their stories—and their hearts."

The audience applauded, and Abigail heard Lyman clapping behind her.

"One more thing," Abigail said, "and then I'll sit down and let you get back to your food and drinks." She used her laser pointer to circle a couple in the front row of the photograph. The bride wore a full-length gown, and her veil blew over the face of the man next to her, partially obscuring it. "You can't see his entire face, but I know exactly who this couple is. They are my grandparents."

Gasps followed by applause exploded from the room. A woman at a nearby table wiped away a tear.

"They were married sixty-five years until they passed away within weeks of each other. My mother had a copy of this group wedding picture, which was how I got interested in the project for the historical society in the first place. I didn't know then that I'd be involved in bringing it to life again, but I love a good story, especially one with a happy ending that stands the test of time."

Abigail gave a little bow, acknowledging the crowd, and turned to walk down from the podium. Lyman took her arm and leaned in. "You were amazing. Fantastic."

"This is what I do," Abigail said. "Bring the past to life."

Except for her past with him. That had already had one disappointing ending, and she was wiser now, having learned from history.

CHAPTER TEN

#NiagaraFallsHoliday

THE SATURDAY MORNING after July Fourth, Abigail had booked a special history tour focusing on patriotic celebrations at the falls going back two centuries. It was a jam-packed weekend, because a lot of people had booked a long weekend, to include the Fourth itself. Hotels were full, restaurants were doing a lively business and Abigail felt as if the whole city was vibrating with excitement. As it should be. Every day and every weekend. The more she could do to continue bringing people to the falls, the better.

She'd offered this same tour the previous summer and had six participants. This year, fifteen people had signed up. Was it her face and name recognition from the #CatchTheBride hashtag or the #FallInLoveAtTheFalls campaign and now the #100weddings tag that had caught fire? She didn't want the attention to be a flash in the pan, a sensation for a few weeks before everyone forgot about the city she loved with its beauty and rich history. She had to grab this wave and hope it continued to build.

Abigail put up her red, white and blue umbrella and took her post at the entrance to Niagara Falls State Park. "You're in the right place," she said to a woman who showed her a QR code on her phone with her ticket to the event. A family with two older teens approached, and the mom showed tickets for four on her phone. "Coffee and pastries in room A," Abigail said. "We'll start with a slideshow and then go on a walking tour."

She waited, gathering and directing the next ten participants. Abigail was accustomed to a slightly older demographic for her history tours, but there were six people under eighteen and even one young couple among the participants. This was a good sign. She didn't think she was cashing in on the misfortune of her canceled wedding, exactly, but if a happy ending wasn't in the cards right now, she could at least share her love of history and other people's stories. It was better than nothing.

Abigail closed her umbrella and turned to follow her fifteen tour group members.

"Is there room for one more?"

Lyman strode up in a United States Coast Guard T-shirt, navy blue shorts and a blue ball cap with the Maid of the Mist logo on the front. It was the most casual she'd seen him in the month she'd...associated...with him. He'd usually been in his captain's uniform or dressed up for a date or an event. In shorts and a T-shirt, he reminded her very much of the Lyman she'd once known.

"I don't believe you have a ticket," she teased.

He held up his phone. "I was a late entry, just this morning."

Abigail scanned the code with her phone, and it pinged its acceptance. Did she want Lyman along on her tour? She was working, and she took her work seriously. Would attention be diverted from her carefully curated stories about the history of the holiday to the upcoming mass wedding? She didn't want distractions for her guests.

Or herself.

"Did Macey set this up?" Abigail asked. The woman from the tourist board had said she wanted to get Lyman out on a tour with her, but neither Macey nor Sam was present.

"No. This was my decision," Lyman said.

He'd chosen to spend a Saturday morning traipsing around and learning about the history of a place where he didn't want to be...or at least hadn't wanted to be.

"Aren't you working today?" she asked.

Lyman shrugged. "My boss gave me the day off to start off the long weekend. He said it was to thank me for my service, but I have the feeling I'll be pressed into plenty of service with fireworks cruises in the next two days."

"And you want to spend your day off going on a history walk?"

He smiled. "Do you ask all your guests why they want to go on your tour?"

"Of course," she said. "I build rapport with them by asking them about their interest in the area or history. It's a way to connect with them, and I can also focus on a special area of interest they might have. For example, perhaps one of my guests used to work for the local power company, and in that case I would be sure to include extra details about the role of power generation in the development of Niagara Falls."

"I'll think of a good answer when the time comes," Lyman said.

Okay, so he was coming along. She could handle this just fine. "Follow me."

"Right behind you," Lyman said.

Abigail turned and headed through the sliding glass doors of the state park visitors' center. Cool air-conditioning sent a chill over her. The door to room A was open, and the scent of coffee wafted out. She approached the podium and leaned her umbrella against it while she surveyed her group. An older man and woman were still at the refreshment table, but everyone else had found a seat in the three rows of chairs set up in a semicircle, all of them with a good view of the screen where the logo of the Niagara Falls History Museum alternated with an image of the falls.

Lyman went to the table and picked up a plate. He used the silver tongs to select a pastry, then filled a paper cup with coffee and took a seat in the last row. Removing his hat, he hung it on the back of his chair. His dark hair glistened as if it was still damp from a morning shower. Had this really been a last-minute decision, and had it really been his own?

"Good morning," Abigail said. "It's nine o'clock and everyone is here, so I'd like to honor your time and get started. Please continue to enjoy the refreshments during this twenty-minute presentation, and then I promise I'll get you out there in the sunshine for the truly fun part of the tour.

"In honor of the Independence Day weekend, our tour today will highlight various events commemorating the holiday throughout the years, and you'll also get an overview of local history in case you're new to the area or just want to know more. Of course, I'll be happy to answer any questions throughout the tour, but I have one for you as we get started. Would anyone like to share why you've chosen this tour today or what brings you to Niagara Falls?"

A man in the front row raised his hand. "We're from Florida and we just retired, so we're spending the summer touring a cooler climate instead of baking down there. It's our first trip to the state of New York and the falls."

"Welcome," Abigail said. "You couldn't have

chosen a more refreshing location. The breeze and mist off the falls always make it feel cool, even in July."

A boy who was about ten or twelve raised his hand. "I have to do a report about something I did this summer. Can I take pictures with my phone?"

Abigail smiled. "Of course. You can take pictures of the screen and anything on the tour, and I can give you the email address for the historical museum if you need any further information once you start writing your report."

Ten seconds went by and no one else raised a hand, and Abigail was about to move on when Lyman lifted his hand in the back row. Given his position in the room, no one else was likely to notice his hand up, and she could probably get away with ignoring him. But he'd given up a Saturday morning to be here, and she wanted to know why.

"Yes?" she said, nodding toward him.

"This is my hometown," he said. "I've been away for years, but now that I'm back, I'm realizing how little I actually know about the history of the place I grew up."

Everyone turned to look at him.

"Were you in the service?" a man asked, pointing to Lyman's T-shirt.

"Yes. Six years, and now I have two more in the reserves."

In all her conversations with him, he hadn't mentioned two years in the reserves. Not that she'd asked, and not that she'd been willing to talk about the future. The past was too emotional—for her, at least—and the future? They didn't have one. So, they'd stuck with the nice safe present as much as possible.

"Thank you for your service," the man said, and several other people nodded.

"You look familiar," a woman said. "Like I've seen your picture."

The teen girl with a family in the second row held up her phone. "This is cool. You two are the ones on the signs and online."

Abigail felt a stone sink from her throat to her stomach. Great. This was what people were going to remember from their time with her today. That she was the jilted bride and he was the handsome boat captain. Like they were both cartoon characters instead of real people with depth and issues and...history.

She needed to take control of the narrative.

"Like my friend Lyman in the back, I'm from here, and I love Niagara Falls for its beauty and its history. That's why I'm here to share those stories with you."

She picked up her clicker for the slide show, but as she glanced at the back of the room, she saw Lyman mouth the word *sorry*.

If he hadn't intended to steal the spotlight and draw attention to their ad campaign, why had he shown up? His statement about learning more about the history of his hometown didn't ring true somehow. The Lyman she'd once known hadn't wanted to stick around back then, and as far as she knew, this Lyman wasn't planning to stay any longer than necessary, either. So why had he come?

There were only two reasons she could imagine, and they both gave her an unsettled feeling.

He wanted to know more about Niagara Falls and was changing his tune about it.

Or he wanted to spend time with her.

ABIGAIL'S SLIDESHOW DIDN'T present many surprises for Lyman. He'd been around for fireworks shows plenty of times. How different could they look over the course of a hundred years? Fireworks were fireworks, and the falls were the falls. The picnic and parade images on the screen showed people in clothing from different time periods, but the fire trucks and floats—despite the evolving designs—were a mainstay. The usual things. Abigail told a few stories that made it interesting, though. Like the great food poisoning disaster of the early twentieth century, which had landed hundreds of people in local hospitals after a poorly executed picnic lunch. And the American bicentennial parade from 1976 that had people going all out in their sequined tops and bell-bottomed pants.

Would history look back on this summer's parade and picnic with anything more than a shrug?

Lyman didn't know, but he suspected that Abigail would find something interesting to say about it.

"And now for something special to end the show," Abigail said. "This isn't technically part of the Independence Day celebration, but it is history." The photo of the fifty wedding couples appeared on the screen, a photo that was now familiar to Lyman. Judging from the gasps in the audience and their rapt attention, he doubted anyone else in the room had seen it.

"We're planning to double this number with a mass wedding on August 15. We need all the help we can get, so if you know someone getting married or thinking of getting married, please send them our way." Abigail put up a slide with contact information for the historical museum and encouraged everyone to snap a picture with their phone.

"Ready to get moving?" Abigail asked. She took off her green-framed glasses and picked up her umbrella. "I'm happy to say this is just for navigation today, as we have sunny skies forecast for the entire weekend. You may see rainbows, but it won't be because it's raining."

Lyman tried to stay in the back of the group. Maybe he shouldn't have come along. When he'd discovered he had a free Saturday—the first all summer—he'd gone online and searched for fun things to do in Niagara Falls. He didn't know what had possessed him to do that. Shouldn't he know all the things his hometown had to offer? Among the golf, helicopter tours and boat rides, he'd found the history museum's tour schedule. It was only two hours, so he'd be home for brunch with his parents and could spend the afternoon with his dad. Let his mom shop or visit friends— whatever she did with her spare time.

He hadn't been home for a long stretch of time as an adult, and seeing the city without looking for its flaws was a new experience. Looking at Niagara Falls without searching for the exit...that was different. He needed a home base for his two years committed to the Coast Guard reserves, but that could be anywhere, especially anywhere he could find work on the water.

The tour group moved slowly, forcing him to take baby steps to remain in the back without stepping on anyone's heels. He could still hear Abigail's clear voice at the front of the group. Her experience leading tours was obvious. She didn't miss a beat or a step as she kept up an interesting narrative, the attention of the group riveted on her. Even the teenagers shoved their phones in their back pockets and appeared to be listening.

"Picture spot," Abigail announced when they came to a scenic overlook where they could almost reach out and touch the raging water right before it went over the falls. Lyman remembered visiting the same spot many times and marveling at how easy it would be for someone to jump right in. Unfortunately, he knew some people had, and the consequences didn't include a happy ending.

"While you take a few shots, I'll tell you about a Fourth of July tragedy that took place right here over a hundred years ago. There was a family of daredevils called the MacNeals. Their act included a high-wire walk across the gorge and attempts to go over the falls in a barrel. The story goes that the daughter, Iris, was the bravest among the children, but her parents wouldn't allow her to participate in the act. Her brothers got the fame while she helped her mother sew their costumes and appeared at events for the newspapers."

Abigail paused. "People thought she was just a pretty face, but that's not how she saw herself. One day, which happened to be the third of July, her brothers were preparing for a spectacular attempt at going over the falls in a specially designed boat. We have pictures of the boat." Abigail paused again. "Before and, sadly, after. You see, Iris decided to upstage her brothers and attempt the daredevil trip over the falls on the day before the holiday. She had a friend help her move the boat to this location overnight, arranged for a photographer from the newspaper to capture the entire thing and climbed in the boat right where we're standing."

People stopped taking pictures and focused on Abigail. Lyman felt himself holding his breath even though he suspected where this story was going.

"Iris was brave, certainly as much as her brothers, but she didn't know that the special boat wasn't quite finished. They'd planned to add reinforcing bars, like a modern roll cage, later in the day before their Independence Day spectacular. Iris stole the boat a day too early, and she paid the price with her life."

"Too bad her brothers didn't include her in their plans," a woman in the group said. "She might have made it."

Abigail smiled. "I'd like to think so. As a historian, I learn about so many stories from the past, and every single time I'm hoping for a happy ending. It seeps over into my present life, too, and I'm always hoping—"

She caught Lyman's glance and stopped. Were her cheeks pink? She swallowed and gazed back over the falls. "If you'd like to see the photographs of her magnificent launch right here, where she looks like a queen climbing into that boat, you can view them on the history museum's webpage. I add new pictures and stories as often as I can. Sadly, that page also contains the only known photograph of the fragments of the boat, which were found on a rock downstream."

"But other people have made it over the falls, right?" a boy asked.

Abigail smiled at him. "Yes, but I wouldn't advise it. There are a lot more tragic endings than happy ones."

Lyman wanted to ask about the happy ones, but he was afraid to say anything. This was Abigail's tour, and it was bad enough that the group had already identified him and Abigail as the #Catch-TheBride couple.

Abigail popped up her umbrella so everyone could see easily to follow her and started down the path, and the group followed her. After a few minutes of walking and another story about a special Independence Day speaker decades ago who happened to be a presidential candidate, they came to the area of Bridal Veil Falls, where Abigail's wedding should have taken place just over a month ago.

The location—especially the one near the railing—where he'd caught her midair was seared into his brain. Did Abigail bring tour groups here a lot, and did she always spare a moment to think of the groom who didn't show up? Or…did she think of Lyman showing up unexpectedly after six years of silence?

"Here we are at the famous Bridal Veil Falls. This platform gets you close to the falls, but it was also the location of a famous Votes for Women demonstration here on July 4, 1918. If you recall from the slideshow, I showed you the picture of the stage and the women all wearing white gowns and sashes. Suffragists always wore white, because that color came to symbolize their movement. The white gown…" Abigail said. Her voice trailed off for a moment.

Lyman remembered her white gown, the way it spilled over his arms and draped across his legs as he'd held her. Her look of surprise mingling with sorrow. Her groom had caused that sorrow, a much worse one than he himself had created when he'd left her at the end of a summer romance. He'd never made her any promises. Had made no plans for the future. Had made it clear his future was somewhere else.

And yet here he was.

"Now that," Abigail said, returning her attention to the group, "is a story with a happy outcome. Of course the women succeeded, after years of effort, in securing the vote, and the Nineteenth Amendment was ratified in 1920. They returned here a year later to march in a parade celebrating their success."

The group dispersed to take pictures, and Abigail directed them to be ready to move on to their next stop, Terrapin Point, in five minutes. She walked over to the railing where she would be out of the way of photographs and leaned against it, looking down at the falls. Lyman didn't need to take any touristy photos. Instead he walked to the railing and leaned next to Abigail. Not touching her, but assuming her same posture and turning his face to see the same view.

"For real, why are you here?" Abigail said.

"There's a good view. Even a rainbow." He pointed to one of the ever-present rainbows visible on the edge of Horseshoe Falls touching Canada.

"I mean on an early-morning history tour."

"Maybe I…" He paused, trying to construct his thoughts and words at the same time. "Maybe I don't want to feel like a fraud, promoting this historical event when the truth is that I don't know much about the history of Niagara Falls."

"We learned about it in school. Local history was the whole eighth-grade social studies curriculum."

Lyman laughed and turned toward Abigail. "I was a middle school boy. Do you think I was really paying attention?"

"I was," Abigail said, her voice soft. "I loved those stories even back then. Still do. I love the idea of being able to tell people's stories."

"Especially the ones with happy endings?"

She frowned, a line appearing between her eyes. Again, he fought an impulse to run a gentle finger along that line and smooth it away.

"You must think I'm a fool for trying to look on the bright side all the time and cling to the idea that…well, things will work out for people, even when it seems like they won't."

He needed a minute to unpack that statement and figure out how the moving pieces all fit together, but it wasn't a boat engine. There was no instruction manual on people's thoughts and dreams.

"Can I take your picture together?" a voice asked behind them. "This is the spot, isn't it?"

They both turned and saw one of the women from the tour, her phone held out. "Where he's holding you in your wedding dress—the picture that's on the billboards and all over the internet."

Lyman swallowed. "This is the spot, but I'm not here in an official capacity, just as a fellow tour guest, like you."

"But there's something between you two, right? Just like the hashtag says? You make a great couple," the woman said. "Are you getting married?"

Lyman couldn't breathe. There was so much wedding everything in the air. The #CatchThe-Bride hashtag, the mass wedding coming up. Was bridal fever contagious? If so, Abigail might be accustomed to it, since her mom and best friend ran a wedding business. But he hadn't given a single thought to white dresses and champagne toasts all the time he'd been in the Coast Guard.

"I'm sorry," Lyman said, "but I don't want Abigail's history tour to turn into—"

"Go ahead," Abigail interrupted him, smiling at the woman. "Just promise me you'll tag the history museum if you post it on social media." She took Lyman's arm and flashed him a radiant smile.

Just like the woman who'd climbed into a barrel to attempt the unthinkable, he'd gotten him-self into this by buying a ticket on a day when he could have been doing anything else.

CHAPTER ELEVEN

#WillTheyWed?

MINERVA HELD OPEN the door of the church while Abigail carried in a huge box of ribbons and flowers—patriotic colors for the July Fourth weekend. The morning service had ended and the parking lot cleared only moments earlier, and then Minerva, Ginny and Abigail moved in to get the church ready for an early-afternoon wedding. Most of their weddings were falls-related, but sometimes they had an indoor church wedding coupled with pictures at the falls and an outdoor reception.

"I confirmed with the horse and carriage," Ginny said as she took a bundle of flowers from her daughter. "They'll be waiting outside at one thirty. We'll get pictures, and then we'll hop in the car with the photographer and follow them as they ride through the state park to take more pictures. This is a big one."

Abigail smiled at her mother. She thought every

wedding was big. Even the ones with five guests and a minuscule budget. Marriage was a big deal to Ginny, and Abigail had always assumed it was because of her happy marriage. Although Abigail's dad traveled frequently as a civil engineer to work on projects, his homecoming every single time was a big deal. Her mother made a cake or his favorite cookies—peanut butter—and arranged her schedule so she could be the person picking him up at the airport or waiting at the kitchen door. Abigail had never told anyone, but for quite some time after Lyman had gone off to join the Coast Guard, she'd imagined herself picking him up at the airport.

She was glad she'd never revealed that to anyone, even her mother, who would understand but pity her. She didn't want to be an object of sympathy. That was why she'd taken control of the narrative about the photo with Lyman.

"I'm nervous about the heat," Minerva said. "I don't want the cake to start sliding."

"We'll hurry up and serve it if we see any sign of that," Abigail suggested. "As long as the bride and groom get pictures with the cake and then cutting it, it won't really matter in the long run if it's served early in the reception."

"Good point," her mother said. "They wanted an outdoor reception in July, so they acknowledged the risk."

Minerva laughed. "That's the *only* risk. These

two are one of my greatest matchmaking successes, and all I had to do was throw them together with the barest hint of a suggestion. I knew it would be fireworks if I just got them out of their comfort zones."

Abigail knew the story about Minerva getting a local reporter, Pete, to go on the new zip-line adventure on the Canadian side with a very pretty local girl she and Abigail had gone to high school with. Minnie had persuaded Pete that the pictures would be more interesting if he did a tandem zip, and he might as well take someone photogenic. A two-minute thrill had turned into a year of dating, and now here they were putting red, white and blue ribbons on the ends of church pews and hoping the red flowers on the wedding cake wouldn't start to bleed into the white icing.

"If the party lasts long enough, they'll have actual fireworks," Ginny said. "Although our permit for the tent in the park expires at dusk. I'm sure they'll make do somehow."

"They're in love," Minerva said with a little sigh.

"Ooh, the mass wedding thing," Ginny interrupted. "Macey told me when I saw her at the coffee shop this morning. There were thirty couples signed up within a few days of the announcement."

Abigail tied a fussy bow on a flower arrangement on the altar. "Only seventy to go."

"You'll get them," Minerva said.

Abigail held out a hand, palm up, and Minerva wordlessly handed her a pair of scissors. They'd done this countless times.

"I was hoping you'd use your matchmaking magic and help find more couples," Abigail said. "It's early July and we only have until August 15. Surely you know some couples who are just one zip line or bottle of champagne away from a proposal?"

"You act like it's so easy," Minnie said. "Matchmaking takes planning, precision and patience. Knowing just when and how to strike is the secret."

"And does this apply to your own love life?"

Minnie took back the scissors and cut a neat angle on a wide blue ribbon. "I rely on the element of surprise, and it's not likely I'd be able to pull off surprising myself, now is it?"

Ginny laughed. "I surprise myself sometimes, but I think it's age. For example, the dress I wore to the fireworks last year doesn't fit the same this year. I haven't gained a pound, but I think it's the menopause shift. Like everything is moving a bit north, south, east or west."

Abigail regarded her mother, who was still beautiful and vibrant in her early fifties. She'd gone through a few phases in which she'd tried to let her gray grow in, but she'd given up and gone back to dyeing her hair a pretty medium brown each time. Abigail got her blond hair from her dad.

"I think your geography is just fine, but you could get something new if you want," Abigail suggested. "We could go to the new boutique by the casino."

"We can go shopping, but you're getting something new, not me. You're going to the fireworks with Lyman, and there will be lots of pictures."

"It'll be dark," Abigail said. "No one will care what I'm wearing."

She planned to wear something white, as usual, to keep the bride theme going. Lyman typically wore blue, a color in which he was very attractive. For the camera, of course.

"People care," Minerva said. "Even the history museum's social media accounts, which are usually a bit quiet, if you don't mind my saying so, have gotten a big bump since Lyman showed up on your tour yesterday morning and people posted pictures."

Abigail felt a stab of guilt. She'd allowed people to post pictures and shamelessly asked them to tag the museum. The museum building needed renovations to improve the parking area, entrance and restrooms. She dreamed of making it a destination for tourists where they could get a coffee and linger over the displays, asking questions of the full-time staff the museum might be able to afford someday. It was a classic chicken-or-egg scenario—they needed funding to make improvements, but they needed to prove they were a big draw first…which required funding.

If she had to hustle and use her campaign with Lyman to do it, it would be worth it. If that hustle also helped her mom and Minerva's wedding business, it would be even more worthwhile. Abigail was in this for the people she loved, and pretending to fall for Lyman was a small price to pay.

As REQUESTED, Lyman waited on the viewing platform that extended over the Niagara River. Elevators taking visitors down to the Maid of the Mist dock took up the center part of the long platform, but the rest was open and offered an incredible view of Horseshoe Falls, the American Falls and Bridal Veil Falls. From the other side of the platform, he could look down at the Maid of the Mist dock and down the length of the Niagara River gorge until it disappeared around a bend.

There was usually a small fee for entrance onto the platform, but tonight, for the July Fourth fireworks, it was free. A section on the end affording a perfect view of the fireworks location was marked off with a barrier and a sign that said Reserved. There was a bistro table with a cooler tucked underneath, two chairs and a vase of red, white and blue flowers. Not exactly a private date, but it would look great in the pictures.

Standing out among the hundreds of tourists

attempting to claim a spot for fireworks viewing was Abigail, wearing a white top and white pants and posing by the railing as the now-familiar photographer from the tourist bureau snapped photos. Had Macey also texted Abigail with instructions on what color to wear? Maybe not. He'd already picked up on the theme. Abigail wore white for each of their official interactions. He got the symbolism.

He'd also picked up on an increased level of enthusiasm from her since the addition of the mass wedding thing and its connection to the history museum. He didn't blame her for wanting to get something out of the campaign, something that would outlast the summer. She was invested in Niagara Falls in a way he would never be.

Lyman let out a long breath and then strode to the reserved area, preparing to force a smile. However, when Abigail turned and saw him, her long blond hair, worn down tonight, blowing out behind her on the breeze, he found himself smiling without any effort. Was she as genuinely happy to see him as she seemed, or was she making a champion effort for the photos?

The crowd seemed to notice, too, their focus landing on him now. He paused midstep. It was only the attention from strangers that had his heart beating faster. All he had to do was cross the platform and follow instructions. He'd been following instructions for years.

"Happy Fourth of July," he said as he took Abigail's hand and leaned in to kiss her cheek. This was how Macey had suggested he greet her. She'd called it something like "slow burn," describing a lead-up to something bigger, like a real kiss. There was still a lot of summer left, and he didn't know where that real kiss would be in the instructions. He liked the sound of slow, but he wasn't sure about the *burn* part.

"Can you do that again, but on the other cheek?" Sam asked. Lyman noticed that Macey was standing right next to Sam, her arm practically brushing his. "It would look better in the picture."

Abigail smiled at him and did a little eye roll, and Lyman laughed at their moment of shared feelings. He backed up ten steps and prepared to kiss her other cheek, now anticipating how soft her skin would be under his lips and the hint of flowers from her hair. That would be just the same no matter what side he was on. She hadn't changed much at all in six years—not physically, anyway.

Along with the official photos, Lyman noticed tourists taking pictures, too. Did the tourists recognize them from the #CatchTheBride and #FallInLoveAtTheFalls campaign, or did they just think Lyman and Abigail must be special because they had a reserved section in a prime viewing location for the holiday fireworks?

The sun was gone, leaving only a faint streak

of red in the western sky, which seemed appropriate for the holiday. At the halfway point of summer, Lyman should be glad his tour of duty helping his parents and piloting the Maid of the Mist was also approaching halfway—even though he'd technically left everything open-ended depending on his dad's health, a potential call up from the reserves and what he decided to do with his life. He'd had a reprieve upon finishing his six years of active duty, but his reserve weekends would begin soon.

"You look very serious for such a happy holiday," Abigail said.

Lyman chuckled. "What if I think it's a very serious holiday?" He had just been having serious thoughts about the holiday's placement in the grand scheme of his summer and life.

"I think most people celebrate this holiday, they don't ponder it seriously," Abigail said.

"There's sparkling grape juice in the cooler and some glasses," Macey said, inserting herself between them. "Park rules prohibit anything stronger, even on a holiday."

Lyman opened the cooler and twisted the cap off the bottle. He poured the bubbly liquid into the clear glasses and handed one to Abigail.

"A toast to having a date with a historian on a historical holiday," he said as he gently clinked his glass against hers.

"Do that again," the photographer said.

Abigail gave him a broad smile as she touched his glass and held the pose just long enough for several pictures.

"What's your favorite part about the holiday?" Lyman asked. He sipped the drink and turned toward the railing, where the view changed from red to blue to white waterfalls illuminated for the nightly show.

"The historical context, the Declaration of Independence, freedom," Abigail said, then she grinned. "But I also like hot dogs, pie and fireworks. Best of both worlds."

"I like pie and fireworks, but hot dogs are forever ruined for me. We had a company picnic my second year in the service, and then we got called out on a missing boater in rough seas. Very rough."

"Uh-oh," Abigail said. "Were you seasick?"

"Not me, but we had a new recruit who must have eaten ten hot dogs at that picnic, because… well, I won't torture you with the details, but the only saving grace of that day was finding the missing boater alive."

"I'm glad your suffering was worth it."

"Always," Lyman said.

"You were on my tour yesterday, so you know that picnics are risky. There's historical record to support the fact," Abigail said.

"Some are fine, like the one you brought aboard the Maid."

"It had a very short time frame, and I made safe choices," Abigail said.

Lyman wondered if that was a metaphor for the two of them spending time together—keep it short and stick to safe topics. For him, that meant simply following orders and acting in the best interest of the mission, no matter what his personal feelings were.

They finished their drinks and stowed the supplies back in the cooler. Macey and Sam reviewed the pictures on Sam's camera screen and also on Macey's phone, their heads close together. Macey looked up, smiled and gave them a thumbs-up.

"Did you know there's a new hashtag?" Macey asked as they entered the five-minute countdown to fireworks.

"Is it about the history museum and the mass wedding?" Abigail asked. She looked hopeful, and why not? Of course there would be direct benefits to the things she cared about if the campaign and mass wedding were successful, but why shouldn't she cash in? No one would begrudge her that. He didn't stand to gain any personal benefit aside from pleasing his boss and leaving open a door for future employment if needed, but that didn't matter. He was in it for the greater good.

And he had a heck of a place to watch the fireworks.

"The new hashtag is #WillTheyWed," Macey said.

"What?" Abigail asked.

"You two are the they, and I believe it's refer-ring to the mass wedding. Something that hap-pened due to your spontaneous attendance at the history tour, Lyman—which was pure gold, by the way—sparked this question that seems to be asking if you two will be one of the hundred cou-ples getting married on August 15."

"We're not," Abigail said quickly.

"Of course not," Lyman agreed.

"But it's fun making people wonder," Macey said. "Isn't that part of the deal? Falling in love is all about the wondering and uncertainty. Why not let people in on the fun?"

"No one rushes into a wedding only two months after being jil—"

Abigail's words were interrupted by the first burst of fireworks over the falls. The crowd pressed against the railing and Lyman squeezed up against Abigail. Even with their reserved spot, the competition for the view made it more con-venient for Lyman to put an arm around Abigail to save a little space.

"Look at each other so I can get your faces in profile with the fireworks in between," Sam said between loud bursts of color and noise. "Perfect."

"I hate my profile," Abigail said. "My nose always looks too short for the rest of my face." Despite her concerns, she faced Lyman and held still for the camera.

"Your nose is perfect," Lyman said. Was it the holiday atmosphere or his desire to follow orders that made him blurt that out?

Abigail turned to face the fireworks, and Lyman watched the vivid colors play over her face. He kept a hand on her shoulder, and the scent of her hair mingled with the fresh smell of the water from the falls. The breeze blew the smoke away from them.

Lyman felt his phone buzz in his pocket. It was probably someone from the Coast Guard wishing him a happy holiday. His parents were home watching a holiday program on television, and the Maid of the Mist boats were safely docked. No one could need him. He ignored his phone.

It was nice having someone to spend a holiday with. Was it his imagination, or did they have some level of comfort between them, sort of like an old friend? He liked being here with her, his arm around her.

Of course, she might view their status as old friends differently, because he was the one who had ended things and left without a backward glance. But they were kids then. It was water under the bridge. Now they were sort of like colleagues, partners, a team.

Even over the noise of the fireworks and the crowd pressed around him, he heard his ringtone interrupting his thoughts. Someone was calling him.

Abigail must not have heard his phone, because

she looked up in surprise when he took his arm away and dug in his pocket for his phone. She frowned when she saw what he was doing, probably concerned he was wrecking their photo op, even though Sam had certainly taken enough pictures already. How many fireworks photos did they need?

He saw his mom's number on the screen and stuck a finger in one ear to block out noise while he answered it. He could hardly hear what she was saying, but he knew he heard the word *hospital*. "I'll be right there," he said. "I'll call you from the car."

Lyman palmed his phone and gave Abigail a quick wave.

"Wait," she said, grabbing his arm. "Are you okay? Is everything all right?"

"It's my dad, I think."

"Andy?"

Hearing her say his dad's name made everything seem more personal.

"I have to go."

"I'll go with you," Abigail said. "I can drive you."

"I can drive."

"Well, then, I'll just go along for moral support."

"You should stay and enjoy the fireworks," he said. They were wasting time. He couldn't hear his mother's words, but minutes could count with his father's history of heart disease.

"I can't," Abigail said. "Not like this." She

grabbed his hand and began to push through the crowd. Lyman could only follow with her unrelenting grip on his hand. He should be in front, burrowing through the people, because he was a lot bigger than Abigail, but her determination seemed to make up for her size. In moments, they were at the entrance of the observation deck and were leaving the crowd behind. They wouldn't even have to worry about traffic, since the fireworks were in full swing.

"Mine's right here," Abigail said. "I got here early enough to get a good parking spot."

Lyman didn't argue. He waited for Abigail to unlock the doors, then he got in the passenger seat. He told her which hospital it was, then called his mom. It went to voice mail.

"No answer?"

"No."

"The hospital has bad cell service. When I broke my arm three years ago, Minnie went with me and left my mom in charge of a wedding, but she was panicking because she couldn't get a call through and she wanted to tell my mom something important about the wedding cake delivery."

"You broke your arm?"

Abigail gave a little shrug as she pulled out of the parking lot and got on the road. Everyone was watching fireworks, so the streets were deserted.

"How did it happen?"

"I was using a ladder to hang up a decoration

at the reception hall, and I leaned out a little too far and lost my balance."

"Which arm?"

"Right."

"At least that was good, since you're left-handed."

He didn't know why he remembered that detail about her, and her quick glance toward him demonstrated that she was surprised, too.

She cleared her throat. "We'll be there in five minutes. You should try calling your mom again."

This time, the call connected. "What's going on?" He listened as his mother gave a quick, concise overview of the previous hour, beginning with an assurance that his dad was okay and it was just a scare.

"Dad's okay," he whispered to Abigail, though his relief lasted about twenty more seconds when he registered what his mother was saying. His dad had discomfort in his chest and pain down his left arm, and that had been enough for his mother to dial 911. It wasn't until they got to the hospital that he admitted he'd done something he shouldn't have. While Lyman was at the history tour the previous morning and his mom was at the grocery store, Andy had decided to help out around the house and had mowed the tiny front lawn.

"When I got home from the tour, he told me the neighbor kid had come over and mowed it," Lyman said, exasperation in every word. "What was he thinking?"

"You know your father," his mother said. "He wants to help, and he's tired of everyone waiting on him. So, long story short, the pain is probably muscular and has nothing to do with his heart. It's just been a long time since he's pulled like that, and he shouldn't have been doing it."

"I should have mowed the lawn. That was my responsibility."

"Just get here and give us a ride home, all right? You can beat yourself up later over it. Love you, honey," his mother said.

"Love you, too," he said and disconnected. He sat silent for a moment. He could see the lights of the hospital up ahead. "I guess you heard most of that."

"Not everything, but I did hear your mom threatening to beat you up," Abigail said.

"No, she said—" He paused and laughed. "Okay, you know what she said. Worse yet, I left my truck back at the park, so do you think you could drive my whole family home and then give me a ride back to my truck tonight? It's okay if you can't. I'll call someone."

"Don't you dare," Abigail said. "I'm going to take your dad's side. I'll tell him how I tried running the sweeper with my arm in a cast. My mom had a fit! It'll make the car ride to your house more fun."

"I owe you."

"Good. Then you can explain to Macey why

we ran away during the fireworks and ruined her PR event."

Lyman took off his seat belt as Abigail pulled into a spot near the emergency entrance. He reached over and put his hand over hers. "Thank you."

"We're a team," Abigail said lightly, but she let Lyman's hand linger over hers for a long moment.

CHAPTER TWELVE

#FallsLoveCanada

ABIGAIL HAD CROSSED the Rainbow Bridge, which linked the American city of Niagara Falls with the Canadian city of the same name, hundreds of times. This time was different. For one thing, she was usually in a car with her mom or a friend making the border crossing to enjoy the shops, restaurants and beautiful hotels on the other side. Sometimes they went to Niagara-on-the-Lake, just a half hour's drive into Canada, to visit the quaint village or see a play or musical at the Shaw Festival.

This time, she was on foot, using the pedestrian lane of the bridge, and she was with Lyman.

"We're almost halfway," she said. "I hope you brought your passport." She patted her purse, where her own passport was zipped into the outside pocket. "Or do you have some special military ID?"

"That's only if I'm on official military business," Lyman said. The sunshine glanced off his light blue Niagara Falls T-shirt depicting a waterfall and the flags of both countries. Abigail wore a similar T-shirt in white. Macey had provided them a few days ago in preparation for this event. "Unless there's a boat in distress on the Canadian side, I'm off duty."

Abigail laughed. "Let's hope not. We have enough to think about today, and we are very lucky to be let out without a chaperone."

"You don't miss Macey and Sam following us around?"

"No. And I hope our selfies prove we can be trusted on our own."

Abigail meant, of course, that they could be trusted to fulfill the PR mission on their own. They didn't need a chaperone in the traditional sense of the word. They were well past their teen years, and there was nothing romantic between them. They were well past that, too.

"It was her idea to make our photos from today seem more personal. She used the word *intimate*," Abigail said. The word felt odd hanging in the air between them. She had made every effort to treat Lyman as a coworker on a shared mission rather than an ex-boyfriend, a jilted-bride catcher or even a friend. But the night she'd driven him to the hospital had shifted something between them. It had been the impulse of a moment, her desire to be helpful and practical. But it had also felt like the action of a friend. An old friend who knew his family and what they were going through.

"Does she want to review the pictures before we post them?"

Abigail shook her head. "Strangely, no. She wants us to do this on our own as a subtle way of freshening up the campaign now that we're half-way through it. I think she wants us to take the reins."

Lyman walked next to her. She was on the side of the bridge closest to the water, while the line of cars waiting to go through Border Patrol were on the other side of Lyman. It was a sunny Friday morning, and they were making the trip across the bridge to draw on the Canadian connection. Macey had received some feedback about not making the campaign a "competition" with Canada and instead highlighting tourism of the whole area for the benefit of all. Abigail suspected she was hoping some Canadian couples would join the mass wedding so they could add the word *international* to the promotion.

"I think the new hashtag makes it pretty personal," he said. "'Will they or won't they?' I was even asked about it at work twice this week."

Abigail nodded. "A visitor to the history museum asked me about it, and a wedding guest peppered my mother with questions this week, too. I guess that means the campaign to fall in love at the falls is working." She shrugged. "Who knows.

Maybe history will show that it was a good thing when I got jilted."

She couldn't believe she'd said it out loud. She was equally astonished that such a thought had crossed her mind and that her mouth had betrayed her by saying it. Especially in front of the worst person in the world to admit it to. If she'd blundered into that statement with her mom or Minerva, it would be different. They would assure her that what happened was terrible but she deserved better and, in time, she'd heal and find someone who truly loved her. They'd said as much.

But she'd just blurted this in front of Lyman. Who stopped walking. She sensed this rather than saw it, because she closed her eyes and gripped the handrail. She stopped walking, too. What if she hadn't been jilted and was, instead, now married to Josh? The thought was impossible. Josh didn't love her. She knew that now, but what if she didn't know it and he'd gone on pretending and even gone so far as to marry her?

It would be terrible. She opened her eyes and breathed in a deep lungful of misty air. The height of the bridge over the gorge made her dizzy for a moment, and she concentrated on filling her body with a big, refreshing breath. For the first time in over a month, she was glad she had been prevented from making a terrible mistake—not by her own perception or wisdom, but by someone else's.

Would she ever be able to trust herself again?

"You shouldn't say that," Lyman said when she finally turned to him as he stood motionless on the sidewalk behind her.

The skyline of the American side was behind him, with its casino building rising over some low restaurants and hotels. People went there to take their chances, knowing there was a much greater chance of losing than winning. Was that life? Was she ever going to be ready to take a risk again?

"What happened to you was terrible. You deserve better."

The words were like a warm embrace for a moment, so much like what her mother or a friend—someone who truly loved her—would say. It was nice that Lyman would say those words. But then, he had also chosen to leave her behind. It wasn't the same, of course. There had been no promises, no ring. But at the time, she'd thought in her heart that their summer love was a beginning, not the final chapter Lyman seemed to consider it. Running into each other now wasn't the sequel to their story. It didn't mean anything.

"So what do you say to them?" Abigail asked. "The people who ask the hashtag question?"

Lyman cracked a small smile. "The first time it happened, I stared at the person for so long they probably regretted asking it. I didn't mean to be rude, but I was put on the spot and didn't know what to say. I thought I was good at thinking fast in an emergency."

Abigail laughed. "I'm sure you are." She thought of the way he'd caught her on her wedding day and held her securely in his arms. She'd felt safe for just a moment, as if she was a stranded swimmer and had latched on to something solid.

"But I thought about it, so the next time it happened, I had an answer ready."

"What was your answer?" Abigail asked. They stood in the middle of the wide bridge, surrounded by two countries and one of the natural wonders of the world, but all she could think about was Lyman's prepared answer to that question.

"I told the next person that the summer has been full of surprises so far, and I don't know how it will end."

HE WASN'T LYING. The summer *had* been full of surprises, and he truly didn't know how it would end. He'd planned to stay as long as his family needed him to, and then he'd figure out where to go from there. He had the option to re-enlist with the Coast Guard for another period of time, and that option would remain open throughout his mandatory two years in the reserves.

He was on reserve. In a holding pattern. Ready, but not necessarily needed. It was a strange place to be. Was that why he found himself feeling exposed and vulnerable, as if he was looking for a landmark or an anchor, something to tell him where he should be?

He knew who he was. An only son, a veteran, a boat captain and a participant in a strange campaign that brought him face-to-face with his past—a past he'd never examined too closely, and one in which he didn't look too good, at least not to Abigail.

"We should take pictures on the bridge," Abigail said. She unzipped her purse and took out her phone. "Unless you want to wait until later and get them on the return trip."

"Now's good. The sun will be higher when we come back, and it will cast shadows."

Lyman moved behind Abigail as she held up her camera and carefully framed a shot with the falls in the background. "Smile," she said. He did as directed, and she took several shots. "We should do a fun picture next," she said. "We could make faces or stick out our tongues, something fun that friends would do."

"We are friends," he said.

"As far as our audience knows, yes," Abigail said.

Only for an audience? Not because they really were friends? She snapped a picture, and Lyman knew she caught his frown.

"You have to look like you're having fun," she said. "Not like you're trying to figure out a calculus problem."

"My math face would be much more serious than that."

They both laughed, and Abigail snapped some more pictures. He hoped he looked happy in those, not as if he was forcing a smile or posing. Just a happy guy out for the day with an old friend. Two hometown kids reunited for a good cause.

"Will you send me these pictures?" he asked. "Even the ones you don't decide to post?" He wanted to have some of the pictures of the two of them that were just for his and Abigail's own use, not to be shared with everyone. Didn't they have a right to keep some of their summer experience and adventures just for themselves and not put it out there for public consumption?

"We should decide together which ones to post," Abigail said. "We'll find a shady spot on the Canadian side and go through them so we can post some throughout the day. That way it will seem authentic in case anyone is following along in real time."

It would only seem authentic. Of course it would, Lyman thought. Their time belonged to the campaign, not to them.

CHAPTER THIRTEEN

#FunDayAtTheFalls

"WE NEED A lot of pictures with the American Falls in the background," Abigail said. "The best view of the American Falls is from the Canadian side, so it's a nice crossover between the countries."

Mutual benefit, she thought. Just like the hashtags and events. They posed along the edge and took selfies, and a few fellow tourists offered to take their picture for them in exchange for the same. Lyman used a silver-haired man's phone to take a picture of him with his grandchildren. It all felt so normal, being out and about enjoying the scenery.

Wouldn't it be nice if they were a real couple... of friends.

"I used to love the restaurant tucked into the gardens by the bridge," Lyman said. "It has a view and shade. What do you think of brunch?"

It wasn't in the official plan. They were just going to go snap a bunch of pictures. But it was late morning, and they had been walking a lot.

"I could eat," she said.

They climbed the terraced steps and walked through a formal garden complete with a fish pond and an amphitheater, and then they found the entrance to the outdoor seating area, where mulberry trees and umbrellas shaded tables that had a view of the falls.

Lyman went straight for the menu when they sat down, but Abigail looked out over the garden. "This always reminds me of my favorite book from when I was little. Did you ever read *The Secret Garden*?" At the shake of his head, she said, "It's about a girl and a boy who both resolve their struggles by working together to bring a forgotten garden back to life."

It was a personal thing to share, the kind of thing they might have discussed back when they were dating for real. She'd read that book over and over. The children in the stories had a happy ending, which they worked hard to create, and knowing that happy ending was coming was what had Abigail picking up the book over and over.

"I liked pirate books," Lyman said. "But knowing what I do now about actual pirates, I believe they were seriously misrepresented in kids' books."

"Did you encounter real pirates?"

"Only once directly, but we heard a lot about them. We don't operate very far outside the U.S. borders, but sometimes pirates get bold enough to come close. They're treacherous, not at all like the fun movies with the talking parrots and peg legs."

Abigail wanted to ask more, but Lyman laid his menu down and announced he was having the big breakfast platter because he was starving. It was her cue to make a choice. They did have goals for the day and couldn't linger too long over brunch.

She laid her menu on top of his, and their server came over.

"You first," Lyman said.

"Big breakfast platter with Canadian bacon, eggs over hard, whole wheat toast and hash browns," Abigail said.

Lyman smiled at her and then toward the server. "Same for me."

"I usually eat that amount of food throughout an entire day," Abigail said.

"But brunch is the ultimate cheater meal. It's technically both breakfast and lunch, so you can eat twice the food." Lyman grinned. "You see the logic, right?"

"Strangely, yes. And this place has a reputation for an amazing breakfast. Since we're here, we might as well enjoy it."

"Exactly," Lyman said. "So my view of pirates was exposed as a fraud, but how about your thoughts about gardens. Did you ever try making a walled garden in your backyard?"

"It has walls already."

"I remember a wood fence for the dog you had in high school. Does that count as walls?"

Anything could count as a wall, Abigail thought, including things you couldn't touch, like history or emotional barriers. She had walls.

"It counts, even though that fence was to keep him in and not invaders out, but I did try to plant bulbs in a patch in the one corner. The grass always wants to creep in, but I pull it out every year and let the tulips and crocuses have their space."

"Maybe I should live up to my favorite books and put together a pirate costume for Halloween. It wouldn't have been funny in the Coast Guard, but I could get away with it here."

"But you won't be here at Halloween, will you?" Abigail asked. And then she wished she hadn't. It was none of her business, and she didn't want him to think it mattered to her. She'd gotten over him leaving once, and this time her heart was clearly not involved. What he did or did not do made no difference to her.

"I don't know my plans," he admitted. "My dad mowed the lawn, as you know, and yesterday he drove himself to the trolley office to say hello to his friends at work. He was dead tired when he got home, but he's definitely getting better. I doubt they'll need my help much longer."

"But you'll stay until the big wedding," Abigail said. She wished her voice didn't have a note of desperation in it. The project had to be successful. She was committed. *They* were committed.

"I said I would, and I don't go back on my word," Lyman said.

"That's true. I remember last time you left town. You'd warned everyone you were going. You'd said it all summer. But for some reason, I... People were still surprised."

"I was truthful with you back then," he said.

"Of course you were," she said lightly. "Which is why I was fine with your leaving back then and it doesn't matter either way to me now. I just want to be sure we finish this job."

The server brought wide plates of food, thank goodness, so Abigail could take some time to round up her thoughts. She'd meant it when she said his actions did not affect her—she just wanted to make sure he knew she meant it. She was tempted to bring it up again and nail down the point, but would that have the opposite effect?

LYMAN ATE HALF of everything and then went back for a second pass at the giant plate of breakfast food. It was a strategy he'd perfected while serving on boats: eat half and decide if you wanted to top off the tank. Depending on the wind and the waves, sometimes you did and sometimes you didn't.

Judging the weather and hazards was a lot less clear when it came to his relationship with Abigail. He was afraid to touch on anything from the past or the future, but she'd been the one to bring it up. Was it because she was fearless about it or the opposite? He'd known guys in the service who wanted to talk a lot about the things Lyman had finally figured out scared them.

"Aside from pictures, we don't have a script to follow, do we?" Lyman asked.

Abigail shook her head with her mouth full.

"So we could deviate and tour something I've always wanted to see?"

She swallowed. "What have you always wanted to see?"

"The fort on the Canadian side. I've seen the American one dozens of times. My parents used to take me there on picnics for my birthday. But we never got to the one close to Niagara-on-the-Lake."

"Fort George," Abigail said.

"Have you been there?"

"Years ago. I've read a lot about it as I've studied local history. Its history is closely linked with the American fort. I could tell you all about it if you like."

"Maybe this is a bad idea if you've already seen it. I don't want you to be bored," he said.

"I'm never bored by history. But we don't have a car, and Fort George is about a thirty-minute drive from here."

"Oh. Is there a trolley like on the American side?"

He thought of his father and how much he would like touring the fort. Why hadn't they made the short drive across the bridge and up the Niagara River Parkway when he was growing up? His parents had passports and loved a day trip. It reminded Lyman that summer days went fast. Life was short and you had to make the most of it. He'd seen other lives cut short in his time in the service, and his father's health issues were making him think twice about…everything. Especially the way he treated people he cared about.

"They have a bus system," Abigail said. "But I don't think it goes all the way to Fort George."

"Another time," Lyman said. "I've gone this long without seeing it and survived."

"We could take a rideshare," Abigail suggested. She held up her phone, the Uber app open on her screen.

Abigail seemed anxious to make the trip happen. Was she trying to make him happy, or was she just relieved to have something concrete to do with their time? She loved history. Maybe it was as simple as that.

"I don't think it will make for romantic photographs," Lyman said, giving Abigail an opportunity to back out. "If you think it would be a waste of our time, we could wander around the flower gardens and sip overpriced fancy drinks. The kind of things people post pictures of on social media all the time."

Abigail laughed. "Is that your impression of social media? Wandering around in gardens and taking staged photos of food and drinks?"

"Am I wrong?" Lyman asked.

"Not entirely. And we missed our opportunity to take pictures of our food, because we just dug in."

"So is it too risky and off topic to go to the fort?"

She shook her head. "Since we're volunteers doing this for the local good, I think we can do what we want today. My only request is that I get to pop into a few of the shops in Niagara-on-the-Lake after we tour the fort."

"Will I need to take pictures of you in boutiques or be the pack mule for all your purchases?" Lyman asked.

Abigail laughed. "No. But we better get moving if we want to have time for both."

In the car on the way farther into Canada, Lyman read up on the history of the fort on his phone. "It's hard to believe Canada and the United States were on opposite sides of a war," he said. "Did you know the fort was really important during the War of 1812, when—" He looked up and noticed the expression on Abigail's face. He shut his mouth, and they both laughed. "Sorry," he said. "One of us is a local history scholar, and it's not me."

Abigail smiled and put a hand on his arm. "It's nice to find an interest we have in common after all…well, after all the history we seem to have."

Although they were on their way to tour a place that was all about the past, Lyman felt very interested in the present as he rode with Abigail and heard her sweet voice and smelled the floral aroma of her hair.

Maybe it was because the present was all they had—and all they'd ever have.

CHAPTER FOURTEEN

#InLoveAtNiagara

THE HASHTAG HAD changed again, Abigail noticed when she picked up her phone. From #CatchThe-Bride to #WillTheyWontThey to, now, #InLove-AtNiagara. It was a reaction to their fun day out in Canada three days ago. Unlike the other ones, this one had started small and grown instead of starting with a lot of reactions and then dwindling after a day or two.

She was in love *with* Niagara and all the scenic beauty and history. But in love *at* Niagara? That was different.

"I love the picture of Lyman trying out the beds at the fort and finding out he would have been way too tall to live there," her mother said as she put down the laundry basket on a hallway table outside Abigail's bedroom. The small two-bedroom, two-bath home had a laundry area in the garage, but they always sorted their clothes here. It was a familiar mother-daughter activity, and they'd had many conversations while pairing socks.

"There were lots of good pictures," Abigail said neutrally. "Canada is lovely, and the weather was perfect."

Her mother had never been a social media fan, but she'd discovered it this summer and now had three different apps on her phone. She followed dozens of accounts related to Niagara Falls and had become a junkie for anything wedding-related, especially sites showing decorated outdoor venues. Ginny Warren was serious about giving her weddings a magical touch and had found a treasure trove of ideas now that she had a reason to engage online.

"His expression was so funny, and his feet hung off the bed by at least six inches," her mother said as she folded a T-shirt with much more precision than it needed.

"People were, on average, shorter a few hundred years ago," Abigail said, "but Lyman is tall even for modern times."

"I wonder if he grew more after he left town," her mother said. "I don't remember exactly how tall he was when you two were dating."

They'd hardly spoken of it. Her mother, although known to blunder into sensitive topics in a well-meaning way, had been almost perfect in her record of not bringing up Abigail's first heartbreak.

Especially given the jilted-bride situation. And Abigail was grateful for it.

"Do you remember?" Ginny asked. "How tall he was?"

Until now, apparently. Was this because of the new hashtag? Every one seemed to shove their relationship a bit harder toward something real and meaningful. Was everyone really fooled by the pictures?

"I don't remember exactly," Abigail said. She did remember putting her head on Lyman's shoulder at a school dance. Recalled the picture she still kept where she was standing two steps above him on the stairs leading down to the falls near the Bridal Veil viewing platform. The two-step advantage had put them at equal heights, and they were both grinning in the picture, as if there were other hidden jokes to be discovered.

In fact, they'd recreated the picture during their tour of Fort George, using steps leading to one of the buildings. But she hadn't posted it. Instead, she'd kept it on her phone without even sending it to Lyman. He wouldn't remember that picture from six summers ago anyway. He wouldn't get the joke.

"I need to tell you something," her mother said. She scooped the last sock out of the laundry basket and paired it with one in her own pile.

Abigail could guess it was serious from her mother's expression. Her first thought was that her mom knew her feelings about Lyman were getting a bit muddled. Arms-lengthing had worked so well for the first month. The night of the fireworks had reminded her they could be—and had been—friends. And the day trip to Canada had given her a taste of how fun that friendship could be. If her mother was about to lecture her about guarding her heart and keeping things all business between herself and Lyman, Abigail was already there, one step ahead of Ginny. She'd given herself the same lecture.

"He came to me first because he wasn't sure how you'd feel about him," her mother said.

"Lyman?"

Ginny's face twisted with surprise. "No. Josh. He's back in town for a week, and he contacted me and Minerva late this afternoon—you know he had our numbers because of the…uh…wedding planning—and he wanted to know if you'd be willing to talk to him or if you were too mad and never wanted to see him again."

Abigail sucked in a breath and held it. Josh was back in town and wanted to see her. Had even been thoughtful enough to check first with the two people she loved most, just in case.

"Why does he want to see me?"

Her mother touched her shoulder. "I asked him that, too. Of course, I hoped he'd changed his mind and was here to beg you to take him back."

"You did?" Abigail said. How could her mother

think she'd take back a guy who left her like he did, without even the courtesy of telling her himself? "Mom, I—"

"Because I thought you deserved the satisfaction of telling him to get out of town and take his apology with him," Ginny said.

Abigail laughed. "Is that what you told him?"

"No. I told him I would give you his message and it would be up to you to decide if you wanted to see him."

Abigail gathered up her pile of clothes and hugged them to her.

"I don't know," she said. "I need to think about it."

"He's here for a week. Said he had to clean out his apartment since he's decided to move to Colorado permanently."

"So he's just been visiting there for over a month, just hanging around and..." She was startled to realize she hadn't thought about him much. Had driven past the apartment he'd rented while he worked a temp job at a local business. She'd been tempted to see if the landlord would let her in so she could get her favorite jacket, which she'd left over a chair in his dining area. If she'd had a key, she might have taken Minerva with her and gone to get it.

But he'd never given her a key, even though she was going to move in with him after the wedding. And she had never actually packed up her stuff at her parents' house, thinking there would be plenty of time for that later.

Had they been doomed and she hadn't even known it until everyone else found out in a dramatic way?

"It hasn't been that long," Ginny said. "And maybe he's found a job there. You never know."

Of course she didn't know. And she shouldn't care. She'd moved on with her life and found a strong role and purpose. Her exhibit about the mass wedding was going to be fabulous, even if it was a bit ironic that it got a big boost from her own failed wedding. Lemons to lemonade.

She'd gone through the stages. Shock first. Then anger and betrayal. Then a gut-wrenching feeling of not being good enough and being, somehow, to blame. And then where she was now—the wondering. It had been over five weeks, and she'd arrived at wondering what role she'd played in the failure. Had Josh also gone through those stages, or was it different for the person who did the leaving?

She'd never been the one to leave. Suddenly, she thought of Lyman and wondered what he would think about her meeting up with her ex.

"You should think about it, but don't feel you have to see him," her mother advised. "I was prepared to welcome Josh as a member of the family, but after what he did, I don't give a fig about his feelings, and I wouldn't blame you if you didn't, either."

"I'll think about it," Abigail said. "And thank you for giving me the message. You could have told him to get out of town yourself."

Her mother smiled. "Believe me, I thought about it. You're the most precious person in the world to me and your father, and your happiness matters most."

Abigail took her laundry to her room, resolving to sleep on the question of Josh and not think about it until the next morning.

I would like my jacket back, ABIGAIL TEXTED JOSH the next morning. I heard you were back in town and it's the only thing I want from you.

Okay. Where can I bring it?

That was it? No request for her time or a plea to at least give him a chance to explain or apologize? Just *where can I bring it?*

Fine.

I'm meeting a tour group at the visitors' center steps at ten o'clock. You can bring it then.

Having him stop by a public place was a safe choice. If he had something to say, it would have to be brief, and she'd have the added bonus of reclaiming her jacket.

From the moment Josh showed up, Abigail knew

it wasn't going to be a quick custody swap of the clothing. He brought coffee, with two creamers and one sugar, how she liked it. She thought it sweet at first, but then she remembered they had almost been married. Was it such a stretch for him to know about her coffee preference? Cindy at the Tim Hortons knew, too, and she hadn't pledged her love to Cindy.

"I just wanted to see you and assure myself you were okay," he said.

He wanted to assure himself? This was about *his* feelings?

"Of course I'm okay," she said. She was still eating and breathing and working, and she hadn't spent every summer day since the jilting crying over him in her bedroom. She hadn't cried very much at all. Maybe it was because she'd immediately gotten busy with the tourism promotion and then the mass wedding plans.

In fact, she was pretty sure she'd shed more tears at the end of the summer Lyman left to join the Coast Guard. She was older and wiser now, and her entire self wasn't wrapped up in whether some man wanted her or not.

"I should have told you in person and called it off before the last minute," Josh said. "I'm sorry about the way I did it."

Abigail tilted her head and looked at him. She opened the coffee's lid and set it on a low stone wall and then took her time putting creamer in and stirring it. "You're not sorry for doing it, but just the way you did it."

"That's not exactly what I mean."

"It's what you just said," she pointed out. "You don't want to feel guilty about it. Fine. Don't feel guilty."

Tourists were gathering and mingling around them, and the breeze coming from the falls lifted her hair and blew a strand across her eyes. It reminded her of her wedding veil blowing across her face at a spot not far from where she and Josh stood. It seemed an eternity ago.

A family still wearing their blue Maid of the Mist raincoats walked past. They must have been on an early boat, and she wondered if Lyman would be their captain.

"You should go," she told Josh.

"I thought we could talk."

Abigail regarded him, his sunny good looks and lanky frame. She'd fallen in love with his carefree manner and go-with-the-flow attitude that was so different from hers. She'd thought he was a breath of fresh air, always thinking about the future and uninterested in the past, like she was, but now she realized he was more like something caught on that breeze, floating wherever it was pushed. Had she pushed him into marriage? Should she give him a chance to tell his side?

"Maybe sometime while you're in town this week," she said.

"Lunch?"

Today? She needed more than a few hours' notice if she was going to sit across a table from him and rehash what had gone wrong.

"I have a tour coming any minute." She checked her phone. Where was the family group of ten she was supposed to be meeting? Had they gotten the location mixed up?

There was a message from the manager of the history tours.

Family emergency. Group canceled the tour.

Abigail's shoulders sagged when she read it. Now she'd have no excuse to send Josh on his way.

But Josh didn't know that. As far as he knew, there were a dozen people counting on her to make their vacation complete by revealing the hidden stories of Niagara Falls' history.

Maybe it was a sign that she should get this conversation with Josh over with. But what was there to talk about?

She swallowed a sip of coffee. "Actually, that tour has been rescheduled. I have a lot of work to do on a display I'm working on—"

"The big wedding thing?" Josh asked.

"Yes."

"I saw all the posts about having another mass wedding. Looks like your idea has really caught on."

"It wasn't entirely my idea, but I'm part of it."

"I know," he said.

His two little words implied that he knew all about the #CatchTheBride photo that had sparked the whole promotional and wedding campaign. A ripple of anger went through Abigail. Of course he knew about it. He was the reason she'd been running alone toward the falls in the first place. If he'd shown up and married her like he was supposed to—

Then she'd be married to him right now.

And that thought made her feel like a leftover balloon after a party. Sagging a bit, perhaps being kicked around the dance floor.

He'd done her a favor, but not out of the kindness of his heart. He'd been saving himself, too.

"I don't want to have lunch with you, Josh."

"Why not?"

She faced him and met his gaze head-on. "Why didn't you want to marry me?"

He flinched but then seemed to steady himself. "I did, at first. When I said yes, I meant it. It sounded like a good idea. We were having fun, and I really cared about you."

"But then?" Was she foolish for asking? Why open a wound that had been healing over the last six weeks? Why give Josh space in her head and her heart when it had taken him six entire weeks to contact her?

She hadn't contacted him, either, though. Had he been waiting to hear from her? She wanted to shake her head. What was the natural order of things? Did the jilter or the jiltee open the line of communication and offer an olive branch?

"You know I was only living here temporarily," Josh said. "I do temp jobs and move from place to place. I didn't have a permanent home growing up, since my mom was in the Air Force, and the idea of putting down roots... Well, sometimes I get drawn in by the thought, like it's a perfect fantasy. I got sucked in by thinking about a home and...you."

She held up a hand. "Wait. Are you saying I was like some spider in a web who ensnared you?"

"You did ask me to dance at that wedding reception."

"You asked me. You hardly knew your coworker who was getting married, and I was done serving cake."

"You were nice. I didn't know anyone in town, and spending time with you was fun. You knew everyone and everything about Niagara Falls. I got carried away," he said. "And you're always thinking about weddings—"

"I'm not always thinking about weddings," she said.

"That's your job."

"It's my mom and best friend's job. I work at the history museum."

Josh crossed his arms and looked down at her. "Where you were heavily invested in that picture of fifty couples getting married. You tracked down their history and whereabouts like a dog on a scent."

Abigail opened her mouth but couldn't make a sound for a moment. She had to collect her thoughts. She turned her back to Josh and looked toward the falls. The trees blocked most of the view, but she heard the distant thundering sound and saw the mist rising above the trees. The water kept moving. It didn't care what human dramas were playing out on its shores. She'd always found it comforting, part of the musical background of her life. But right now it seemed to mock her. It was rushing and making noise and...going where?

Where was her own life going?

She felt Josh's hands on her shoulders, and her first inclination was to shake them off and step away, but it was easier talking to him when she was looking at the falls and not him. Maybe the falls weren't mocking her. Maybe they were consoling her and telling her they'd be there for the next thousand years, no matter what.

"So what happened?" she asked, of herself as much as Josh.

"I chickened out," he said. He took his hands off her shoulders, but she could sense him standing right behind her. Was he looking at the falls, too? They didn't mean the same thing to him. The permanence wasn't part of who he was. "I chose moving on instead of settling down."

"That's what your friend said when he came to tell me. It was funny—I thought he was the first of your guests to show up for the wedding." She couldn't say *our wedding*. It hadn't belonged to them. As it turned out, she was the one who wanted it, not him. And one person wanting something was not enough. She thought of those fifty couples in the photograph waiting for her back at her office. Were they going into marriage with their eyes wide-open, both parties coming to it with equal enthusiasm? Or was one of them driving the bus, bringing the enthusiasm and commitment that would be enough to sustain the whole thing?

Maybe she had gotten wrapped up in wedding fever and Josh was right there, convenient and appealing. She'd been the driver but he'd only wanted a short ride. Why hadn't she seen that?

"You deserve someone who wants to be here and make something permanent with you," Josh said.

Somehow, that made her think of Lyman. He'd left town, too, but he hadn't made any promises to her or any big statements about her deserving someone who wanted her permanently. Permanent. Like a rock formation. He'd been up front about his plans and then he'd followed through, leaving in search of what he wanted.

There was something about that that she respected, now that she thought about it.

"I'll decide what I deserve," Abigail said, turning to face her former fiancé. "And right now, I'd like my jacket back, please."

She held out her hand, and Josh put down the bag he was carrying and dug out her coat. It was a wrinkled mess from being jammed in the pack, but those wrinkles would come out eventually and she'd forget all about them.

"Goodbye hug?" Josh asked, arms open.

Abigail allowed a brief hug, but she kept her eyes open. Which was when she saw Lyman walking by. He paused and looked at her as if he was asking if she needed to be rescued. He stood, broad-shouldered, a few feet away, but then she shook her head at him and he turned and walked away.

She didn't need him or anyone else to rescue her. She needed to decide for herself what she wanted for her future.

CHAPTER FIFTEEN

#NiagaraTrolleyLove

LYMAN OFFERED ABIGAIL a hand as she stepped onto the trolley at the stop closest to Prospect Point. He'd just gotten off work, and this trolley stop was closest to the Maid dock and the starting point of his next date with Abigail. He'd changed out of his captain's uniform and into shorts and a T-shirt appropriate for a hot July evening. His fellow captains, twins Jackson and Jasper, had attempted to give him dating advice in a grandfatherly way, suggesting everything from flowers to hand-holding to making friends with Abigail's mother.

Lyman had politely listened but declined any further dating tips. No advice, no matter how many decades of experience accompanied it, would help him understand his complicated feelings toward Abigail. It had been two days since he'd seen her talking with the man he assumed was the ex. Was that guy back in town? What was his game?

It was none of Lyman's business. He was here to do a job he'd agreed to. Abigail's love life was her own. The sliver of curiosity, though, felt a bit like jealousy. Perhaps it was because Abigail's spare time belonged to their shared mission, not to some guy who didn't want her.

Not that he could see any reason a guy wouldn't want Abigail, in theory. She was smart, dedicated to her work and those she loved, funny, and her hair caught the sunlight as if it belonged to it.

"Did you have a rough day on the water?" Abigail asked as she took his hand and stepped onto the trolley.

"It was the same as usual," he said. He didn't mean it as an insult, just a fact.

"Well, you look very serious," she said. "And we're supposed to look carefree, because this trolley is eco-friendly and makes eight scenic stops, just like the brochure says."

Lyman smiled.

"That's better," she said. She put a hand on his shoulder, and Lyman tried not to blink when the camera flashed.

"Good," Sam said. "Now sit in the middle row and wave through the open window."

Lyman let Abigail have the window seat, and he leaned over her and smiled and waved at the camera. Were they going to do this at every stop? He knew from experience that two of the eight stops weren't glamorous—just transportation to the parking lots. His father had told him stories about those parking lot stops, with frustrated parents loading strollers and confused tourists not remembering which lot they'd parked in. Of course his dad had stayed late at work many times to make an extra loop and help people find their cars. His dad said he felt he owed them that for the price of their ticket, and he hoped someone would do it for him if he was in unfamiliar territory.

Lyman had grown up watching his father's dedication to serving others, and his mom, too, with her work as a dental hygienist. Serving in the Coast Guard was different, but the same idea—helping people who needed something. Did the people who boarded the Maid of the Mist need something other than a momentary distraction? Maybe some of them did. He saw families spending time together, older people checking items off their bucket list, young people in love.

Now he was getting sentimental. Maybe it was riding the trolley, which reminded him so much of his dad.

"There's that serious look again," Abigail said as she settled into the seat next to him and the trolley rang its bell and started moving. His arm was still across the back of the seat, and he left it there.

"Tourism is serious business," he said.

"My mother would say weddings are serious business," Abigail said. "I guess people think whatever business they're in is important. I hope so. People should love what they do."

"Is history serious business?"

"Asks the man who spent hours at Fort George trying out the bunks and looking through every little opening they fired guns and cannons through."

"That was a fun day," Lyman said. "It was nice to share that interest, you know? Not that I didn't appreciate how you suffered through all those superhero movies with me when we were dating."

"And you helped me take care of my neighbor's dogs for a month while they were in Europe. Those dogs were maniacs. Remember walking them all the time?" she asked.

Lyman laughed. "I do. The little brown one loved me."

"He pooped in your shoe."

"Only once. I wised up after that," Lyman said. "Wasn't going to happen again."

"Sadder but wiser," Abigail said.

"I've been meaning to ask you—"

Abigail turned to him. "You can go ahead and ask. About Josh, right?"

"You don't owe me any explanation. I only paused because of the look on your face."

"What look?"

"I was afraid you were going to shove him over the falls, and I thought I should be on hand to prevent you from spending the rest of your life in prison."

Abigail laughed. "Believe me, that's not what I was thinking about."

"But you did look determined."

She glanced out the window as they approached the next trolley stop. "I was determined to figure out what I wanted."

"And was that… Josh?"

"I thought you said I didn't need to explain anything to you."

"You don't," Lyman said quickly.

Abigail smiled. "I don't want him back. And he didn't come back to town to ask for a second chance. Chapter closed."

Why was he in town, then?

The trolley picked up speed on the way to the next stop. The driver had a radio tuned to the parks service frequency, and quiet chatter from the rangers on duty about the tourist amenities filtered back to Lyman. If there were other people on the bus, he probably wouldn't hear it at all, but the bus had been specially designated just for them, and Sam and Macey, who sat in the front seat.

The breeze through the open window ruffled the white lace on Abigail's sleeve and tickled Lyman's arm, but he didn't move it.

"It's only one month until the big event," he said. "Have you heard how many couples are signed up?"

Abigail frowned. "Only fifty-seven right now."

"That's still a lot. We just announced it a few weeks ago."

"True. And our target audience is a bit narrow."

"People who plan to get married in August," Lyman said, nodding.

"And didn't already have a deposit on a venue and a cake ordered and all the details that go into putting together a wedding."

"So we're down to people who want to get married but didn't have any kind of a plan," Lyman said.

Abigail laughed. "That sounds a bit judgmental. Like you don't approve of people who don't know what they're doing."

Lyman felt the trolley slow as it approached the stop. They were nearing a quieter part of the Niagara Falls State Park, where a big, grassy area sat next to a path leading to three little islands with foot bridges connecting them. Three Sisters Island. He'd played there a lot as a kid, but the infrastructure, including bridges and walkways, had improved substantially in recent years, taking away some of the thrill of the danger of being close to the water.

"I would just wonder what their level of commitment is if they haven't set a date or ordered a cake," Lyman said. "And I wouldn't want them to back out on us if we hope to get the one hundred couples we want for the group photo."

"Even people who have a cake ordered can back out," Abigail said.

"Sorry." Lyman gave her a sympathetic smile.

She shrugged. "It's okay. Really."

A snippet of radio traffic caught his attention with the words *in the water*. Lyman turned an ear toward the front of the trolley. He heard the note of urgency in the dispatcher's voice and the words *child* and *edge* and *fall*. Lyman got up and moved to the front of the trolley. When he reached the seat behind the driver he heard, "Three sisters." He pulled out his phone and called dispatch, a number he had programmed because of his work on the Maid.

"This is Lyman Roberts, one of the Maid captains. Do you have an emergency in the area of Three Sisters Island?"

He felt Abigail slide into the seat behind him, but he focused out the front windshield as they approached the stop. It was evening. How many rangers were on duty and where were they? He might be the nearest first responder.

"Stand by," the dispatcher said. In the background, Lyman heard her giving directions to the rangers on duty. The trolley pulled up to the stop and Lyman shot out the door, having overheard enough to know where he was going. He held his phone to his ear and jogged toward the entrance of the walkway to the three connected islands.

ABIGAIL AND MACEY exchanged a glance.

"What's going on?" Sam asked. "All I heard was something about the water at Three Sisters, and Lyman got on his phone and then ran out the door."

"He's a rescuer," Abigail said. She didn't know what else to say, but she got off the trolley and started running after Lyman. There was no one around in this relatively quiet area of the state park. It was a weekday evening at dinnertime, and the forecast for rain in an hour had driven most tourists back to their hotels, Abigail imagined.

But not all of them.

Lyman raced across the first bridge and then stopped, looking down. Abigail caught up and almost ran into him. He was on the phone with someone she assumed was the park police, but his attention was below, where there was a child in the water and a woman holding on to the boy with one hand and clutching a tree branch with the other. The water wasn't deep, but it was moving fast.

"Talk to them," Lyman said, and he thrust his phone into Abigail's hand as he went over the railing at the end of the bridge and made his way through the foliage to the water's edge. Abigail could barely breathe, but the dispatcher was talking to her, asking questions.

"I'm watching it now," Abigail said, her eyes and her heart following Lyman's quick, sure movements. He didn't hesitate, and confidence radiated from him. "There's a woman, and she's on the edge of the water but not drowning, and she has hold of a little boy who is floundering in the water, but she can't get a better grip because she's trying to hold on. The water is moving fast. Lyman is almost to them."

"The park police are on the way. Do you have any rescue equipment?" the dispatcher asked.

"No. Just a trained Coast Guard guy who— Oh, he's reaching for the little boy. He has hold of a tree and he's…he's got him. He's swinging the boy back onto dry ground, and now he's reaching for the woman, who—"

"Who what? Are they still in the water?"

Abigail started moving as fast as she could. She cleared the end of the bridge and crashed through some bushes and small trees until she got to the little boy, who was alone because the woman had lost her grip on the tree and fallen face-first into the water. Abigail didn't know how to help rescue the woman, but she could make sure the child didn't go back in.

"Are you there?" the dispatcher demanded. "Hello?"

Abigail scooped the boy up with one arm, murmuring, "I've got you," to him. Into the phone, she said, "I have the boy and—" A member of the state park police brushed past her, a rope in his hand.

"The police are here," she told the dispatcher in a hoarse voice. "I think they're attempting to rescue the woman. And Lyman."

She could barely watch as she held the boy close to keep him warm and stop him from seeing what was happening. The woman was on her knees in the water, but the current had her flailing and she couldn't get up. Lyman was in the water, too, moving toward her and fighting to stay upright. As Abigail watched, the park police threw Lyman a rope, and he caught it and tied the end around the woman's waist as he knelt next to her.

"They have ropes," Abigail said to the dispatcher.

Water battered Lyman as he helped the woman to shore, aided by the rope being reeled in by the park police. It was over in less than a minute, and Abigail sank to her knees in front of the boy. "Are you okay?" she asked. The child's face was smeared with tears and mud, but he nodded timidly. "It's going to be okay," Abigail said.

Lyman and the boy's mother trudged up the bank along with the park police, and the mother ran to her son, clutching him tightly. Abigail imagined the child would get a lengthy lecture about not climbing over railings ever again, but she doubted the mom would be willing to let go of him for a long time.

Abigail was damp and muddy herself, but Lyman was soaked through as he approached her.

He had a cut over one eye and a deep scratch on his bicep. Abigail wrapped her arms around him and held him tight for a moment.

"You saved them," she whispered, overcome by emotion.

He held her for a moment before untangling himself. "The park police saved us. I shouldn't have gone in without a rope, but I… Well, I did. I didn't think she could hang on any longer."

There was clapping from the bridge, and Abigail and Lyman spun around and saw Sam, Macey and some tourists gathered there, obviously happy about the outcome. Abigail looked at Lyman, whose face was thunderous. "It's not a show," he said. "It's someone's life."

"I know," Abigail said. "I'll make them delete those pictures."

Lyman turned back to the park police and helped them get the woman and child back onto the bridge, where paramedics had parked. Abigail followed the group, and Lyman turned to offer her a hand as she climbed onto the bridge. He put an arm around her to help her and then winced.

"Sorry," he said. He'd smeared blood on her white shirt.

"I don't care about that," she said. "But you should have the paramedics look at your arm and your head."

"A tree and a rock got me, but I was lucky overall," he said.

Everyone was lucky, Abigail thought. Lucky that the trolley radio caught Lyman's attention and they happened to be nearby, and very lucky that Lyman was a trained rescuer, clearly unafraid to take action.

"Thanks for holding on to the kid," Lyman said. "I don't know what I'd have done if he wandered back into the water while we were trying to get his mom out."

"I was glad I could do something." She didn't want Lyman to see she was still shaking.

Lyman sat on the edge of the bridge while the park police talked to the woman and the paramedics. Abigail sat next to him and waited while the police made their report, took some photographs and asked a few questions. After a minute, one of the paramedics crooked a finger at Lyman, and he went over to their vehicle, accepted a small white towel and wiped off his cuts.

Sam and Macey sat next to Abigail, Sam's arm around Macey's shoulders. "Not what I expected to happen on the trolley tour," Sam said.

"You can't use those photos."

"I didn't take any," he said. "It seemed wrong, and I was honestly too scared to even pick up my camera."

"Good. Lyman doesn't want any pictures out there."

Macey shook her head. "We weren't the only people on the bridge, so I can't make any guarantees. Tourists came running when they saw the park police blazing in, and they can post pictures if they want, I guess. I'd like to think they'd use discretion, but… I'm not hopeful."

Lyman returned from the ambulance. "Think our trolley is still waiting for us?" he asked. "I could at least use a ride to the parking lot so I—we—can go home and change."

Abigail looked at her summery white eyelet top. It was a mess. Lyman reached down and picked off a leaf that had gotten stuck to her knee. Abigail was so happy Lyman had been in the right place at the right time, and that she'd been there with him.

"Will your dad be furious he wasn't driving the trolley tonight and missed all the action?" she asked as he took her hand and pulled her up. They started walking back across the bridges.

"I'll never hear the end of it," Lyman said.

The adrenaline created by all the excitement suddenly left her, and she felt as if her legs weighed a thousand pounds each. She slowed her step, and Lyman turned to her, concern on his face.

"I didn't ask if you were all right," he said. "Are you? That's a hard thing to witness, let alone be part of."

He was concerned about her. After all that had happened, she was the center of his focus at the moment. It felt good, like the feeling of his solid chest when she'd put her arms around him. They'd kissed as teenagers, but the contact was different now. It had aged along with them, and its meaning was deeper.

Not that she would admit that to him…or herself. She'd trusted her emotions with Josh, and now she wasn't sure she trusted herself.

"Shaky legs," she admitted. "That's all." Lyman put an arm around her waist and guided her back to the trolley, where he assisted her up the steps and made her sit in the front seat. He slid in next to her and put a hand on her knee, and she didn't feel that she needed to say a word all the way back to the parking lot because Lyman had been there, too, and he understood.

CHAPTER SIXTEEN

#ChristmasAtTheFalls

Lyman's boss, Tom, was waiting for him the next morning when he got to work, and Tom was wearing his serious military face.

"You took a big risk," he said.

Lyman juggled his thermos of coffee, his lunch and the key to his work locker. "The trolley is perfectly safe—tourists ride it all day long and there's never been an incident. At least that's what my dad says, and he might be exaggerating, but I don't think he'd cover up anything dangerous."

His boss's expression relaxed into a half smile. "If you keep on being a hero for the cameras, you may have to quit this job and become a full-time tourist attraction."

"Right place at the right time," he said, echoing the words he'd used with Abigail the night before. He'd forgotten for a moment, in the heat of the rescue, that it would look different to Abigail than it did to him. He'd evaluated the scene, calculated the risk versus opportunity for success, used his strength and training, and then participated in the paperwork. Abigail had been shaken. Was it her fear of what could have happened to the mother and son, or to him? He liked the thought that she cared about him in particular.

It wasn't a good idea or fair to her to invite her attention. His life was in a holding pattern, and he didn't want her to get caught up in the decisions he'd have to make. He'd left her once—she'd never been part of his decision-making then—and she'd just been left at the altar. She would be wise to guard her heart. Everyone should. It was the most private and important thing anyone had.

Tom put a hand on Lyman's shoulder. "I'm proud of you—you make a fine addition to our team here. But don't go getting involved in any dramatics on the Maid. They say any publicity is good, but we prefer to stick to only the suggestion of danger, not the real thing."

"That sounds like a perfect world to me," Lyman said.

"Have you seen any of the pictures those bystanders posted online? They give the wrong impression," Tom said. "The picture of you helping Abigail over the bridge made it look like she was the one you were rescuing, especially since the ones of you actually in the water were farther away."

"The news article should make it clear it was someone else," Lyman said.

"That's what I thought. But first impressions, you know. People see what they want."

Lyman unscrewed the lid on his coffee thermos and took a swig.

"What's next for you and Abigail?" his boss asked.

"Christmas in July," Lyman said. "We're doing a tree lighting thing and then highlighting the workers who bring the colored lights on the falls to life every night. Sort of a behind-the-scenes tour of the magic."

"I don't remember Christmas in July being much of a thing in the past, but you two are bringing all kinds of good attention to this area. I hope you're having some fun, too, and it's not all work," Tom said.

Lyman suspected his boss was indirectly asking if there was any real romance between him and Abigail.

"We're partners on a mission, that's all," Lyman said.

His boss nodded. "Well, you've got a good partner, and it doesn't look like a hardship working with her."

It wasn't a hardship. The fact that it was easy to be with Abigail, though, made it seem somehow more deceptive. Not for everyone else, but for themselves. What would happen when the campaign and the summer came to an end?

Lyman put on his captain's jacket and hat from his work locker and strode out to the boat to go through the standard morning routine. It was a familiar and comforting habit. Engine check, lights, dials, safety equipment in the pilothouse, lifeboats and life jackets on the passenger deck. Rescue rope. Flotation rings to throw overboard. Everything in place. He knew water safety, and the drill was designed to make everything automatic.

He'd acted automatically but with training and judgment the night before, jumping in to help that woman and child. He didn't want pictures circulating online because in the pictures he was dressed as a civilian, a bystander. The waters around Niagara Falls were rapid and dangerous, and most people would be putting themselves at serious risk if they tried to help someone else.

He hadn't come home to be a hero, hadn't even thought about using skills other than piloting a boat. Was there a way to find purpose and meaning in his life if he...stayed?

"Good morning," he said, greeting the seasonal workers who handled the dock ropes and guided tourists onto the Maid of the Mist. "Slippery deck this morning from the dew."

"Yes, sir," the teenager said, giving him a thumbs-up instead of a salute that would have been common in the service.

Sir. He was twenty-four. He'd just seen a few things in the years since he was that kid's age. He'd wanted adventure and to see what was outside Niagara Falls. What did he want now?

Hours later, Lyman finished his shift, then dashed home and mowed the lawn before his dad got any more ideas about trying that again. He didn't have time for dinner, so he grabbed a protein bar, took a quick shower and dressed as instructed for the evening event. If he didn't have the fake dates and pictures with Abigail, what would he be doing with his evenings and free time? His parents needed him—at least, they had needed him for the first few months he was home—but each day his dad got better and his mom breathed a little easier. Soon, his dad would get back on his feet the rest of the way and Lyman would be free to go wherever he wanted.

Wherever that was, he thought as he drove to the tourism office at half past five to meet with Abigail and Macey about the progress toward finding one hundred couples to get married just over twenty days from now. From there, he and Abigail would go on to their scheduled event with the ever-present photographer in tow.

"I've talked to the Illumination Board, and they're in," Macey said as they sat down in her office. The lobby closed at five, so now there was only the quiet hum of the air-conditioning.

Lyman knew vaguely that a board oversaw the

lights on the falls every night and that it was a joint effort between Canada and the United States, since the lights had to be projected from the Canadian side to light up the American and Horseshoe Falls.

"Do you mean the behind-the-scenes tour of the lights?" Lyman asked. "I thought that was already set up."

"It is. You're doing the tree lighting for the Christmas in July event and then going right over to the Canadian side and meeting the two people on duty overseeing the red and green lights."

"Good," Lyman said. He was happy to follow orders, but he liked clarity.

Macey folded her hands on her desk. "The falls will be red and green tonight, and that's great. We'll get pictures, and you'll highlight the lights on the falls and associate the lights with all the hashtags we've been using."

"I feel like there's more," Abigail said.

Lyman exchanged a grin with her. They both knew something more was coming. Macey was tireless in her enthusiasm for promoting the falls, and Lyman respected that. She worked hard with a goal in mind. He'd operated under many leaders in the service, and he admired Macey's energy and determination.

Did Abigail feel the same way? She shifted in her chair next to Lyman. She had abandoned her usual choice of white clothing and chosen instead to wear a red top with dark jeans that stopped just above her ankles. She wore red sneakers and a red headband.

Lyman had worn a green polo shirt, but he knew he didn't look as festive as Abigail. She was the photogenic one who kept people following the hashtag.

"They light up the falls for special occasions all the time—New York sports teams making the playoffs, holidays, charitable events. Why not light it up to draw attention to the mass wedding?" Macey asked. "Who knows? There may be a couple somewhere in the crowds who see the lights and either get engaged right there or decide to move their wedding to August 15, right here." She gave a one-shoulder shrug and a grin. "It could happen."

Lyman struggled to picture it. "The lights will be red and green tonight for the Christmas in July thing, right?"

"Yes," Macey said. "And you'll promote it a lot, even tag the Illumination Board so people can find out more. We'll spend two days teasing a special lighting, and then on Saturday night, the falls will be red and pink with, hopefully—" she crossed her fingers as she spoke "—hearts projected like they do snowflakes in the winter show."

"People will think it's Valentine's Day in July," Abigail said.

"Not if we work together to promote the real reason. Love and romance. The Illumination Board is also promising to do the same color scheme on the night of August 15, if the mass wedding gets a hundred couples and goes off as planned."

"It will," Abigail said.

"We're at sixty-five. We have a ways to go," Macey said. "Which is why you two are going to get out there and hustle. Build up the excitement, whatever it takes."

Lyman risked a glance at Abigail and caught her looking at him.

"Whatever it takes," Abigail repeated, not looking at Macey but keeping her gaze on Lyman.

"I think it's time for a kiss," Macey said. "The #FallInLoveAtTheFalls hashtag has flagged a little, and people are anxious for fresh content. The water rescue during the trolley tour was amazing, and you make a great hero, Lyman, but it was off topic."

"We didn't have any intention of using that for publicity," Lyman said.

"I know," Macey said, waving a hand. "That's not what I meant. I just meant we need to keep the focus on the Fall in Love at the Falls motif so people will come for the rainbows and honeymoons and especially the big wedding."

"I don't know about a kiss," Abigail said.

"Just once for the camera," Macey said. "You know, we could do it in front of the green screen and then get a lot of use out of it, like we did those other photos."

"No," Abigail and Lyman said at the same time.

Lyman didn't know what Abigail was thinking, but he was thinking that kissing her in front of a green screen as a setup in a studio would be as unromantic as it got. He wasn't an actor.

"A kiss has to happen spontaneously," Abigail said.

Lyman stared at his shoes, which he'd tied using a complicated knot he'd learned in the Coast Guard. This kissing conversation was making him wish he was standing on the deck of a boat with a strong wind blowing sea spray over him.

"Just make sure the camera is rolling if it does," Macey said.

ABIGAIL DIDN'T KNOW why she'd said it, the comment about a kiss being spontaneous. Her intention was to argue against a setup, but it had come out sounding as if she thought she and Lyman were naturally headed toward kissing.

Which they weren't. Of course.

"So, sixty-five couples," she said as she walked with Lyman toward the large Christmas tree temporarily set up near the entrance to Niagara Falls State Park. It was a hot summer evening. Her mom and Minerva were busy overseeing a wedding reception at the hotel, also with a Christmas in July theme, and Abigail would normally have been hanging around offering to help them or at home working on her research for history tours.

But here she was with Lyman Roberts instead.

He reached for her hand as they approached the entrance. It was part of their ruse. People expected to see them arrive together and be... together.

"Don't be discouraged," he said. "Sixty-five is still a lot, and some couples could easily still join up. Maybe they want to get married but don't even know it yet."

"I'd think they'd know. It's only three weeks away."

"Fast decisions can work out," Lyman said. "Sometimes."

"Do you always know what you're doing weeks in advance?"

Lyman laughed. "That depends if I'm making the decisions or if they're being made for me. For example, I didn't know we'd have pink hearts on the falls in two days and that we'll be doing this evening all over again."

Did he regret getting roped into these shenanigans? She was the one who would more directly benefit because of her mom's business and her own display at the history museum. What did Lyman get out of it, aside from a vague sense of duty?

He didn't directly benefit, but he also didn't

stand to lose if the campaign didn't go well. The stakes were much higher for her than him.

"I had an idea about the mass wedding," Lyman said.

"You do?" Lyman was thinking of ideas now instead of just going along with the plans?

"Yes, but I didn't want to tell Macey before I ran it past you first."

"Why?"

He tugged at the collar of his shirt. "I respect Macey and the mission, but I'm more...invested... in *your* opinion, I guess."

She wasn't the expert on publicity and media. Why did he think her opinion had more value?

She didn't want to admit to herself that there might be a reason that was, well, personal. Did their friendship rank higher to him than the job they were doing?

"What's your idea?" she asked. She slowed her steps to give him time to explain before they got to the Christmas tree, where a small crowd was already gathered.

"It was my mother's idea. She said she wished she could participate in the big ceremony with my dad, but it would be a vow renewal in their case, not an actual wedding."

Abigail stopped and turned toward Lyman. She caught both his hands as excitement raced through her.

"That's brilliant!"

"Do you think so?"

"Yes. I love that. It brings together older couples with younger ones and it celebrates love at not just the beginning, but also the..."

The what? *The what comes after*, she thought. The later years. The reaffirmation of what made people fall in love and stay that way. It was so beautiful, and it hit a nostalgic chord in her. She wondered when her time would come for a first wedding, let alone a renewal.

"What's the matter?" Lyman asked, leaning down and speaking softly. She felt the heat from his face as he nearly brushed her cheek with his own. "You looked happy but then sad."

"I'm happy," she said, unwilling to share her emotions with Lyman because they were too raw. "I'm just wondering how we can convince Macey to do this and how we target those couples who are older. They may not be on social media."

Lyman laughed. "If my mom is any indication, they're on their phones checking their feeds just as often as people our age. They'll find out, and I think they'll be thrilled to be included."

She laughed. "You're right. My mom has followed our romance faithfully all summer."

It was odd calling it "our romance" when the only person close enough to hear was Lyman. It sounded too personal.

He blew out a breath. "Same with my parents.

It's been good entertainment for my dad while he's supposed to be resting."

Entertainment. A spectacle. That was the true essence of their supposed romance. What would people think when they found out the truth? Their close friends and family knew, so maybe it didn't matter what the rest of the world thought. They had a goal.

"Should we start promoting the idea tonight?" Abigail asked.

Christmas music blasted from a speaker near the tree, and Lyman glanced over at the holiday setup. "We better do as instructed right now, but when Macey shows up in a little while, we'll run it by her."

Abigail still held both Lyman's hands. "If I forget to tell you later, Merry Christmas."

Lyman smiled and kissed the top of her head, and a warm, sweet feeling rushed through her. She thought of the kiss Macey had suggested.

"We were supposed to make sure the camera was rolling in the event of a kiss," she said.

"That wasn't for the camera," Lyman said.

Abigail knew Lyman would be long gone by Christmas, but the music and festive lights coupled with the soft brush of his lips in her hair made her feel like celebrating tonight, even if it was all they'd ever have.

CHAPTER SEVENTEEN

#LightsOnTheFalls

LYMAN WASN'T SURE about the whole Christmas-in-July thing. Maybe it was some kind of transplanted holiday nostalgia that had made him kiss Abigail's hair. Or perhaps it was her joy at his suggestion of a way to strengthen the campaign. It was important to her. He didn't want her to be let down. He didn't want to be the one to let her down.

So he followed the program and laid his hand on the switch that would light up the Christmas tree. Abigail put her hand over his. The crowd counted down, flashes from multiple cameras pierced the dusk and he and Abigail illuminated the tree. Decorated with red, white and blue lights as a nod to summer, in addition to Christmas, the tree also had glittery red hearts, blue tinsel arranged to look like waterfalls and ornaments showcasing local attractions. There were miniature Maid of the Mist boats, barrels, a replica of the Skylon Tower and even little green trolley cars.

When the flashes died off and the crowd moved on, Lyman and Abigail walked over to Macey, who waited at the edge of the crowd so she could see the whole event and judge the reaction of the tourists. Sam sat on a bench next to her.

"We need to make it a weeklong thing next year, the Christmas-in-July thing. A one-and-done day doesn't have the bang for the buck," she said. "But you two looked great. Did you hear that person in the crowd chanting 'kiss, kiss, kiss'?"

"No," Lyman said at the same time Abigail said "yes."

An awkward silence followed, but then Macey said, "You have an hour before you're scheduled to do the behind-the-scenes-at-the-lights thing. Of course, it's all computer controlled, but there are always two people on duty just to make sure. It's nice to highlight the people on the ground doing all the work."

"Yes," he and Abigail said together, and then they laughed.

"Come on," Macey said. "I know you two are officially working for the tourism board, but you're having fun, too, right? We've even thrown in free T-shirts, dinners and trolley rides for the privilege of using your pretty faces."

"She's the pretty one," Lyman said. He sucked in a breath. He'd meant to imply that he wasn't there for his looks, just a man doing his duty for the greater good. But Abigail and Macey both gave him a look when he said it.

"And a hard worker," Macey said. "Which is good, because we still need thirty-five more couples."

"Should we tell her now?" Lyman asked, glad to change the subject.

Abigail smiled and nodded.

Macey stared at them. "Whatever you're going to tell me, you two look happy about it. Can I hope you've fallen—"

"We have an idea," Abigail said, interrupting her. "Actually, it was Lyman's idea."

"My mother's idea," he corrected. "It's about expanding our list of couples for the big wedding."

"It's already open to any couple, no limits on who they are or who they love," Macey said.

"I know," Abigail said. "But we'd like to include couples who are already married and want to renew their vows."

Macey was silent a moment, and Lyman was afraid she was going to say no.

"Were there any vow renewals at the 1950 wedding?" Macey asked.

"No," Abigail said. "Maybe they just didn't think of it, or I wonder if it wasn't a thing back then?"

"Well, it is now," Macey said. "This…this could be huge. And it's easier to get people at the last minute because they don't have to do the whole proposal, get a ring, make double sure you really want to be married to this person thing. They're already married. The damage is done," she said and then laughed. "No risk to renewing vows, because it's not like renewing a lease. They already have a life lease. I love it."

Lyman respected Macey's all-business persona, but he did think calling marriage a *life lease* was a bit cold. Marriage was different.

"Do you think the vow-renewal thing will work?" Lyman asked.

"Work? I think we'll easily talk a bunch of locals into joining the fun."

"Starting with my parents," Lyman said.

"And probably mine," Macey said.

"Mine if my dad's in town," Abigail said.

"We've got work to do," Sam said.

"Let me think about teasing a big announcement, and I'll get back to you about it tomorrow," Macey said. "I'll see you at the light station in an hour."

Lyman still held Abigail's hand as Macey and Sam left. He noticed they were walking close together, as if they were talking about something important and didn't want anyone else to hear.

"Your idea might save this event," Abigail said, turning toward him. Christmas lights bounced off the tree and reflected on her shining face. He was tempted to ask for a kiss right this minute, but he was afraid she would tell him it was a waste of time without Sam there to document it.

"We should get going," he said. "There might be traffic on the bridge, and we don't want to be late."

THE NIGHT WAS all about illumination, Abigail thought as she entered the control room for their tour. And the actual lights were only part of it. She felt light within, as if suddenly anything was possible. Lyman's great idea for getting to one hundred couples took a huge weight off her mind, that was all.

"My father worked here," the man who'd introduced himself as Chuck said. "I used to come and watch when I was a kid. It was a whole different ball of wax back then. No quick switches on the colors, no special effects. And boy, is it brighter now with the LEDs. Night and day," he added.

Lyman laughed. "My dad drives the trolley on the American side, and he always talks about the improvements they've made over the years."

"The falls are the same, though," Chuck said. "Thank goodness, or I'd be out of a job."

"How long have you worked here?"

"Since 1985. Long before you two were even born."

Abigail laughed. She wasn't surprised. She knew of people who'd piloted the Maid of the Mist or worked in the gift shops for that long. It was wonderful, rewarding work making sure visitors enjoyed their trip to the natural wonder of the falls.

"Tell us about a typical day in the life of an illumination expert," Abigail said. She was aware of Sam taking pictures as she and Lyman got a crash course from the workers who ensured the light show would go on. Abigail tried to remain on the fringes of the pictures and keep the focus on Chuck and his coworker Dan, who popped in and introduced himself, apologizing about being hung up with a computer he'd had to reboot.

"Red and green for Christmas in July," Dan said. "We do it every year, but I've wondered if anyone really noticed. Something tells me they will this year, thanks to you two."

"We're more responsible for the show in two nights with the red and pink and hearts," Lyman said. "That promotes the mass wedding Abigail and I are hosting as part of the Fall in Love at the Falls campaign."

"It just got added to our calendar," Chuck said. "In the past it would have taken time to set up, but now it's just a couple of mouse clicks."

"We appreciate those clicks," Lyman said.

"Do you mind putting on these Santa hats for a picture?" Sam asked.

Chuck and Dan exchanged a glance and a shrug. "As long as you get my good side," Chuck said.

Lyman stood behind Abigail, with Chuck and Dan flanking her. They all wore Santa hats, but the warmth Abigail felt came from Lyman's hands on her shoulders.

"So, do we get to know any secrets?" Dan asked. "My daughter has been following the hashtags about you two, and she's betting you'll be one of the couples getting married at the big wedding. One hundred and one, right?"

Abigail held up both hands in traffic stop pose. "Our job is to promote Niagara Falls. It's not about us."

Dan shrugged. "Can't blame us for hoping you get a happy ending, especially after you got left at the altar."

He said it kindly, like a beloved uncle might offer advice at the Thanksgiving table. *I know you haven't found the right man yet, Sally, but don't worry, he's out there.* But Abigail felt a bit raw tonight. It had been almost two months since Josh had run away from their wedding. And she'd come to terms with it, and with him. Maybe it was mixing Christmas-in-July emotions with the trajectory of the big wedding that had her tripping over her own feelings tonight.

She attempted a smile that she hoped would fool Dan, Chuck and the photographer. "Maybe that was the luckiest day of my life," she said.

Lyman glanced down and gave her a long, searching look.

"There you are," Macey said, hurrying into the

work area and standing close to Sam. "Sorry I'm late, but I had to pick something up."

"No problem," Sam said. "I think we're about finished here."

"Not quite," Macey said. "Let's get some outdoor pictures. It's romantic."

Sam shrugged, and Macey got behind Abigail and Lyman, shooing them out the door while she thanked Chuck and Dan for their help.

Once outside, Abigail turned to Macey. "Where do you want us?"

"We need the falls in the background but enough light so we can clearly see what you two are doing," Macey said. She directed them a place along a railing where a nearby streetlight provided some light and the falls glowed red and green behind them.

"What are we doing?" Lyman asked.

Macey gave a guilty grin and pulled out a red velvet box. Abigail felt her heart sink when she saw it. It was a ring box.

"I don't think—" Abigail began.

"We need to up our game," Macey said. "Who doesn't love a man on one knee offering a ring?"

Love? Abigail shook her head. This wasn't about true love.

"Hold out your hand," Macey said to Lyman. He followed orders and offered his hand, palm up. Macey put the red velvet box in his hand, and Sam took close-ups. He swung the camera around and got a shot of Abigail's shocked expression.

"Perfect," Macey said. "Like you just can't believe it."

"I can't," Abigail said.

"Yes," Macey said. "This is gold. Take a knee, Lyman."

Lyman looked at Abigail as if he was waiting for her permission. She debated. One nod from her, and there would be a proposal picture making the social media rounds. If she said no—

"We've come this far," Macey said. "Your idea for the vow renewals to help us get to the magic number of one hundred couples is great. I almost didn't pick up the ring after I heard your plan. But I decided a little insurance goes a long way."

Abigail glanced at the falls, spectacular in their majesty. Everyone should come and see them, even if they were lured there by an ad campaign built on a stack of lies. She was doing all this for Niagara Falls, the tourism, the weddings, the people who took home a paycheck because of the magic. She nodded to Lyman, who got on one knee and looked up at her, an open ring box in his hands.

She was glad for the night lighting that captured them in profile, shadows concealing the true heartbreak of a fake proposal from a man for whom she was beginning to feel something real.

CHAPTER EIGHTEEN

#MaidOfTheMistWedding

GINNY WARREN KNELT and stuck her head into the cabinet under the kitchen sink.

"The online video says you can drain the P trap and maybe your ring will fall right out," Abigail said. "Follow the drainpipe and see if there is a little thing to unscrew at the bottom."

"I don't think so," her mom said.

Abigail got down to look for herself using her phone's flashlight. "Nope, no little thing to drain it. So we'll need a bucket, and we can unscrew the things and take off the trap thing."

Her mom laughed. "You just used the word *thing* four times. How confident are we about this video?"

"It's our best bet. You want your ring back, don't you?"

"Desperately. You got it for me for Christmas, and I love it."

"I knew you'd like it, because it has a little sapphire that matches your eyes." Abigail and her mother generally exchanged practical Christmas gifts—hats and gloves for the cold New York winters, sweaters, wool coats. One time, Abigail had gotten her mother new floor mats for her car, and her mother had given Abigail a thick terry-cloth bathrobe. The previous year, they had agreed on frivolous gifts, hence the ring for her mom and a necklace with a heart encrusted with tiny diamonds for Abigail.

"We'll try the video's instructions but agree to call a plumber if it goes haywire," Abigail said. She'd googled "how to get a ring out of the kitchen sink drain" and found mostly references to wedding rings, but a ring was a ring. "Give me a minute to get a bucket."

Abigail retrieved the bucket from the utility closet and also grabbed a towel. This wasn't the first DIY project she'd attempted with her mom while her dad was out of town, and their record was better than fifty percent for fixing things themselves. Except for anything electrical. They were both afraid to mess with that. Abigail ducked past her mom and put the bucket right below the big U-shaped pipe.

"I'm unscrewing the big plastic ring around one side," her mom said.

"Try to do the other one at the same time so it comes off evenly," Abigail suggested. "The video shows it being a nice neat drop into the waiting bucket."

"And things are always exactly as they appear on the internet," her mom said, laughing. Abigail knew her mom wasn't throwing shade on her fake dating with Lyman, because Ginny had been a supporter of the idea from the start, although it would have been a fair example. Things between her and Lyman were not what they appeared online. She heard her mom grunt as she tried moving the fastener around the pipe.

"Need help?"

"I think I've got it."

Abigail sat on the kitchen floor next to her mom's feet. "The Christmas-in-July thing was fun last night. We lit up the tree and then met the guys who run the lights on the falls."

"And?"

Abigail knew what her mother was asking. She wasn't wearing the engagement ring, but those pictures were already online.

"I saw all the pictures this morning," Ginny added. "Your dad called last night and asked if you were really engaged. I told him I didn't think so."

"I'm not."

"And then your dad asked if that was Chuck in that picture. He knows him from years ago."

"It was. Those guys have worked there since the '80s," Abigail said. "They were good sports about the pictures."

"You and Lyman are the good sports. I just hope

you find a way to get back to your normal life after August 15."

Abigail laughed. "I have no idea what normal is anymore."

A clunk sounded, and then her mom said, "I got the thing off, and it's really disgusting, full of murky water and some sludgy brown stuff."

"I smell it," Abigail said. "Ick. Did you find your ring?"

Her mom made a disgusted sound. "How bad do I want this back?"

"Sapphires," Abigail said. "They're your favorite."

A few seconds later, Ginny said, "Got it, but it needs a major cleaning, and so does this pipe. I think we'll take it out in the yard and hose it out."

"The pipe, right?"

Her mom popped out from under the sink and laughed. "I'm not taking a chance on losing the ring again." She handed Abigail the ring, which was, indeed, tangled with hair and brown sludge. Abigail wrapped it in a paper towel and put it in a bowl on the counter.

"Are you going to show me your fake engagement ring?"

Abigail shrugged. "It's upstairs. Something Macey picked out. It's on loan from a jewelry store."

"Don't drop it down the drain, then." Ginny picked up the bucket and headed for the kitchen door that led into a small, fenced backyard. "Your dad missed out on this fun job," her mom said.

"We managed—you managed—it yourself."

"True, but it would have been nice if I could have persuaded him to stick his finger in the yucky stuff to get my ring."

Abigail thought about the man she'd almost married. She doubted he would have taken one for the team and reached into a gross drainpipe. Lyman popped into her head. He probably would have done that and more. But that was no reason for her to get all sentimental about him. She could hire a plumber if she needed one.

Abigail followed her mom into the yard and turned on the spigot. She took the bucket and gooey pipe and flushed them out and then set them in the sun to dry. Abigail sat next to her mom on a bench on the small deck outside the kitchen entrance.

"Your dad posted pictures last night of the project he's working on. It was interesting, but I usually just look at the pictures so I can get a glimpse of him. I just want to know he's okay. Does he have his jacket with him? Does he look like he's eating all right? You worry about people when you can't get your arms around them," her mother said. "I know it's silly to scour the internet just to feel closer to him."

Abigail put an arm around her mom. "The first

few months after Lyman went off to the Coast Guard, I used to peek at his mom's Facebook page."

"I did, too," her mom said.

"Really?"

Ginny shrugged. "I was curious about him. I liked Lyman, and I thought he was... Well, I liked the way he treated you."

"Right up to leaving me and everyone else behind," Abigail said.

"You can't blame him for wanting to see what's out there."

"But he acted·like this place was terrible and he couldn't wait to get away."

"He was eighteen. Maybe he made those bold statements to cover up the fact that he was nervous about leaving. People use cover of all kinds. Some people act like they don't care about things when they actually do."

Abigail met her mother's gaze. Was there a hidden message? Did her mother suspect that all the pretending with Lyman no longer felt like a game?

"I heard one of the older captains on the Maid is retiring," her mom said. "Actually, two of them, the twin brothers."

"Jasper and Jackson."

"Yes. I guess they're both turning sixty-seven and hitting the Social Security retirement age. Anyway, that means a permanent spot could open up for Lyman if he's interested in sticking around this time."

Abigail fought against the bubble of hope and excitement she felt rising up her throat. There was no reason to think Lyman would want to stay. He'd seen the wide world, and it was a lot bigger than Niagara Falls. His dad was getting better. There was nothing keeping Lyman in his hometown. Moreover, he'd never mentioned his future plans, even with all the time they'd spent together.

"What Lyman does is none of my business," Abigail said. "Our friendship is fabricated. It serves a purpose, and then we'll go our separate ways after August."

Her mother gave her a long look. "I wasn't talking about your friendship."

Abigail didn't respond. Talking to her mom about her feelings for Lyman was dangerous. She could lie to herself more easily than to her mother.

"I'm going to go soak my ring in some alcohol and get ready for a last-minute wedding," Ginny said as she got up.

"I didn't know you had a wedding today."

"It was a surprise. A couple came to town for a proposal weekend, and they decided they were going to seal the deal and basically make it an elopement weekend."

"When did you find out about this?"

"Last evening after they got their license at

city hall. I guess Christmas in July is a new romantic holiday."

Abigail thought about the kiss Lyman had brushed against her hair. That had been some kind of friendship, a shared moment. Not romance. Even if it had felt that way with the music and lights all around them and the sweetness of his touch.

"The bride is out looking for a dress this morning, but I think she may be a candidate for one of our loaner gowns. We'll see."

"Where's the wedding?"

"On the Maid of the Mist. I pulled strings with Tom, and he's going to have either Jasper or Jackson do the ceremony, being boat captains and all. That's how I heard they're retiring, talking with Tom this morning. Ever since that couple from television eloped and got married on the Maid, we've had requests. This one is a quickie, though," her mom said.

"Do you need help? I don't have any tours this afternoon."

"Minnie and I have it covered. You should take some time for yourself, because you've been so busy with your job and the new exhibit and the promotional events. Read a book in the garden," her mother said. She picked up the bucket. "Right after you help me figure out how to reattach this drainpipe."

IT WAS THE fourth wedding party he'd seen board the Maid of the Mist, but Lyman had chosen not to get involved in any of the festivities. He was the captain. Ensuring the safety of all souls onboard was his job, not attending weddings onboard or steering the ship so the parties either did or did not get wet.

He didn't get involved, but he did pose for pictures after they docked, if the couple requested it. Why not?

Jasper, in full captain's uniform, strode up to the gangplank. "Don't get excited," he said. "I'm not here to steal your shift. I'm officiating the wedding onboard by special request."

Lyman laughed. "Do you have a license to do that?"

"Of course. My brother does, too. After we retire, we may make it our full-time gig and take up with Ginny Warren in her business, just in case they want very distinguished-looking boat captains to officiate all their weddings."

"Why not?" Lyman asked. "Do you want me to take it slow and give you extra time, just in case you want to give a long lecture on the sanctity of marriage or advice from your two hundred years on the water?"

Jasper laughed and gave Lyman a fake elbow gouge. "It's only a hundred and fifty years, and don't do anything special. By the time we do the vows and a kiss, half the wedding party will be ready to get off the boat, if I've learned anything from doing this dozens of times."

"Here they come," Lyman said. He pointed up the hill, where a small group of people were making their way toward the boat. He recognized Ginny and Minnie, and there was a woman wearing a floating white veil with a tank top and shorts. The man wore a dark suit.

"Looks like they forgot the dress," Jasper commented. "Think she plans to get married in a blue raincoat like all the other tourists?"

"I've given up predicting tourists."

"Wait a minute," Jasper said, keeping a smile on his face for the tourists boarding the boat but leaning in to talk to Lyman. "This is getting interesting. That looks like Abigail carrying a garment bag."

Lyman shifted his focus to a spot farther back on the long pathway that led from the elevator to the dock. Tourists boarded the elevator up on the observation deck and made their way through the raincoat tent and down a pathway to get on the boat.

"I believe it is," Lyman said. "Looks like she's coming to the rescue."

She hadn't mentioned anything the night before about working a wedding. She led tours at least five days a week and split the rest of her time between the history museum and helping out with the wedding business.

The wedding party made it to the raincoat tent, but they didn't come out the other side right away. Lyman smiled and greeted tourists but kept one eye out for a white veil. Time was running short if they were going to make this boat, and he was about to suggest to Jasper that they get on the next one when a bride emerged from the tent and floated toward them in a long white wedding gown.

Minnie and Ginny followed the bride and groom, who didn't appear to have any other people with them. No maid of honor or best man? Abigail followed a few paces behind the bride, too.

"Welcome aboard the Maid of the Mist," Jasper said in his best guest-service voice. Lyman smiled at the bride, but there was something about her that puzzled him. Did she look familiar?

The bride and groom smiled and shook hands with Jasper and Lyman while Minnie slipped Jasper an envelope, which he tucked in his uniform pocket. The whole group went toward the bow of the boat, except for Abigail, who lingered behind.

"To the rescue?" he asked her. "Did she forget her dress in her hotel room or something?"

Abigail shook her head, frowning. "She had to borrow one at the last minute."

"Is that a thing?"

She nodded. "Minerva and Mom keep spare gowns and suits on hand in case of disaster or unplanned events."

"So you had to make a dash to the loaner closet?" Lyman guessed. What was nagging him?

"Not exactly," Abigail said.

"Wait a minute. Now I get it. That was *your* wedding dress, wasn't it?"

She shrugged. "I wasn't using it, and the other dress in the bride's size had a red-wine stain that Minnie didn't notice when she put it away last time. What is it you sailors say? Any port in a storm?"

"Is it storming?" Lyman asked.

"It is for that bride. She wants to get married in a white dress."

"Then why didn't she bring her own?"

"They decided yesterday to turn a proposal weekend into an elopement weekend."

"Hence the lack of guests," Lyman said, nodding.

"And witnesses. So I better get going, because I'm putting my name on the paperwork for them as a witness."

"But you don't know them," Lyman said. He smiled and waved at passengers boarding.

"That's not a requirement, and I've done it many times for couples who just need someone to help make their union legal," Abigail said. She twisted the engagement ring on her finger as she talked, and Lyman wondered what felt worse to her—seeing another bride in her dress or wearing a fake ring.

"Any port in a storm," Lyman said.

"You're catching on." Abigail smiled and turned

toward the front of the boat, where Lyman could see his fellow captain unfolding a piece of paper. Had the couple really decided just yesterday to get married and to do it right away? Was it reckless or was it proof that true love couldn't wait?

"Abigail," he said, raising his voice just enough for her to hear him over the sounds of guests boarding and the engines rumbling.

She stopped and tilted her ear toward him.

"How do you feel about someone else wearing your dress?"

She gave him a small smile. "I hope she has better luck in it than I did."

Lyman nodded, not knowing what to say, and Abigail joined the wedding party while he continued to welcome passengers. This bride already had better luck, because the person she wanted to marry was standing right next to her on the boat. But he wondered if it had truly been bad luck the day Abigail had leaped right into his arms and changed the course of his entire summer.

He didn't think so, and he hoped Abigail didn't, either.

CHAPTER NINETEEN

#RomanceInTheRain

"HELLO, AND THANK you for joining us tonight," Abigail said. She slipped on a pair of pink-rimmed glasses and smiled at her webcam. Lyman, sitting next to her, waved to the dozens of couples who were in the video chat with them. "We'll start with a little warm-up. Which couple here tonight is farthest away from Niagara Falls?"

It was August 1, exactly two weeks before the August 15 mass wedding, and everything appeared to be going smoothly. Macey had suggested the video meeting as a way to talk with the couples and answer some logistical questions about travel and accommodations. The call was also being recorded, and Abigail expected snippets of it to be shared online in the next day or two. She and Lyman had made two public appearances since the Christmas-in-July event—one to be photographed in front of the red and pink hearts projected on the falls and another one at a local florist, where they were, supposedly, choosing flowers for the complimentary bouquets for the mass wedding participants. In both cases, they had kept things light and brief, posing as directed by the photographer and then going home.

Now they were side by side, and Abigail noticed Lyman's hair was still damp and he smelled like soap. Their legs touched under the table. She remembered a happy afternoon from the summer they were eighteen. They'd gone to a graduation party for someone in their class, held at a golf resort with a pool. They swam and sat by the pool, drying in the sun, and Abigail recalled ignoring everyone else and just talking to Lyman throughout the whole party.

It wasn't possible to ignore the eager couples online with them right now. Plus, she and Lyman were much more mature now—definitely not wrapped up in each other.

One lady on the call raised her hand. "I'm from Georgia," she said. "And my fiancé is from right across the line in Tennessee."

Abigail waited a beat. "Can anyone top that for distance?" She already knew the answer. She had a fact sheet on all ninety-eight couples signed up for the mass wedding, compiled from the online applications they'd sent in.

"Montana," a man said. "I'm Darren, and this is Tanja."

From their little boxes onscreen, other couples waved.

Lyman leaned over and looked at the sheet on the desk between him and Abigail. He pointed to a name halfway down—a couple from California—and looked at Abigail, but she gave him a little shake of her head. Not every couple was on the call tonight, and maybe some of them didn't want to speak up or were unfamiliar with unmuting or using the chat feature.

"Well, wherever you're coming from, we're looking forward to welcoming you to beautiful Niagara Falls in two weeks. Generous support has come in from the community for this event, and there will be complimentary airport shuttles running in the days before and after the wedding from the Buffalo airport. You've already received information about hotel deals and meal vouchers from local restaurants. Suffice to say, you're going to fall in love with Niagara Falls."

The couples smiled and laughed at Abigail's reference to the campaign name. Someone typed the #WillTheyWontThey hashtag in the chat box, and it immediately got likes from other participants. Abigail and Lyman had been told in advance not to worry about monitoring the chat because Macey would do that in real time, so Abigail ignored it. But she saw Lyman staring at it.

"We want to talk about you," Abigail said. "This is a great opportunity to share your engagement story and tell us why you signed up for this once-in-a-lifetime event."

A young couple unmuted, and the man waved. "Honestly, we were planning to come there and elope anyway, but then my mom started following you two online, and she persuaded us to have an official wedding and invite our immediate families."

"I'm glad we were an inspiration," Lyman said.

"My mom is coming to the wedding, and she wants to get her picture with you two," the young man continued. "You'll be there, right?"

Abigail and Lyman both said "yes" at the same time, and a few more likes rolled in on the #WillTheyWontThey message in the chat box.

"We'll be there, but the focus will be on all of you who are making the journey here to celebrate with people who are strangers—or at least they were until this virtual meeting," Abigail said. "Which brings me to my next question. Do any of you know each other?"

Two couples unmuted and tried speaking at the same time, and then they both gave up and typed in the chat box.

"Sisters?" Abigail said. "That's fantastic. I wish I had a sister to get married with. Does this make it easier for your families to come along, since they'll be coming to two weddings?"

Both couples gave thumbs-up signs.

An older couple started waving after a moment

of silence, and Abigail unmuted them. "Go ahead," she said. She recognized them and knew what was coming.

"We're one of the couples renewing our vows," the woman said, "and Lyman is our son. We're so proud of him. He served our country and now he's a boat captain on the Maid of the Mist."

Abigail watched the faces of the people on the video chat and saw surprise on a lot of them.

Lyman smiled and waved. "Hi, Mom and Dad. Why do I feel like it's the first day of school and my parents are telling my teacher that I already know my math facts?"

Everyone laughed, and the tension and nervousness dissipated.

"Is this our only parent-and-child pair?" Abigail asked. Her own parents had thought about it, but her dad would be out of town. "Any other related pairs?"

She didn't think there were any more pairs, based on the cities and states people were from, but she didn't know everything about these couples. She thought about the fifty couples in the original mass wedding and all the research she had done about them. She'd spent so much time following their stories before and after their weddings that she felt as if she knew them or even was related to them.

"How about anyone related to or who knows someone from the 1950 wedding?"

Lyman put an arm around her shoulders and also pointed at her, and she could see people leaning in closer to their computer cameras. She elbowed him playfully.

"My grandparents are in the original picture," she said. "I'll share my screen and show you."

Abigail got a lump in her throat when she showed the picture, pointing out her mother's parents. They were older when they got married and had Ginny later in life, so Abigail had hardly known them before they passed away. The wedding photograph made her feel closer to them.

"Question and answer time," Abigail said, hoping to get away from anything emotional and focus on the logistical and practical aspects of the event. "We're only two weeks away, and you can always ask questions in the online forum, but ask away now if you want, because someone else may have the same question."

"How many couples total are signed up?" a man asked.

"Ninety-eight," Lyman said. "So please ask your friends to join us."

"What if we don't get a hundred?" another person asked. "Will it be canceled?"

"No," Abigail said. "It will go down in history as ninety-eight weddings, and future historians will have to dig deep with their research to find out why it wasn't an even hundred."

A lady unmuted. "I bet you two are going to

get a marriage license a day in advance and be ready just in case."

Lyman had already removed his arm from around Abigail's shoulders, but now she felt him inch away and create a sliver of space between them. Was he doing that for himself or for her?

"We love Niagara Falls, and we're willing to do almost anything to make this event a success," Abigail said. She stressed the word *almost*.

"Were you two really high school sweethearts reunited by accident?" another person asked.

Abigail wouldn't have called them high school sweethearts. Didn't that term apply to married couples who dated in high school? They'd dated only one summer, and six years of ghostlike silence had followed.

"It's hard to believe, isn't it?" Lyman said. Abigail admired how he cleverly acknowledged the question without confirming or denying it. Did he see her as his high school sweetheart or just a girl he'd dated the summer he was anxious to ship out?

For the next ten minutes, Abigail, Lyman and sometimes Macey answered questions about places to stay and dine while in Niagara Falls, and they shared specifics on the location of the mass wedding, the flowers, the time everyone should show up and even the menu for the group reception that would be held afterward under a big tent on the grounds of the state park.

"We hope you'll arrive a few days early and participate in the spa days, cake tasting and the bachelor and bachelorette parties," Abigail said. "But if that's not in your plans, we'll see you on the big day—just be sure to have your New York State marriage license in hand at least twenty-four hours ahead of time."

They ended the call, but Lyman didn't get up and move away. It was only a moment until Macey came into the room.

"I certainly hope we get a few more interested couples so I can stop stressing about being short. I'd actually like a few spares just in case of travel issues or cold feet on the big day," she said.

Abigail didn't say anything, but she thought about Josh and his cold feet that had carried him far away from her on their wedding day.

"Hey," Lyman said quietly to Macey, who put a hand over her mouth.

"Sorry," she said. "I didn't think before I said that, I keep forgetting that's how—"

"It's okay," Abigail said. "It's not a bad thing to forget that day."

"Except for the part where you two, you know..."

"We know," Lyman said. "Are we finished for the night?"

After the effort of smiling and cheering on dozens of happy couples, Abigail was suddenly exhausted. She just wanted to go home and get into her pajamas and not have to pretend for anyone.

"All done," Macey said. "I'll text updates and plans, but we're getting close to the finish line."

"Sounds great," Lyman said. He got up and held the door open for Abigail. As soon as she looked outside, her heart sank.

It was pouring rain, huge drops coming down with the force of a garden hose turned on by Mother Nature herself.

LYMAN STOOD NEXT to Abigail in the entrance of the tourist center. It had been a grueling video chat, smiling at the tiny faces on the screen, knowing his parents were watching him and Abigail closely—along with everyone else. *Will they or won't they?* He wished that hashtag would go away. This was supposed to be about Niagara Falls, not him and Abigail.

"You did a great job," he said. "You carried the whole thing."

She smiled up at him. "You chimed in at the right times."

"Will you be glad when this is over?" he asked.

"The big wedding? Definitely. It's a lot of pressure."

He noticed she'd specifically mentioned the big wedding, not necessarily their shared efforts on the whole campaign for the falls.

"I should get home," Abigail said.

"Wait," Lyman said. It was a hot summer evening, and deep puddles were already forming around the sidewalks outside the tourist center. A car went past and splashed their ankles. "Do you remember that time?"

"Yes," Abigail said, without asking him what he meant.

"Me, too." He couldn't help smiling, remembering that summer night when they'd gotten caught in the rain, neither of them heeding their parents' suggestions to keep an eye on the weather and have an indoor date. But they'd planned to walk the whole loop around Goat Island, and they wouldn't let weather stop them. The scenic walkway was just under two miles, and they'd spent most of it carrying their shoes and laughing in the rain.

"We're older and wiser now," Abigail said. "I knew it would rain this evening, and I have an umbrella."

"I also have an umbrella in my truck," Lyman said. "But a little water won't hurt me. I need to get new sneakers anyway."

"My sandals are washable."

"Are those good sandals for walking?"

She smiled. "Good for a few miles."

They stood under the awning at the tourist center, grinning at each other. He knew it would have been easier and smarter to just go home and stay out of the rain. But he didn't mind getting wet. Sometimes, in his work in the Coast Guard, when he'd been soaking wet, his clothes clinging to him and his socks drenched, he'd thought of that care-free summer night.

"Why not?" he said, his words a question.

Abigail shrugged. "Why not."

Lyman stepped out into the rain and let it pour over him. "I'm committed now."

Abigail laughed and stuck one hand out from under the awning, too. "Me, too."

"Wait," he said. He ran over to his truck and came back with an umbrella and a hat. He put the hat on Abigail and tucked her hair into the sides, and then put up the large umbrella, sheltering them both. "Ready."

They crossed the bridge into the state park region and got on the trail that would take them on a loop around Goat Island. There were trolley stops along the way and some cars on the road that ran alongside the trail, but there weren't many tourists out on a rainy evening.

"I can't remember why we were so determined to go out that evening," Abigail said. "We could have waited for a nicer night."

"What's nicer than walking in the rain? Besides, once you're soaked through, you honestly can't get much wetter. No point in fighting it."

"Are you saying we should put the umbrella down?" she asked with a smile.

Lyman looked down at her, her face in shadow under the umbrella, and he felt eighteen again, as if the whole world was waiting for him. But

Abigail was part of that world now, in a way he hadn't allowed her to be before. He hadn't let her into his heart back then because he knew he was leaving. But thing were different now, and somehow being with her felt like a much greater risk.

"Not yet," he said. "We'll make smarter choices this time—at least as long as we can."

As they walked along under the umbrella, Lyman put an arm around Abigail. It made it easier to share the limited space, and she didn't object. Walking next to her with rain drowning out the rest of the world kept taking him back to that earlier summer evening.

"That was a great summer," he said aloud.

Abigail glanced up quickly, then nodded. "I loved my job. It was totally uncomplicated. All I had to do was run the cash register at the history museum selling tickets and T-shirts. Little did I know then that I'd be back every summer until I finally got a full-time job there."

Lyman laughed. "They're lucky to have you. Do you still eat lunch in the little break area between the museum and the gift shop next door?"

"No, I usually grab something between tours. I've had lunch delivered for the summer workers a few times, though, and set it up there because I know what it's like to be in their shoes."

"I got pizza for the dockhands last week," Lyman said. "Same reason. Although I should have done it more than once this summer."

"There's still time."

"True, but it feels like the summer is going too fast."

They skirted around a large puddle on the trail and had to duck so the umbrella would fit under a low-hanging tree near the path.

"What are we going to do, Abigail?" he asked quietly.

"About what?"

"About what people believe to be true about us."

"Does it matter what people think?"

It was a fair question. Did he care that people thought he was dating Abigail and that the hashtags and posts made it seem as if they were falling in love, just like the name of the ad campaign?

He didn't.

He only cared what Abigail thought.

"We only have two weeks left. Do we just go back to being normal people after? Will people stop recognizing me when they get on the Maid of the Mist?"

Abigail smiled and glanced up at him. "That's still happening?"

He nodded. "I get asked almost every day if I'm that guy on the billboard."

"What do you say?"

"That I caught a beautiful bride at Niagara Falls and I'm the luckiest captain on the Niagara River."

She laughed. "Someone interrupted my history tour yesterday to ask me if you were really as handsome as you looked in the pictures."

"I hope you said yes."

She shook her head. "I told them you were twice as handsome as you appeared online."

"Is that what you really think?" They were having a light, fun conversation. It was just two old friends exchanging a little banter. It didn't mean anything...did it?

Abigail paused on the pathway and looked behind them. "It's raining harder. Do you think we should turn back?"

"We're almost halfway, so there's no point, is there?" he asked.

"We don't know what's ahead, though," she said. "The path might be flooded or it could rain harder."

"Or," Lyman said, "there could be a beautiful sunset, maybe even a rainbow."

Abigail resumed walking. "I remember a time when you made fun of silly tourists and rainbows."

Lyman put an arm around her again, holding the umbrella so she was sheltered more than he was. "Well, if it weren't for the tourists and rainbows, I wouldn't have had the luxury of a roof over my head growing up, or a nice boring job now. I learned to appreciate those things when I was in the service."

"Is it really boring piloting the Maid of the Mist?"

Lyman thought about it for a minute as he stepped over a puddle. "Not boring. Predictable, maybe repetitive—all the things my dad loves about driving the trolley."

He couldn't say he loved it, but there was something soothing about settling into life in his hometown. Was it just nostalgia brought on by walking in the rain with his former girlfriend?

CHAPTER TWENTY

#FlightOverTheFalls

"WE'VE HIT FIFTY thousand followers on three different social media platforms," Macey told Lyman when she called him the next morning. "And in honor of that major milestone, the tourism board is giving away a seven-day trip to Niagara Falls, all-inclusive."

"That's great," Lyman said. He held the phone to his ear with his shoulder as he put up a ladder to clean the gutters at his parents' house.

"It's a contest, and people can enter by liking any posts with the contest hashtag, which we're going to add to all the posts you and Abigail do."

"Okay," Lyman said. He kicked down the feet on the ladder and stepped up on the bottom rung to test its stability.

"Which means we need to add an event."

"I hope I don't have to pop out of a wedding cake wearing a tiara," Lyman said.

"Do you know if Abigail is afraid of flying?" Macey asked.

That caught him off guard. Had he and Abigail ever talked about flying? They'd certainly never flown anywhere together.

"If we're being shot out of a wedding cake like it's a cannon, you better ask Abigail first how she feels about flying," he said. It wasn't exactly an answer, because he didn't know the answer.

"I'll call her next, but I wanted to make sure you're free tomorrow morning at eight before I set it all up," Macey said.

"What exactly are you setting up?"

"A helicopter ride over the falls. Romantic, and also gives a great overview of all the amenities the city has to offer. The helicopter company is doing it for free in exchange for the publicity. And of course Sam and I will be going along with you and you'll have a script to read from."

"Of course," Lyman said. "Text me the details and I'll be there. I can't speak for Abigail, though."

"I know she doesn't have a history tour until eleven. I checked the schedule at the museum. If she's afraid to fly, I just wanted your assurance that you'll hold her hand."

"You're assuming I'm not afraid, but I will be happy to hold her hand."

"I was counting on both those things."

Macey hung up, and Lyman scooped two years' worth of old leaves and sticks out of the gutters. When he was on active duty, he'd come home when he could, usually for long weekends, but he hadn't really been around much for the past several years. Maybe that was why he felt he was seeing Niagara Falls with fresh eyes.

He backed down the ladder and got out his phone again.

Abigail picked up on the third ring, but her standard hello sounded distracted.

"Is this a bad time for a call?" he asked. "I'm sorry if I'm calling you during work hours."

"It's early yet, and most tourists are still at breakfast," Abigail said. "So I'm in my office working on my research project for the museum display. I've had either a breakthrough or a breakdown."

She was confiding in him? "Do you want to talk about it?"

"I'm not sure. You remember that I've done research on all the couples pictured and traced what happened to them after their weddings, their kids and grandkids, where they lived, stuff like that."

"You want to tell their stories," Lyman said. "I know."

"But there were two couples whose stories I haven't told. I've dug and dug, and all the usual suspects—official records of marriage licenses, church records for baptisms, birth certificates, death certificates, school records, employment records—all those things revealed a lot about forty-eight of the couples."

"But two are a mystery?"

"They were," she said, sounding dejected.

"Did their story have a sad ending?"

She laughed bitterly. "I think they had a sad beginning, if you count not being legally married a bad thing."

"What happened?"

"They are in the picture and their names are recorded as being part of the mass wedding, but I finally found evidence about them. One of the couples couldn't legally marry because the man was already married and his divorce was never finalized. His first wife outlived him by five years and never signed the divorce papers."

"Wow," Lyman said. "How did they end up in the ceremony?"

"Fact-checking back then wasn't as easy as it is now. Macey is working with a member of the city government to verify everyone has marriage licenses twenty-four hours before the wedding and to make sure the licenses get filed within five days afterward as required. But back in 1950? No computers, no internet searches. I guess they pulled off being illegally married. At least for a while."

"What happened then?"

"They separated, but the second wife wasn't entitled to anything because their marriage wasn't legal, so she died in poverty along with a daughter he never claimed."

"I'm sorry," Lyman said. "That's a sad story, and I feel bad for both wives."

"Me, too. The other couple also wasn't legally married, but for a different reason—she was too young. I wondered why I couldn't find a record of a license, and I started researching both of them and found that she was fifteen at the time of the wedding in 1950. He was only eighteen. They eventually got a license and married in Indiana three years later, and they ended up having five kids and being married over fifty years before he died, but they had a strange start."

Lyman blew out a breath. "I don't know if you feel better or worse having finally gotten to the bottom of all fifty stories."

"I don't, either," she said. "I hope that all one hundred couples at our event are there legally and happily and they don't have any terrible secrets."

"Maybe those two couples didn't have secrets from each other, it was just the rest of the world they were fooling," Lyman said.

There was a long silence on the other end of the line, and Lyman was afraid he'd spoken too honestly. Was pretending to be a couple hurting anyone other than themselves at this point?

"Was there a reason you called?" Abigail asked.

"Macey asked me if you were afraid of flying."

"Why?" She sounded confused.

"And I had to confess that I didn't know," Lyman said.

"Why would you know that?"

"I know your favorite book, what makes you happy and the fact that you always match your glasses to your outfits."

"What makes me happy?" she asked.

Lyman leaned against the wall of his parents' house and held the phone close to his ear so he wouldn't miss anything.

"Stories with happy endings."

There was another long pause. "I'm not afraid of flying."

"That was my guess. And I'm glad. Because the tourism board is setting up a big contest to celebrate lots of followers, and we're going up in a helicopter tomorrow morning to film the announcement. Macey's going to call you."

"She's tried. I saw her number on my screen. But I was busy talking to you." There was a note of humor in Abigail's voice, and Lyman hoped he'd cheered her up after her tough morning.

"You can act surprised when she tells you," Lyman said.

Abigail sighed. "I'm getting tired of pretending."

ABIGAIL WASN'T AFRAID to fly, but the butterflies in her stomach were out in full force anyway. She'd never been in a helicopter, even though she saw them circling over the falls all day long. She hadn't been interested in investing her money in the substantial ticket price for a short-lived thrill.

A few hundred bucks for a ride that lasted twenty minutes? She wasn't stingy, but there were uses for her money that would stretch it a lot farther.

Lyman was already there chatting with the pilot and looking at the rotors and something in the engine compartment. They were talking and nodding their heads as if they were in complete understanding about the mechanics of flight. Abigail grinned. She'd be willing to bet they didn't know the history of flights over the falls going clear back to a daredevil flight a century ago—and she doubted they'd seen the pictures in the archive at the history museum. They didn't know everything, but that was okay. Perhaps she'd tell Lyman all those details later.

As she approached, Lyman saw her and smiled broadly, as if he— Well, it was silly to read too much into it, but it seemed like he smiled as if she'd just made his day. Maybe it was the helicopter and he was giddy about getting to fly over the falls.

"Have you ever flown over the falls?" Abigail asked him as he approached her.

"No. I've flown over a lot of water, but never waterfalls like these."

The way he said that, *waterfalls like these*, suggested he was impressed by them. Was this the Lyman Roberts who couldn't wait to get away from boring old Niagara Falls years ago? She had to give him credit for growing up. Now that she thought about it, he hadn't made a disparaging remark about the sameness and repetition of life in his hometown all summer.

"Me neither," she said. "In fact, I've never been in a helicopter."

Lyman put a hand on her arm as if he wanted to protect her. "It'll be fine," he said. "Just noisy, so we have headgear. I'll be right there by your side."

"That will make the photographer happy."

"It makes me happy, too," Lyman said. "It wouldn't be any fun doing this alone."

Abigail fought a wave of emotion. "You wouldn't be alone anyway. Macey and Sam will be there, and don't forget about the pilot."

Lyman studied her seriously. "You know what I mean. We're partners in this, Abigail." He swallowed and removed his hand as if he needed the distance to help compose his thoughts. "You're an excellent partner."

"I'm timely and I follow orders, just like you," she said.

"It's more than that—"

"Ready for the preflight instructions?" the pilot interrupted. "Is everyone who's going up here?"

Abigail looked around and saw Macey and Sam standing by the small building where tourists purchased tickets. Sam had his camera raised, and Abigail wondered if he'd captured her expression and Lyman's during their short conversation. Each time they talked lately, it seemed as if there was something right under the surface they were both afraid to say. What would be the harm in admitting that she liked him and liked being with him? It wasn't a marriage proposal or a contract requiring him to stick around. She wasn't even looking for a romantic relationship.

But it was nice having Lyman as a friend.

She waved Macey and Sam over, and the pilot gave them instructions for what to expect on the flight. He assigned them seats and headsets, and Macey handed Abigail and Lyman a set of posters they were supposed to hold up.

"I'll hold up notecards with what you're supposed to say through the microphones on your helmets and then you hold up the little posters and we'll get pictures of you two with the posters and the falls in the background," Macey said. "And make sure people can see your ring, Abigail."

"That's a lot going on," Lyman said. "Are you sure you don't want us to dangle from ropes and drop confetti on tourists? Maybe release some doves?"

Abigail laughed. "I'll do my best, but this is my first time in a helicopter—reading off cue cards may be the limit of my ability."

"You'll be fine," Macey said. "You can walk backward and keep the attention of fifteen tourists at a time, no matter the weather. You have skills."

They all buckled in, and Lyman put a hand on

Abigail's shoulder. "You'll love it," he said. "It's more exhilarating than scary."

The engine noise reached a crescendo, and Abigail felt the helicopter lifting off. She leaned over, looked out her window and saw the familiar streets of Niagara Falls speeding away beneath her.

"We're going up the gorge first, and then we'll fly straight at the falls," the pilot said through the headset. "You've never seen them this way before."

Abigail looked over at Lyman, who nodded encouragingly. She looked out the window again, but then she went to say something to Lyman and didn't realize he'd leaned in close to her, and suddenly, with no warning at all, their lips connected in a moment that was pure adrenaline, its intensity matching the thrill of being airborne over the Niagara River.

The moment stretched on. Neither of them jerked backward. Instead, her lips lingered on Lyman's, and she almost forgot she was hundreds of feet in the air. The wild feeling of flight was just the helicopter ride, she told her racing heart. She drew back slowly, and in her peripheral vision she saw Macey raising both fists in the air in a victory gesture.

They'd finally had the kiss. And Abigail had no doubt Sam had captured it.

"You were…going to say something?" Lyman asked.

"I was?"

"I thought…"

"I forgot what I was going to say," Abigail said. Had it been some comment about the way the Maid of the Mist dock appeared tiny below them? Or was it something about the mist in the morning sun?

"Going to hover here as planned," the pilot said through the headset, clearly oblivious that something had just changed in the air between Abigail and Lyman.

They'd kissed before during their sweet romance, fleeting like the summer. But this kiss, although accidental, was different. They were grown-ups. Their relationship had grown up, too, even if it was stained and battered a bit by choices they'd both made or had made for them.

She wanted another kiss. The thought hit Abigail out of the clear blue sky, but she didn't have time to process it. Macey handed over a microphone on a long cord and held up a cue card with text about the big giveaway written in bold black letters. Even without her glasses, Abigail had no trouble reading the cards, but her mouth wouldn't connect with her brain.

Lyman put an arm around her shoulders and angled them so the camera would get them in front of the side window, through which there was a clear view of the falls. He was doing it right. Was he more composed because of his experience in helicopters? Or hadn't the kiss affected him as it did her?

Lyman read the cue card and held up the cardboard poster printed with hashtags and announcements, still keeping his arm around Abigail. She forced a smile but let him do the talking. She'd done most of the talking in their other PR events. If their online fans thought it strange, they could always put out a story that Abigail was a nervous flyer. No one had to know it was the kiss that had her befuddled and speechless.

Macey changed her cue card, and Lyman dutifully read it with enthusiasm. Because Abigail was very close to him—close enough to kiss in the confined space of the helicopter, with his arm around her—she could see the red on his neck and cheek and feel the nervous twitch of his fingers on her shoulder as they opened and closed, as if Lyman wasn't sure how tight to hang on.

She could sense those things, but the camera probably wouldn't.

Macey held up one finger as if to imply one more thing and switched to the next cue card. It said, "Who will be the one hundredth couple at the wedding? We're saving that last spot for someone special—could it be you?"

Lyman read slowly, looking right at the camera. The way he dragged out the words left room for the video to do its magic and imply the last spot could belong to someone very special. Macey handed him a fresh set of posters, and Abigail recognized the hashtags they'd been using all summer long, written large on colorful cards. Lyman handed the cards to Abigail, and she held them up one at a time.

#CatchTheBride

#FallInLoveAtTheFalls

#WillTheyWed?

Lyman pressed a kiss to her cheek, the touch of his lips taking her back several minutes to when their lips had touched in a kiss she'd be thinking about long after the hashtags faded from their moment in social media time. All summer long, she'd looked for traces of the boy she'd known in the man he was now. Six years made a difference. Six years changed the meaning of a kiss and the impact of a strong arm around her shoulders.

But they wouldn't change the future.

Macey waved her hands at Abigail to catch her attention, and she made a "smile" gesture by dragging up the corners of her own mouth with her index fingers. *Look happy*, she mouthed.

Lyman drew back so he could look her in the face. He raised his eyebrows in a silent question. Abigail wasn't sure she could muster a smile for the camera, so she did the next best thing that would make the viewers happy. She leaned in and pressed a kiss to Lyman's lips.

If he asked her about it later, she'd claim she was overwhelmed by the helicopter ride and the cue cards, so she'd needed a quick distraction.

Right. That was what she'd tell him.

CHAPTER TWENTY-ONE

#PlusOneAtNiagara

It HAD BEEN three days since the helicopter ride. Choppers were nothing new to him. Kissing Abigail wasn't exactly new, either. But those teenage kisses hadn't been the kind that kept him awake at night. Now, though... The first one had been an accidental meeting of their lips. The second one was no accident.

He hesitated over the text message. There was no official reason for him to see Abigail tonight. No need to pose for the camera or pretend they were falling in love at the falls.

No need to pretend.

Are you free tonight?

He hit Send and waited. His break between departures on the Maid of the Mist would last another five minutes. He leaned on the railing, phone in hand.

The private cruise to celebrate the retirement

of twins Jasper and Jackson would go upriver, piloted by one of Tom's friends who was a retired boat captain but came in to substitute or take shifts during busy times. That way, the other captains of the Maid would be free to enjoy the party onboard.

Dates weren't mandatory, but Lyman felt somehow more comfortable having Abigail by his side. She was great at conversation, loved the area and knew the people. She'd appreciate the historical aspect of the long-serving twin brothers retiring from the Maid of the Mist, which was itself an important part of local history.

Yes, but I don't think we have plans, the text came back.

We don't, but we could. Would you like to go to a retirement party for Jasper and Jackson?

He checked his watch. Two minutes left on his break.

It's onboard the Maid with free food and drinks, he added.

What time?

I could pick you up at six.

Are we going as ourselves or as the people on the billboard?

This text was accompanied by a smiley face emoji.

Just ourselves, he replied.

I'll be ready.

The thought made his heart race. He didn't have an official reason for asking her to the party. And she didn't have an official reason for saying yes.

"Captain?"

One of the summer deckhands paused near him at the rail. "Everyone's onboard."

"Thank you," Lyman said. He shoved his phone in his pocket, inwardly berating himself for thinking about Abigail instead of the hundreds of tourists whose safety he was responsible for. He remembered daydreaming at his summer job as a teenager when he'd been a deckhand on the Maid. He'd taken that job just seriously enough, always believing there was someone higher up the food chain who was actually responsible.

Now he was the guy who was responsible. He went into the pilothouse, double-checked the safety manifest, gave the usual directions and commands to the deckhands, and steered the boat away from shore. As the currents tugged at the vessel and he navigated, Lyman thought about Jackson and Jasper, who were his age decades ago. Had they wondered how long they would be there at the helm of the Maid, or had they just taken things day by day?

"THIS SEEMS LIKE an actual date," Minerva commented as she scrolled through pictures from recent summer weddings. Abigail sat in the comfy chair in the corner of the office Minerva and Ginny used, just off the lobby of the hotel where their wedding business had a partnership.

"He needed someone to go to the party with," Abigail said.

"Yes, and he chose you."

"He asked me. Maybe he already asked five people before he got to me."

Minerva looked up and stared at Abigail. "Of course, he has friends in town, since he grew up here, but I highly doubt you were call number six."

"Maybe we'll take some casual pictures and it will help the cause. We're still looking for couples ninety-nine and one hundred."

"You need two couples?"

"One backed out," Abigail said. "Cold feet. I guess it was better to do that over a week in advance and not...you know."

Minerva swiveled in her office chair and faced Abigail. "Speaking as the local matchmaker, I can say with some authority that the hardest thing to do is open your heart again once it's been bruised."

"It's safer not to," Abigail agreed.

"But you never know what you could be missing out on. You've been my friend since kindergarten, and I always thought you were brave and smart. But I've been impressed by how you've embraced this whole fake-dating-for-the-greater-good thing. At first, I thought it was just a good distraction and it would be nice to take your mind off Josh and how he weaseled out on you."

Parking herself in the corner of Minerva's office may have been a mistake, Abigail thought. She should have chosen to sit on a nice rock in the state park. "I thought you were busy updating your website with recent pictures," Abigail said.

Minerva ignored the interruption. "Then I thought you might be having some fun with Lyman. He's a safe choice—you'd already dated him and done the breakup thing, and the parameters were clear. Not a real romance, not a real risk."

"Uh-huh," Abigail said. She intended to sound uninterested in the conversation, but she had to admit to herself she was curious about what Minnie was going to say. Her friend knew all about her long-ago summer with Lyman, the few guys she'd dated since then and, of course, Josh. Abigail believed she was doing a decent job of fooling everyone. The general public was sure she and Lyman were in love, while the people who knew her best believed there was nothing real between her and Lyman.

Didn't they?

"But things are different now between you and Lyman than they were years ago."

It wasn't a question. Minerva folded her hands in her lap and waited.

"Of course they are. We were young and having fun the summer after high school."

"Twenty-four isn't old," Minnie said.

Abigail smiled at her oldest friend. "But it's wiser than eighteen."

"I have no doubt you're wiser, although I'm not sure I'd say the same for myself. And Lyman? Is he better at knowing what he wants now?"

"You'd have to ask him."

"Are you going to?"

Abigail shook her head. "I'm not interested in whatever he has planned for his life after our campaign ends. He doesn't owe me any explanation, just like he didn't back then, even though we were dating."

Minerva rolled her chair closer. "Sometimes I think we get too focused on the happy ending— at least the wedding, which I guess is more of a happy beginning. It's easy to forget there are a lot of sad ones out there."

"I try to ignore those," Abigail said.

"Me, too," Minerva said on a sigh. "If I dwelled on those, it would hurt my ability to push other people to the altar."

"And you're good at that," Abigail said. "Although I can't blame you for the Josh thing. I pushed myself into it, and I pushed him, too."

"You wanted to have someone. Everyone does."

Abigail rested her head on the high back of the chair. "You know, even though I knew Lyman was leaving at the end of that summer and our relationship wasn't going anywhere, I still let myself hope. I let myself get hurt, even though he had been clear from that first kiss a few weeks before graduation."

"The unfortunate brain-heart disconnect," Minerva said.

"And then with Josh. Ugh. Looking back on it, I think that relationship was what I wanted."

"And now with you and Lyman?"

"Now I know better, which is why it's fine that I'm going along to this party tonight. Once again, he's probably leaving at the end of the summer. But this time I believe it, and I've kept my heart and head above water, no matter what the hashtags say."

"Good," Minerva said. "Now, what are you wearing?"

Abigail smiled. Minerva was a good friend. She knew what questions to ask and also when to stop asking.

"Anything but white," Abigail said.

CHAPTER TWENTY-TWO

#PartyAtTheFalls

IT WAS LIKE a first date. Lyman felt heat under his collar every time he tried to think of what he'd say when he got to Abigail's house. He was only a block away and time was running out. Should he thank her for coming along? Comment on the weather? Ask her if she thought they should tell Macey about this and even take pictures, just in case anyone doubted they were in love?

He parked in the driveway, not the street this time, right behind Abigail's car. Her mom's car was there, too, and he felt like he was eighteen again. He wondered if Ginny would be watching out the living room window.

He stepped out of the driver's seat, his heart racing. Abigail came down the three concrete steps that led to the aluminum storm door on the front porch.

She smiled broadly. "Oh, good," she said. "You're casual. I debated about what to wear to a retirement party, but since it's on the Maid, I hoped something like this would work."

He nodded. "It works."

Abigail wore a green dress with short sleeves and a ruffled skirt that swished around her legs when she walked toward him. She wore flat sandals and had her hair pulled back in a ponytail.

"Very well," he added.

"You look nice, too," she said, giving his striped polo shirt and knee-length shorts a once-over.

"Thank you." He cleared his throat. "And thank you for coming to the party as my…guest."

"I'm happy to be your guest."

If her mom was watching out the front window, she was seeing two people struggling so hard against awkwardness that it was probably painful to watch. Lyman decided on action. He walked back to his truck and opened the passenger door. "Boat leaves the dock at six thirty."

"The Maid dock? Do we have time to park and go down the elevator?"

He shook his head. "The maintenance dock upriver. We can park right there."

Abigail settled into her seat. "I've never been there."

"I'll give you a tour, but don't get your hopes up too much," he said. "It's not that exciting."

She gave him a curious glance. "I won't."

Lyman got behind the wheel. "How was your

day?" he asked as he backed down the driveway and turned onto the street.

"It was fine," Abigail said. "Morning and afternoon tours, and I hung out with Minnie at the wedding chapel in between."

"That sounds nice." *Ah, polite conversation.* The saving grace when navigating around the elephant in the room.

"She's updating the website with pictures from this summer's weddings, with the brides' and grooms' permission, of course."

"Of course."

"And how was your day?" she asked.

He couldn't tell her he'd spent all day trying not to think about asking her to the party and then trying not to think about how he was going to get through an evening with her without wondering how it would feel to kiss her again. Just them. No cameras or script to follow. Had that been a real kiss on the helicopter or was it only his imagination? There was no way to ask that question.

He cleared his throat. "Fine. The usual day shift on the Maid. We had a large group of tourists from Europe."

"That's nice," Abigail said.

"When I was a kid, I always wondered why people from other countries wanted to come here. I used to think they should go to New York City or California or even Las Vegas. Someplace exciting."

"And what do you think now?"

"I think it doesn't get much more exciting than a zillion gallons of water falling hundreds of feet every second of every day."

Abigail laughed. "When I was a kid and I heard people speaking all different languages throughout the parks, I thought it was proof that this was one of the most special places in the world."

He turned down a road, and Abigail said, "I thought I knew every road around Niagara Falls, but I don't know this one."

This summer was full of new things mixed with the familiar, he reflected.

"What do you plan to do at the end of the summer?" she asked.

"At the end of the summer I'll still have twenty months to go in the reserves," Lyman said.

"Do you have to be stationed somewhere in particular?"

Was she curious about life in the reserves, or could he hope she had another reason for asking?

"Not really. I'll owe them a weekend a month and need to be ready in case my service is needed."

It was a nonanswer, but he was being careful.

He didn't say another word until they pulled into the maintenance area for the Maid of the Mist boats, just up the river from the tourist dock.

"I'd be glad to give you a tour of this area another day," Lyman said, "but right now we should park and get on the Maid so we don't miss the party."

"You don't have to give me a rain check on that," Abigail said. "I don't want you to feel obligated to tie up any more of your time with me."

Was that how she really felt? Asking her to be his date for the evening was far from an obligation, but he didn't know how to convince her of that.

"I'll get your door," Lyman said as he parked.

"I got it." Abigail got out before he could make good on his offer. She walked beside him toward the dock, leaving just enough distance between them so he couldn't reach for her hand.

THIS WAS HIS first time enjoying a trip on the Maid with no responsibility. He wasn't shadowing the captain as he had his first week on the job. He wasn't in charge of anyone's safety, unless he counted his own as he navigated a tightrope with Abigail. Most of the people on the boat had their own assumptions about his relationship with Abigail.

Even if his fellow captains knew the initial picture of him and Abigail had been unplanned and the whole thing had snowballed, he thought they were buying in to the social media suggesting that love had blossomed—again.

"We have a photo booth," Kirsten said as he and Abigail boarded. "In case you two aren't already sick of having your picture taken."

"I was hoping to have my picture taken with the guests of honor," Lyman said.

Kirsten laughed. "There will be plenty of that. Those two are already in party mode. The way they're celebrating their retirement, you'd think they can't wait to ditch all of us."

"Leaving is a double-edged sword," Lyman said. "You want out, but then you miss things."

He stopped and noticed Abigail's look.

"Something I learned about the service," he added quickly. "I thought I'd never miss being out in bad weather and sharing tight quarters on boats, but sometimes I do anyway."

"Lucky for you," Kirsten said, "we have bad weather here sometimes, and the Maid can get pretty crowded on summer days."

Lyman grinned. "A perfect substitute."

He put a hand at the small of Abigail's back and steered her toward the center of the boat, where tables and chairs were set up in the area where hundreds of tourists usually jockeyed for position in their blue raincoats. This was different—peaceful.

The horn sounded, and Abigail jumped and put a hand on her heart.

"You get used to it," Lyman said. "Although that's a lot easier when you're the one blowing the horn. Looks like we got here just in time."

He felt the vessel move under his feet and kept an arm around Abigail to steady her, just in case her sea legs weren't as experienced as his. "Want to get something to eat?"

She nodded and dropped the hand that was over her heart. As soon as she saw the caterer, Abigail broke into a smile and strode toward her.

"Hi, Susan," she said. "Now that I know you're doing the catering, I'm really glad I agreed to come to this party."

"Should I be offended?" Lyman asked. He extended his hand to the woman in the white apron. "Lyman Roberts."

"I'm Susan Nickles, and I know who you are. Everyone does. You and Abigail are the most famous couple in town."

"Not for long," Abigail said.

Susan tilted her head, and Lyman heard Abigail catch her breath as if she'd just said something she didn't intend to say.

"I believe she means that pretty soon there will be a hundred couples going down in history at the mass wedding and we'll be a drop in the bucket," Lyman said.

Abigail nodded. "Yep. We'll stop hogging the spotlight after that."

"Well, I like seeing you two in the spotlight," Susan said. "Try the chicken. It's the best thing on the menu tonight and goes well with the wine they're serving."

"That was a smooth save," she said to Lyman

as they walked away. "Thanks for covering my blunder."

"I surprised myself by pulling that off," he admitted.

Abigail laughed and seemed to relax at last, and they filled small plates, each of them taking a piece of chicken under the watchful eye of the caterer, and then they moved to a table where Tom and his wife were already seated.

"Join us," Tom said. "Have you met Patty?"

They made their introductions, and Patty said, "We're having so much fun following along with this romance you two have cooked up this summer."

"That's...great," Abigail said. "We're looking for people to join the fun. I wonder if you and Tom might want to renew your vows in the big ceremony next weekend."

Patty shook her head. "Can't. Our son and his wife are going on a tenth anniversary weekend, and we promised to drive down to Erie and babysit while they're gone. They have a three-year-old and a six-month-old. It'll be a handful for us, but we love seeing the kids."

"That's really nice," Abigail said.

"We'll keep looking for the last two couples we need," Lyman said. "The quest is part of the fun."

Abigail turned and gave him a little smile when he said that. "The quest, huh?"

He shrugged. "Seems like as good a word as

any. *Hunt* sounds predatory, and *search* makes it seem like they're lost somewhere. *Quest* gives our mission a big feeling, like it's bigger than just us."

Patty laughed. "Who's this guy?" she said to her husband. "You didn't tell me your summer captain was a philosopher."

Tom took a sip of his drink. "Lyman's always been that way, even when he worked here as a teenager. Always thinking there was something big out there waiting for him."

"And did you find it?" Patty asked.

How in the world had he gotten himself into this conversation, with Abigail sitting there absorbing every single word? She certainly wouldn't appreciate rehashing his attitude after high school graduation, when he'd basically said there was nothing interesting keeping him in Niagara Falls.

He'd been a fool. Maybe it was the gift of fresh eyes after six years, but he wished he could erase some of his previous words.

"Yes, I did," he said. "I'm sure Tom can tell you that being in the service is life-changing and it makes you see things you'd never seen before."

"I've heard his stories," Patty said.

Tom gave her a look.

"And they continue to fascinate me every time."

Abigail laughed and then cleared her throat. "This chicken is delicious. My mother's wedding business often uses Susan to cater when receptions are part of the package. She does cakes, too, if she has enough notice. Sadly, I've seen a few brides with a grocery store cake when they make the last-minute decision to get married."

"Here in the land of rainbows and honeymoons," Lyman said, exchanging a smile with Abigail.

"So they tell me," she replied.

"You two are adorable," Patty said. "And I hope now that Lyman has reconnected with you, you'll be able to persuade him to stick around and fill a permanent opening as a captain."

"Honey," Tom said, putting a hand over hers.

"Oh, have I spoken out of turn?" she asked, looking mortified.

"Not at all," Lyman assured her. "Tom asked me about it last week. And I told him I would think about it."

Lyman could feel Abigail's eyes boring into the side of his face. It was true. His boss had offered him a permanent position with a decent salary. Winter would be slow, but there would be some work as long as the weather allowed, and there was always maintenance work he could help with. It was also true that he'd told Tom he'd think about it. So much had changed for him, and he didn't want his thinking clouded.

He risked a glance at Abigail, but she looked away quickly and began to cut her chicken into neat little pieces. The conversation turned, mercifully, to roasting Jasper and Jackson about what they were going to do with themselves in retirement as they sat down at the adjacent table and their wives diverted Patty's attention to talk about a mutual acquaintance who'd just had twin granddaughters.

Abigail nodded along with the conversation, but Lyman noticed she was barely touching her food. He was glad when Kirsten, who was acting as the emcee for the event, called for speeches. The boat had motored slowly upriver away from the falls and was anchored in the late-evening summer sunshine.

Lyman and Abigail moved to a spot along the railing as a retired colleague took the mic to honor the brothers. Lyman put a hand on the railing behind Abigail, and she stood in the crook of his arm.

"I'm sorry about all the workplace talk during dinner," he said. "I didn't really think about that when I asked you to be my date tonight."

"You didn't think boat captains would talk about boats?"

"I only thought about you," he said.

Abigail moved away an inch. "You have a lot on your mind, with your dad and the reserves and all the decisions you have to make. Not to mention our joint project to bring romance to Niagara Falls."

"True," he acknowledged.

"Which means we could use this as a two-for-one deal and take some pictures of us right now," Abigail said.

"That's not what this night is about," he said. He knew he was on the brink of saying something he wasn't ready to admit yet, but he hated the thought of being practical and professional at the moment.

"Then…what is it about?"

"We never talked about that kiss," he blurted.

Abigail's cheeks colored, and she moved away another inch.

"That was for the camera," she said.

"Not the second one."

Abigail turned and looked over the railing at the swirling water of the river, deceptively calm on the surface but rippling with tension underneath.

"You're right," she said, turning back and facing him. "It was impulsive, and I shouldn't have done it. I apologize."

"I didn't mind."

She took a long breath and faced the water again. "Maybe it was a good opportunity to get that out of the way. I know it sounds silly, but it was a relief to check that off."

"Why was it a relief?"

She still didn't look at him. "It satisfied my curiosity. I know for sure there's nothing romantic between us and it's safe to consider you a friend without there being any weirdness. That's good news, right?"

"I...guess so." It was nice being considered a friend, but there was definitely weirdness between them. How could it be otherwise, given their history and their present partnership? Maybe Abigail was the smart one to be drawing clear lines now.

"I thought you'd agree. And it's great we had this little chat. Now we can both relax and enjoy the party." She turned a smile on him, the one she used for the cameras, but he couldn't respond likewise. The brief touches, a hug, a kiss, kindness, understanding, friendship...had he blown them all up to mean more than they did? Was he making a mess of all of it?

"I care about you, Abigail." Saying the words aloud took almost all the courage he'd developed in the Coast Guard.

"Of course you do," she said. "We've known each other for years. You'd park my car for me or pick up doughnuts."

"Or hold an umbrella over you," he said.

Abigail paused, and her expression softened. "See, that's a good example. Teamwork. That's what we have."

Her response told him everything he needed to know. She didn't want more from him, which meant he had to get his feelings under control. He couldn't ruin all their efforts. One week to go. He could continue pretending Abigail was only his coworker as they pretended to be falling in love at the falls. Double pretending. Did two negatives make a positive?

"The party ends at nine, and you're stuck on-board with me until then," Lyman said. "I'm sorry."

"Are you sorry you asked me to come tonight?"

"No," he said softly.

Abigail turned away, but he saw the hitch in her breath. Music from the DJ onboard started up, an upbeat song slow enough to dance to. "We have to do something for the next hour. Should we practice dancing together in case we have to do it at the big event?"

She hesitated a long time and then took the hand Lyman was offering.

CHAPTER TWENTY-THREE

#OneWeekUntilTheWedding

IT WAS LATE Friday afternoon, one week before the big event, when Macey messaged the group chat. Sometime during the past few weeks, Sam had been included in the chat, a fact Abigail hadn't found strange considering that Sam was practically glued to Macey's side at every event they did. Sam had even turned down a photography job with Falling for You Custom Weddings because he said he'd promised to help Macey sort through images.

We have 101 couples! Confirmed. Travel plans made. Most licenses in hand. Yay for us!

Abigail read her message while she rode with Minerva to Prospect Point, where a bride and groom would be exchanging vows in just under an hour.

"We have all the couples plus a spare, everyone confirmed," she told her best friend.

"And your mom and I are in overdrive helping

with arrangements. We've contacted all the usual officiants and spread the wealth among the four different florists we use—same with bakeries."

"One hundred different cakes?" Abigail asked as she responded to Macey's message with celebration emojis.

Minerva pulled into the state park. "It's taking four different bakeries to share the load and make the cakes. Each couple will have their own—three tiers, chocolate, white, chocolate, with the frosting down in a waterfall theme down the side. All the same, but who cares? They can take pictures with it and then cut it up and eat it."

"It takes the stress out of planning," Abigail said.

"That's what we do. Couples just have to show up in the clothes they want to be wearing, and they'll be handed flowers and assigned to a group with an officiant. We'll go under the big tent, and they'll find their table for ten with a cake right in the middle of it as a centerpiece."

Abigail laughed. "It's almost like you've done this before."

"We had a double wedding once, but never anything like this. Now we just hope for good weather."

Abigail checked her phone again and saw a thumbs-up from Sam.

"I wonder who the final couple is," Minerva said. "Whoever it is made an almost last-minute decision, but sometimes those are the best."

"Has today's wedding been planned for a while?" Abigail asked as they parked in a loading zone so she could unload a cart and supplies from the minivan Minnie and Ginny used for official business. It had *Falling for You* painted on the side, with hearts and a three-tiered cake painted on the back.

"Seems like forever, but it's probably been six months. We've gone back and forth with this bride, who seems nice but has fussed over every single detail as if the width of ribbon in the bouquets will make or break her marriage."

"It'll all be over soon," Abigail said.

"The wedding, but let's hope not the marriage," Minnie said. "Although our company makes no guarantees."

Another message arrived on Abigail's phone as she juggled boxes with boutonnieres and bags of supplies. Abigail put her stuff on Minnie's cart and followed her friend toward the falls, pulling out her phone as she walked.

Let's meet up somewhere for a drink tonight. I'm buying.

Sam immediately liked the message from Macey, but Abigail hesitated. She knew Lyman wouldn't be there, and it wouldn't be right celebrating without him.

Sorry, I'm out of town this weekend.

The message was from Lyman. He didn't explain where he was to Macey and Sam, but Abigail knew. He'd told her in advance about his Coast Guard reserve weekends that had just begun and would last two years. Not that he owed her an explanation for his absence. He was being courteous since they were partners, teammates.

Rain check, Macey responded. Lots to celebrate next weekend.

Lyman liked her response but offered nothing further.

"What?" Minerva said as she pushed her cart along the walkways, avoiding tourists and strollers.

"Macey invited me, Lyman and Sam out for a drink tonight to celebrate achieving our goal, but Lyman is out of town."

"Where?"

"Somewhere on the East Coast with the Coast Guard reserve. Our first guests for next weekend's wedding arrive Monday, so the official lead-up events aren't starting this weekend. We sort of have the weekend off."

"Well, forty-five minutes until the wedding, and then we'll sample the cake. Did I mention you're serving it?"

Abigail laughed, but her smile faded quickly when she saw her mother running toward them, hands waving in the air. Ginny Warren went to workout classes with her friends three nights a week, but Abigail hadn't seen her mom run in a long time.

"Runaway bride," Ginny said breathlessly, bending over and gasping for air.

"No way," Minerva said. "This bride was all over this ceremony like sea gulls on French fries. She's not walking away."

"See for yourself," Ginny said, pointing to a woman standing far away from the rest of her wedding party, her white gown and veil flapping in the breeze. "She told everyone to leave her alone for a minute because she needed to think."

"So she's not actually running," Minnie observed.

"Thinking can be good," Abigail added.

"Oh, no," Ginny said, waggling a finger. "You should have seen her face. She's thinking of not going through with it."

"Okay," Minnie said. "That's her choice. She already paid the final deposit with us, so we're not out anything if she cancels it. We'll eat the cake ourselves."

"This is serious," Ginny insisted. She glanced over at the bride, who had taken off her veil. "The veil is off. Now do you believe me?"

"Let me go talk to her," Abigail said.

Both Minerva and Ginny turned to stare at her, neither one of them looking like they thought it was a good idea.

"It'll be fine," Abigail said. "I'm not going to

suggest throwing the veil over the falls or anything."

"We didn't think that," her mother said.

Abigail smiled. She could guess what her mom
and best friend were thinking. "I'm just going to
go listen. Maybe that's what she needs."

Before anyone could stop her—including herself—Abigail strode toward the veil-less bride. It
had been over two months since she'd felt very
alone in her own beautiful gown standing near
the majestic falls. She might understand better
than anyone else.

"I'm Abigail," she said as she approached. "My
mom and best friend run Falling for You Custom
Weddings."

"Oh," the bride said. "I'm Victoria."

"Your gown is beautiful."

"Thank you. It was the third one I put a deposit
on. I kept changing my mind."

"Understandable," Abigail said.

"Expensive. I lost the deposits on the first two.
And it was stupid. The first one was the one I
honestly liked the most, but I was afraid of missing out on something else that I might like even
better if I just kept trying on dresses."

Abigail started to get a sense of what the problem was.

"Jimmy and I were engaged once a long time
ago," Victoria continued. "When we were kids.
He grew up across the street, and I thought I'd

never love anyone like I loved him. The first ring was a twist tie from a loaf of bread, but we took it seriously."

"How old were you?"

"Eleven."

"You two have some history," Abigail commented. She didn't want to insert her opinion, but she did want to keep the bride talking.

"Then we both went to college and dated other people, but I didn't really give anyone a chance because I was always comparing them to Jimmy."

"He must be a great guy."

"The best," Victoria said. She examined the beads and sequins on the elaborate tiara fastened to her veil.

"So—"

"See, that's exactly the problem. Whenever I think of Jimmy, I think he's the best and I'm never going to find anyone better, but what if I'm wrong? There are a million men out there. What if I'm just grabbing Jimmy because I'm afraid?"

"Do you think you're rushing into this?"

"We've been engaged for three years and I've known him for twenty-seven."

"So, no," Abigail said. She sighed. "I rushed into a wedding once."

"What happened?"

"The groom didn't show up. He was smarter than I was, although I didn't see it that way at the time. He backed out just before the ceremony."

"Did you just stand there at the altar?" The bride looked horrified, and Abigail didn't have the heart to tell her it was at a nearby location with a very similar view.

"That's a long story, but it involves me sort of ending up with a guy I used to date when we were teenagers," Abigail said.

"Is it a second chance for both of you?"

Abigail was going to say something flippant, but instead, she found herself saying, "It could be, if I let it."

"Why wouldn't you let it?" Victoria asked, pointing at Abigail's ring finger.

Abigail grinned at the bride. "I thought we were talking about you."

Victoria laughed and held up her sparkling tiara and watched the gauzy veil float on the breeze off the falls. "How do I know if I'm making the right choice?"

Abigail leaned on the railing next to the bride and watched the water rush over the falls. She envied this bride, this woman who was taking a good long moment, no matter what anyone thought, to make sure her decision was right for her.

"You have to trust yourself," Abigail said. "Go with what's in your heart."

"It's almost too easy to marry Jimmy, the love of my life, and be done with it."

Abigail laughed. "Nothing about love and marriage is easy. Look at how hard you worked to find that dress."

Victoria quickly reeled in her veil and clutched it to her chest. "That's it. You just made me realize something. Jimmy is the first dress."

Abigail cocked her head, afraid she'd done more damage than good as the bride wrinkled that beautiful veil.

"I was afraid to settle for it even though it was perfect." She looked down at herself. "It was so perfect. I should have held on to it. But here I am in dress number three, which is honestly okay, but not…the one I wanted."

"And Jimmy is the one you want?" Abigail asked slowly.

"Yes. And so is this veil. It was the first one I picked out."

Abigail reached for the veil and began smoothing out the layers. She motioned for Victoria to duck down, and then she fastened the tiara back into place and fluffed out the tulle around the bride's face.

Victoria looked ecstatic for a moment, but then a horrified look crossed her face. "What if I'm Jimmy's dress number three?"

Abigail pointed to a spot down the railing, where a man in a black suit waited, hands clasped, as if his life depended on something. "I think he considers you dress number one," Abigail said. "But you could ask him."

Victoria broke into a radiant smile as she looked at her groom. "I don't need to ask." She started toward her groom, but then turned to Abigail.

"What are you going to do about the guy? The one who left you but came back?"

It took Abigail a moment to realize the bride meant Josh, not Lyman. Lyman hadn't really come back for her. That wasn't why he was there for the summer. And she'd made it clear to him at the retirement party that she had no feelings for him and that kiss meant nothing.

He hadn't argued.

"Make sure he knows how you feel," the bride said. She smiled. "And go with your heart on the wedding dress when the time is right."

CHAPTER TWENTY-FOUR

#BachelorPartyAtTheFalls

THE FRIDAY BEFORE the mass wedding was going down in history, Lyman thought. He had to captain a boatload of bachelors later, and here he was now at the Niagara Falls courthouse signing his name to a marriage license he wasn't going to use.

"It's just in case," Macey insisted to him and Abigail. "If only ninety-nine couples show up tomorrow, you have to save the event. We'll get it annulled—quietly—on Monday and no one needs to know."

Macey had arranged for a private meeting with the clerk, but Sam had taken pictures of Abigail and Lyman entering the courthouse. This was all part of the ruse, a tease to make people wonder if their hashtags were right and he and Abigail would join the big wedding.

"This feels like fraud," Abigail whispered, tapping her foot. "Signing a legal document with no intention of fulfilling it."

"Plenty of people get marriage licenses and don't go through with their weddings," Macey said.

Abigail stopped tapping her foot.

"Sorry," Macey said.

"It's fine," Abigail said. She pulled out a pair of purple glasses that matched the flowers on her white dress so she could inspect the paper in front of her. She took the pen the clerk held out, signed her name and then handed Lyman the pen.

He felt as if he'd been offered the sword of a surrendering army officer. Did it cross her mind, even for a moment, what it would be like to be married to him? And the sudden push for them to get a license wasn't the only thing weighing on him. On his reserve weekend, he'd met up with an old friend who was now working for the Coast Guard in Florida, and that old friend had given him something new to consider.

"I'll file this and you can get married any time after eleven tomorrow," the clerk said cheerfully. "The twenty-four-hour rule, you know."

It would all be over in twenty-four hours. Lyman gave Abigail what he hoped was an encouraging smile, and then they posed for pictures with the other couples as they signed for their licenses.

Hours later, Lyman watched the bachelors boarding the Maid of the Mist. He was more in his comfort zone here than at the courthouse, but he wasn't a bachelor party kind of guy. Lyman had been to exactly two bachelor parties in his life. One had been fun and involved eighteen holes of golf and then pinball games and burgers in the clubhouse. The other had involved some younger members of the group looking for trouble and coming close to finding it. The bachelors boarding the Maid for the first round of evening fun didn't look like troublemakers. Ranging in age from around twenty to past retirement, the men who'd come to Niagara Falls for the big wedding were not much different from him under their blue raincoats.

Except that they were making the ultimate commitment, or renewing their promises to uphold that commitment. And someone was waiting for them at the altar. He'd almost told Abigail how he felt about her. Maybe he hadn't tried hard enough, tongue-tied by the fact that he was afraid she wouldn't believe him anyway. Maybe the problem was that he didn't quite believe himself. Was he really sure he was falling for her?

Fifteen of the grooms had opted out of the party on the eve of the big wedding, and Macey had texted Lyman and Abigail to tell them it was because they were older local guys who were renewing their vows and didn't care to come out and party.

Mostly.

There were two couples who hadn't made it to

town yet, and Macey's text had been accompanied by nervous emojis and question marks.

"Good evening," he said to the men boarding. "Name tags would just get wet, so I'm calling everyone Buddy tonight."

"Thanks, Buddy," one of them said as he walked past.

Several men pulled off their shirts, stuffed them into plastic bags and then put on their raincoats.

"That's not the worst strategy," Lyman told them. "But only acceptable because it's a special event tonight with no kids and families onboard."

"My fiancée said I was supposed to try to stay dry," one of the men said.

"Good luck, Buddy. You can choose your location on the boat strategically, but inside the pilothouse is the only guarantee."

"Any chance?" the man asked.

Lyman laughed. "Authorized personnel only."

"Sheesh. I don't know why she talked me into coming to Niagara Falls. My glasses have been a blur ever since we came to town. We could have gotten married back home in Cincinnati at the courthouse."

"One thing I learned from traveling a lot," one of the other men said. "Happiness is who you're with, not where you are."

Lyman felt those words as if they had the force of a hurricane. *Happiness is who you're with, not where you are.* Not a bad philosophy. Was he happy in Niagara Falls because of Abigail?

"This is my hometown," he found himself saying to the man who was wiping his glasses on a tissue from his pocket. "I was anxious to get out of here as a kid, but I'm glad I came back."

"I'm glad to hear you say that." Tom stood next to him near the gangplank, surprising him. "Does this mean I can expect a commitment from you, or do I need to start looking for another boat captain?"

"Can I get back to you after the wedding weekend?" Lyman asked. He thought about the pros and cons list on his phone's notebook app, inspired by the offer from the Florida Coast Guard officer he'd met in the service and then reconnected with recently. Beaches and sunshine. A shared condo with an ocean view.

"Yes, but if you wait too long to make a choice, sometimes you find that choice gets made for you. And you need to do what you want—be the captain of your own ship," his boss said, speaking slowly and emphasizing the last sentence. "Metaphorically. This isn't your ship, but you know what I mean."

The summer he'd left town, he'd operated solely on what he wanted without regard for anyone's feelings. He hadn't thought he could manage both a relationship and the service, and cutting ties had seemed simple. He'd resisted letting Abigail into his heart and letting emotion guide his future. If he waited too long now to tell her how he felt, would that chance slip away?

He had to tell her he cared about her enough to want to stay in town, but he needed to find the right way. If she told him again that they were just teammates, it would break his heart.

ABIGAIL SURVEYED THE room filled with brides-to-be celebrating the night before their wedding. Their ages spanned fifty years, and they were all in love and excited to be there. The casino had set aside a big conference room for them, and there were stations set up for manicures and pedicures behind screens at one end, and drinks and desserts at the other end of the room. In between, comfortable sofas and chairs provided a place for the participants to get to know each other before joining their fates at the big wedding.

The grooms-to-be would join them after their bachelor cruise on the Maid of the Mist. Abigail wondered if Lyman was talking selfies with dozens of nervous grooms at that very moment. When Macey had divided the group in two and assigned Abigail and Lyman to their halves, Abigail had wished she was involved with the Maid of the Mist event. After all, she loved the outdoors, the stunning views of the falls and the swirling mist and rainbows up close. She couldn't captain the boat, but she'd been on it so many times this summer she almost felt like a crew member.

It might also have helped erase her unease from her last trip on the Maid, which had left her not feeling very good about herself. Whatever Lyman might have wanted to say about that kiss, she had stopped him cold and assured him she'd felt nothing. It was as if she had erected garden walls like in her favorite childhood book. She loved that book about the closed-off garden, and Lyman loved forts. Maybe they were both good at putting up walls.

"Look at these nails," Minerva said, flashing both hands as she maneuvered to the dessert table. "And I don't even have to get married. They didn't ask to see my marriage license at the mani table."

Minerva moved on, and Abigail went back to thinking about what was happening at that moment on the famous boat ride under the falls. They were getting a spectacular view while she stood in the wings of the conference center. But if she were on that boat, what would she say to Lyman? She wasn't going to tell him she'd fallen for him again and beg him not to leave.

She'd done that once. Six years ago, almost to the day. She had more pride now and more wisdom. You couldn't make people feel or believe something. After the humiliation with Josh, she'd finally gotten the message.

"Can I get my picture with you?" a woman

asked. Her name tag said Catherine, and she was a tall brunette with a few freckles and wrinkles. "I've been following you all summer, and you inspired me to give this a try."

"Oh," Abigail said. "I'm glad I was an inspiration."

"After getting jilted, you ran into your ex, quite literally, and you were brave enough to date again. I'm telling you, I don't think I could have done it."

Abigail wanted to come clean and tell the woman that things were not as they appeared. What if she and Lyman accidentally inspired someone to get married and that turned out to be a mistake?

"It's not quite as simple as that," Abigail protested, but she smiled for the picture and the woman moved on to the velvet couches where other brides-to-be sipped on fruity drinks and balanced plates of chocolate torte, vanilla bean mousse and chocolate-covered strawberries. Minerva walked over with a plate filled with one of each.

"I'm volunteering my bridal organizational skills," she said. "But I don't think three desserts and a manicure is out of line for my professional services."

"Not at all," Abigail said. "There's plenty, and some of the brides are here for the beauty treatments and not the desserts."

"This is great," Macey said, joining them. "Although I'm realizing too late that an outdoor venue near the falls would have been better. Looking at these pictures, these women could be anywhere, at any nice hotel. It doesn't really say 'Niagara Falls.'" She did air quotes on her last two words.

"On it," Sam said as he came jogging up to them carrying a big square cutout with *Niagara Falls* printed across the top and *Fall in Love at the Falls* across the bottom. "I have a photo backdrop depicting the American Falls and props. Just wait."

Macey put a hand on his arm. "You're the best."

Sam blushed and then moved to a well-lit corner of the room, where he began unpacking his gear. Macey watched him go, but Abigail exchanged a glance with Minnie and noticed her best friend's grin.

"Macey, maybe I have matchmaking and weddings on the brain," Minnie said, "but is there a little spark between you and Sam?"

"Oh," Macey said. "No, no. We're just… Well, you know we've worked together—closely—all summer on this campaign."

"It's only been a couple of months," Minerva said.

Two months and two weeks, Abigail thought. Long enough for a person to fall in love.

"Which is practically all summer," Macey said. "And I didn't really know Sam until we started… collaborating on the Fall in Love campaign."

"And now?" Abigail asked.

"And now I know he's single, has a nice condo,

likes anything strawberry-flavored and once had a photograph published by a national newspaper, which is a very big deal."

Abigail and Minnie waited without saying anything.

"Autumn is his favorite season, he's terrible at telling jokes because he rushes the punch line and he holds hands at the movies," Macey added.

"Common knowledge," Minerva said, laughing. "I'm sure everyone knows that about Sam."

Macey smiled and shook her head. "I hope it's not just this ad campaign bringing us together all the time that makes me think there's something between us."

"Did he actually hold your hand at the movies?" Abigail asked.

"Twice."

"Then I don't think it's your imagination or the campaign."

Even as Abigail said the words, she recognized the irony—or was it hypocrisy?—of her thoughts. She'd held hands with Lyman. She knew where he lived and could probably order for him at a restaurant. But none of that was real. And him saying he cared about her? It didn't mean what he apparently thought it did. She cared about the night custodian at the museum, Cindy at Tim Hortons who knew her order by heart and her friends and family.

There was caring, and then there was falling

in love. Lyman hadn't said a word about that, and he'd dodged all conversation about the offers for a job that would keep him in town.

Macey snapped back into business mode. "We have an hour until the bachelors join us after their ride on the Maid of the Mist. We'll have the mani-pedi stations removed and the dance floor and DJ set up by them."

"Should I grab more desserts before the men show up?" Minerva asked.

"No need to rush," Macey said. "There's a whole round two coming with sliders, chips and a s'more station just for fun. It's a nice departure from cake, since there will be plenty of that tomorrow. And don't forget, Abigail and Lyman are drawing names for the grand prize at the end of the party. I wanted to hold the drawing at the big reception, but Sam suggested doing it tonight to draw out the excitement instead of having it all packed into tomorrow."

Minerva nodded. "Good advice. Weddings take forever to plan, and then it seems like they're over in the blink of an eye."

"I'm nervous about what happens when this is over," Macey admitted. "Maybe I should find another project I can work with Sam on."

Minerva shook her head. "Why not just call him and tell him you want to eat strawberries and go to movies and then you'd like to hear bad jokes afterward?"

"I'm afraid he'll say no," Macey admitted.

"Then you should be careful," Abigail said.

Macey tilted her head. "I guess," she said, and then she strode toward Sam and started helping him set up his photo booth.

Minerva laughed. "She's not going to be careful. I'm proud of her."

"But what if she's setting herself up for disappointment?" Abigail asked. She pictured Macey standing there at the movies with two tickets in her hand, waiting for someone who wasn't showing up.

"And what if he's the one?" Minerva countered.

Abigail suspected they were not talking exclusively about Macey and Sam, but she didn't want to think about how she would feel waiting for Lyman to show up if she let herself dream about him.

Abigail linked arms with Minerva. "Let's go chat with the brides and see if anyone needs help with gowns, shoes or jewelry."

"Okay, but our emergency closet can only go so far," Minerva said. "That dress with the wine stain is a goner."

An hour later, the other half of the group arrived, looking a bit damp, but Abigail thought they also looked happy. Lyman was smiling—perhaps because he was the only truly dry person—and calling everyone Buddy.

"You seem like a natural at being the host of

a big bachelor party," Abigail said as she walked over to greet him at the door. Lyman put an arm around her and kissed her cheek. The way he did it made him feel like an old friend, which had become increasingly more comfortable as the weeks passed—and dangerous.

"I had the easy job of driving the boat and then directing everyone to the charter bus to bring us here."

"Next you'll be stealing my tour director job," Abigail said.

Lyman laughed. "I've been offered a job here that's much more in line with my skills."

She'd heard it mentioned at the retirement party and knew what he was talking about.

"I'm sure you have plenty of offers," she said carefully.

Lyman's expression became more serious. "I do have one other good offer. But it's not in Niagara Falls."

"There you are," Macey said. She slid in between Lyman and Abigail, taking both their arms and towing them along with her. "Sam is excited about the photo booth he set up. I want to get pictures of you two before you get distracted by everything else. You are the main event, of course."

"I thought that was all these other couples," Abigail said, sweeping a hand to indicate the couples who were hugging and kissing as if they'd been separated for days, not just two hours. Was Lyman really going to leave again?

"Of course, but your picture needs to go out first so it makes sense. It's how we'll reel out the story of tonight's prewedding party—you two kissing in the photo booth first, and then as many other couples as we can get."

Abigail had thought about that kiss in the helicopter with Lyman, but she'd doubted there would be another good opportunity to test whether or not it was just the physics of flying that had made that kiss feel so topsy-turvy. There was only one way to find out, and it might put her mind at rest if she could prove to herself it was physics and not chemistry.

"Let's do it," she said. She took Lyman's hand and pulled him toward the photo booth. They faced each other in front of the Niagara Falls backdrop. Lyman held the cardboard frame with the hashtags and waited, his eyes on hers.

"Ready?" he asked.

"If you are."

His lips curved up at the edges, which made him look very kissable. Abigail stood on tiptoes and touched her lips to his in a kiss that should have been short, sweet and practical. But it wasn't. It went on for at least five seconds longer than it needed to and reminded her of summer days and butterflies and Lyman giving her his hat to shield her from the sun.

Maybe it was just the bright flash of the camera.

"Got it," Sam said. "That's a great picture. You two are convincing as a couple."

Instead of putting down the frame and separating, Lyman leaned in for another kiss, and Abigail let herself remember, finally, that beautiful sunset evening when they had said goodbye for the last time.

When she thought of the way he'd said goodbye, as if he couldn't wait to get away from her... as if she was part of the prison keeping him in Niagara Falls...she pulled back and dropped down to her heels.

"I think we have all the pictures we need," she said, and then she backed away and went to see if Minnie had set aside any desserts for her. She could always count on her best friend to tuck something away in the kitchen to ensure a happy ending for Abigail, no matter how the event had gone.

Abigail needed chocolate right now so her lips would stop buzzing with the feel of Lyman's and her mind could let go of the memories that crowded in on her and wouldn't let her forget that he'd broken her heart once and would do it again. If she let him.

CHAPTER TWENTY-FIVE

#WeddingDayAtTheFalls

THE NIAGARA FALLS STATE PARK truck pulled up, and a park ranger got out. "I was told to bring chairs," he said. "All the folding chairs we have." He held out a work order, and Abigail took the clipboard.

"Am I supposed to count them and sign?" she asked.

"I'm on it," Minerva said as she hurried over. "I put in the request a month ago when we did the facility permit. Thank you, Ranger Grant."

"Ranger Hampton. My first name is Grant."

"I know," Minnie said. "I just wanted to hear you say an entire sentence. You usually won't talk to me at weddings."

The ranger shook his head. "It's your show," he said. He waited for Minerva to sign the paper and then tossed the clipboard through the open window of his truck.

"I'll find someone to help unload these chairs," Abigail said.

The ranger nodded. "That'll make it go faster."

Abigail used the group chat to text Sam, Macey and Lyman, who had gone to pick up flowers using Lyman's truck.

Can you hurry back and haul chairs?

Lyman was the first to respond with a thumbs-up. Abigail started helping Minerva. The park ranger stood in the truck bed and handed chairs down to them.

"Getting a workout," she commented to her friend.

Minerva laughed. "When this huge wedding is over, I may take a break from weddings for a little while."

"You don't mean that."

"I do. I'm taking three days off from even thinking about white veils and corsages. Our next scheduled wedding isn't until the end of next week, and all the plans are firmly in place, so unless we have some surprise elopements or spur-of-the-moment decisions, your mom and I can escape the world of matrimony."

"There's no escaping it in the land of rainbows and honeymoons," Abigail said. She heard the park ranger chuckle, but when she glanced up his expression was all business.

Lyman pulled in just five minutes into the un-loading work and immediately started taking chairs, two under each arm, from the truck to the semicircle they'd set up for wedding specta-tors. While they had asked each couple how many guests they expected, there was no way to predict how many tourists might sit down and enjoy the event. And why not? They were doing all this to promote the falls as a destination.

"I'll be back," Ranger Hampton said.

He drove away, and Minerva grinned at Ab-igail. "He's a man of few words. You'd hardly guess we've worked with him at least a dozen times on wedding setups."

"Is he bringing more chairs?"

"I'm sure. My request was for four hundred, which is probably not going to be enough as it is."

"We'll help out by being too busy to sit down ourselves."

"Which is a shame," Minnie said. "Because this is a once-in-a-lifetime thing. I doubt I'll ever see one hundred couples getting married at the same time again."

"Ninety-nine," Macey said as she walked up. She held up her cell phone. "Last-minute cancel-lation from two couples, so my one hundred and one is down to ninety-nine."

Minerva and Abigail froze.

"Does this mean you have to marry Lyman?" Minnie asked, turning a shocked face to Abigail.

Macey shrugged. "Honestly, Abigail, if you're not comfortable with it, that's okay. I might have pushed you two a little hard yesterday, but I'm not worried about having exactly one hundred anymore. We've achieved our real goal, which is national attention. Did you see the truck from the cable news network? We usually only get local news channels out here, and that's only if someone goes for an unexpected swim. We're getting press coverage, the hits on the tourism site are through the roof and at least ninety-nine couples will post all about it on social media and so will their friends and family. Mission accomplished."

Relief rushed over Abigail. She wouldn't have to marry her fake fiancé. Wouldn't have to pretend all the way to the altar. It would be nice to have one hundred couples for the picture, a symmetrical update to the beautiful photograph of fifty couples from the original wedding.

However, Abigail realized that even if she did carry out a fake wedding with Lyman and pose for the picture, she would know the truth every time she looked at it. It wasn't a real solution.

Abigail sat on a big rock marking the edge of the pathway. Lyman came back for another load of chairs, paused when he looked at her and her friends, and then scooped up four chairs and went back to work.

"There's still time," Macey said. "Someone could jump in at the last minute."

"Not without holding a license for twenty-four hours first," Minerva said. "Our only hope is a vow renewal couple, because that doesn't require a marriage license—not a new one, anyway."

The backup alarm on a truck interrupted their conversation, and Macey and Minerva resumed their task of taking chairs from the park ranger.

"Everything okay?" Lyman asked Abigail. "You seem upset."

She forced a smile. "Do you think spectators will notice if we're one couple short?"

Lyman sat on the rock next to her. "Someone backed out?"

"Two couples."

Lyman was silent a moment, but Abigail noticed his breathing quickened as he sat next to her. He clasped his hands together, twisting them nervously.

"Does this mean we're getting married?" he asked.

"No." She shook her head. "People shouldn't get married if they're not truly committed to it." She let out a long breath. "I believe I learned that the hard way."

"What happened wasn't your fault."

She shook her head. "I'm sure it was—my share of it, anyway. I should have seen it coming. I could have saved a lot of money on a wedding dress."

Lyman smiled. "And a bouquet, although your overhand throw was fantastic."

"Softball in high school."

"I know."

Of course he knew. He'd gone to her games. She remembered looking over at the bleachers and seeing him sitting by her parents. Water under the bridge.

"We should get back to work," she said. "I want to finish setting up, run home for a quick shower and change, and then we're back here at eleven o'clock to emcee the ceremony."

Lyman put a hand on her arm. He was sitting very close to her on their shared rock, and even though they were surrounded by nature and the rumble of the waterfall and tourists and her friends setting up for the big wedding, it felt intimate.

Too intimate.

The thing she had worked hard for all summer was only hours away from the finish line, and she was already sorry it was ending. She hated endings. Maybe that's why she liked weddings so much. Beginnings.

"Abigail, there's something I want to tell you, and I think you're really going to like hearing it." Lyman stood up as if he needed courage to say whatever it was.

She knew what she wanted to hear. Three little words. Those words had been circulating through her heart for weeks. She'd resisted them at first, refusing to let love for Lyman Roberts surface again after letting it lie dormant for so long.

"I'm going to take the job on the Maid of the Mist," he said, the words coming out triumphantly, as if it was a big declaration and he was really proud of himself.

"Oh," she said. "Congratulations."

He looked deflated but soldiered on. "I've thought about it a lot, weighed the pros and cons with that job in Florida I was offered while I serve out my reserve time." He laughed. "I even made a pros and cons list on my phone. Want to see?"

"I...don't need to see that," she said. She didn't want to see a list he'd made about which job was better. She felt like she had that summer, like she didn't factor into his decision at all.

"But are you, I mean, at least a little happy that I'm...not leaving?"

"I'm happy for you if that's the best decision for you."

His brow wrinkled, and he looked as if he was searching for words. Was he going to pull out his phone and show her the notes app with his stupid list?

"Abigail, this has been a strange summer. I never expected to get back together with you—"

"Are we together?" she asked.

"I told you I care about you. And we've been together all summer."

"We worked together."

"But what about that kiss last night in the photo booth?" he asked.

Abigail stood up so he wasn't towering over

her so much. Lyman was saying everything except what she truly needed to hear.

"We were in the photo booth doing what was expected for the campaign. Weren't we?"

All he had to say was that he had fallen in love with her. He needed to be the one to say it. She'd said it first with Josh, had willed that whole engagement into existence, and look what had happened. For once, wouldn't someone fight for her love? Did she always have to be the one writing the happy ending?

"I thought you'd be glad I'm not leaving again," he said. He raked a hand through his short hair. "That I'd be around if we need to do anything else with the ad campaign or anything...like that."

Abigail felt physical pain in her chest and looked over at Minnie, hoping her friend would see her and come to the rescue.

"I already said I was happy for you if this job is what you really want."

"I want to be here in Niagara Falls," he said. "I didn't know it back then, and it wouldn't have been true when I was eighteen, but it's true now. I want to be here, Abigail, and I just wanted you to be the first person to know. I haven't even told my parents or my boss." He reached for her hands and held them both. "I thought that was what you wanted to hear."

He wasn't going to say it. He wasn't going to tell her he wanted a real relationship with her, that he loved her. She let her hands linger in his for a moment, and then she said, "You should get back to hauling those chairs so our guests can watch ninety-nine weddings."

"We could still get married," Lyman said. "And make it an even one hundred couples for the picture."

Abigail shook her head. "No. I love Niagara Falls, but I won't go that far."

Lyman swallowed and looked at his feet. "Maybe someone will show up," he said. "Don't give up on your history display."

Abigail looked over at the falls and watched the puffy clouds of mist rise into the morning air. "I don't give up, but I've also learned that I need to be happy with endings that aren't the ones I would have written."

CHAPTER TWENTY-SIX

#WillTheyWed?

LYMAN HAD CHOSEN his suit for the wedding and made a plan for getting there plenty early. Thank goodness he had a script to follow and a specific role to play for most of the day. That way he could avoid making a mess of things with Abigail.

Why hadn't she leaped into his arms when he said he wasn't leaving? She was the reason—at least the main reason—he wanted to stay. He was sure he'd made that clear, he thought, as he straightened his tie in the bathroom mirror at his parents' house.

"We're ready when you are," his mother said. She wore a dress and his dad was in a suit. He hadn't seen his dad in a suit since his high school graduation.

"You both look great," Lyman said. "Are you sure you want to go through with this? What if you're making a big mistake?" he asked with a grin.

His dad put his arms around his mom's shoulders. "I'm just hoping she'll say 'I do.'"

Lyman laughed. "It's a vow renewal, so I don't think there's any question of that."

"I hope you have a nice time at the wedding," his mom said.

Lyman frowned at himself in the mirror. "I hope so. I think Abigail is mad at me. I told her this morning that I'm planning to stay in town and take the job on the Maid."

"You are?" his parents said at the same time. They both came into the bathroom and hugged him.

"We're so glad," his dad said.

"I am, too. I needed to go away, but right now I'm happy to be home. I think happiness isn't where you are, it's who you're with."

His dad put a hand dramatically on his chest, and both Lyman and his mother gasped.

"Relax," his dad said. "I'm not having a heart attack. I'm just glad to hear you say that. Even though I know your mom and I are only part of the who."

"Hard to say," Lyman said. "When I told Abigail I was staying, she basically said that's nice and she hopes I'm happy. Like I'm a stranger or something."

"Did you tell her why you want to be here?" his mom asked.

"Yes. I mean, I think I did? I said I was sorry about leaving her years ago and never getting in touch, I told her about the pros and cons list I made on my phone, and I said I thought she'd be happy I was staying."

His parents exchanged a glance.

"What?" Lyman asked.

"You didn't tell her she was the reason you were staying, or at least one of the very compelling reasons?" his mother asked.

"You didn't tell her how you feel about her?" his dad asked.

"I told her I cared for her, and I thought—"

"You thought she should know that you love her?" his mom asked.

Lyman nodded.

"And do you know exactly how she feels about you?" his dad asked.

"Obviously not."

"There's one way to find out," his mother said. "And the wedding may be the best or worst place for it, but you better do something."

His phone pinged with a text message, and he read it on his smartwatch. It was from Macey.

Wear your Maid of the Mist dress uniform

Lyman blew out a breath and faced his parents. "Macey wants me in my captain's uniform."

"That'll be nice," his mother said.

"But it's at work. I have time to go get it, but that means we should drive separately and meet at the wedding."

"Not a problem," his mother said. "As long as we all get to the wedding on time. And even though we'll be busy renewing our vows, we'll be there for you if you need us."

Lyman smiled. When he'd first come home, it had been out of duty. But being there for his parents and fellow captains...everyone in Niagara Falls...it now felt as important to him as the camaraderie he'd experienced in the service.

Ten minutes later, Lyman parked in an employee space as close to the Maid complex as he could. He'd have to hurry, but there was just enough time. Even though she seemed disappointed in him, he couldn't let Abigail down by being late. She'd been left at a wedding before.

When Lyman entered the Maid's headquarters, he felt the tension in the air. Tom was on the phone and crooked a finger at him to come over.

"Weren't you supposed to be babysitting this weekend?" Lyman asked.

His boss put a hand over the receiver. "Grandkids are sick and they changed their plans. We have bigger problems right now."

Lyman stood at attention out of habit. He wanted to know what was going on over the phone, but it was already half past ten and the wedding was at eleven. He should be there already.

"I can send out our smaller boat," he said. "Uh-uh, uh-uh, yeah, I got a guy, Coast Guard trained. We'll get him in there."

Lyman froze. What was wrong? He was desperate to do the right thing by the ad campaign and Abigail, but there was clearly something going on.

"We can use the Maid to grab that other boat. On it," he said and pockctcd the phone. He motioned to Lyman without bothering to explain and hustled him toward the elevator down to the docks.

In the elevator, Tom gave him a ten-second explanation. "Got a guy sitting on a rock over by the observation platform that comes out from the power plant tunnel on the Canadian side. I wondered when they opened that deck up if it would be too tempting for people looking to do something stupid."

"He's on the rocks and not in the water?" Lyman asked.

"Yeah, but that's not all. We've got a boat in trouble. Local rescuers went to get him off the rocks and they lost an engine, which means they can't get in close enough without getting in a lot of trouble themselves—not with the currents, you know."

"And the guy can't get himself to safety?" Lyman hated arguing about it, and normally he'd be the first one jumping in a rescue boat, but... Abigail. He had to get to her. She was counting on him to show up, and a growing feeling of desperation resonated in his chest. He had to tell her how he felt about her.

"If he could, he probably would. Maybe he hurt himself, maybe he intends to hurt himself, we don't know," Tom said. "Sorry to wreck your wedding plans, but there may be no time to lose."

Lyman nodded. "Of course I'll do it. So you're sending the Maid to grab the boat, and I'm going over to the guy on the rocks?"

"That's the size of it. You're overdressed," Tom said, slapping him on the shoulder. "But you're perfect for the job."

Lyman met his fellow captain Kirsten near the smaller boat they used for maintenance and transporting things other than tourists. She already had a life jacket on and handed him his. Tom strapped on his life preserver and got in the boat.

"I'm driving, you're rescuing," Kirsten said.

Lyman hopped into the boat, threw off the lines and buckled his flotation device. He wanted to pull out his phone and text Abigail to tell her he'd be late, but the small boat was moving rapidly and he didn't want to lose his phone over the side. He saw the Maid just upriver toward the falls. It was a strange sight, totally empty of tourists, heading into the mist. There was another boat ahead, bright orange, spinning in a current. Lyman saw two rescuers aboard the smaller boat. As he, Tom and Kirsten sped toward the falls, he saw one of the rescuers catch a line thrown from the Maid.

"Who's on the Maid?" he asked Tom.

"The twins. It's their last day, and they're going out with a bang."

Lyman almost smiled, picturing the two brothers working together, probably seamlessly and without words, to get close to and tow in the foundering boat.

He glanced up toward the American side, where he knew hundreds, maybe thousands of tourists were gathered for the usual sightseeing plus the special event. Abigail was up there. Did she know what was going on? He knew the views from Terrapin Point, knew there was a clear view of the new observation deck at water level on the Canadian side, close to the edge of Horseshoe Falls. He passed by it every day on the Maid and frequently saw dozens of people enjoying the up-close encounter with the falls. If Abigail or anyone else up there looked over the edge, they'd see what was going on below.

"How are we doing this?" Kirsten asked. "I've done some training with the local fire department, but not this close to the falls, and not involving someone sitting on a rock."

"You're in charge of the boat. All you have to do is get us close and hold it steady."

She grinned. "Easier said than done, but I can do it. And how about you?"

"I'm hoping we can do this the easy way, but that will take a lot of cooperation and some bravery from whoever is sitting on a rock tempting the fates. The hard way will involve me showing up to the big wedding soaking wet."

As they approached the viewing deck on the Canadian side, Lyman saw all the tourists on the platform pointing and then zeroed in on the man who was sitting on the edge of a big rock, his toes in the water. In his time in the Coast Guard, he'd participated in enough rescues to know that people had their reasons for putting themselves in danger, but the reason could be sorted out later.

"Take this," Lyman yelled as he held up a life ring attached to a long rope. He made sure the man saw him and understood his intent before he threw the life preserver straight at the man, but at a point just beyond him so he wouldn't be tempted to lean forward to catch it and fall in the swirling water.

The man didn't make a move to catch it. Was he deliberately avoiding rescue or just paralyzed with fear? Lyman reeled in the rope and life preserver.

"Try again," he yelled over the noise of the falls. He knew he had the attention of dozens of tourists on the viewing platform nearby at water level.

"Second chance," he said again to the man on the rock. "You can do it. Just grab it."

He held up three fingers and gave the man a countdown, and then he threw it. This time, the boat made an unexpected turn and his aim was off as he tried to balance himself. He felt Tom holding on to the back of his life preserver.

"Sorry about that," Kirsten said.

"You're doing the best you can. You have the harder job."

"Thanks," she said, making an effort to steady the boat using the throttle and steering. "Ready."

Lyman threw the rope again, and this time the man caught it. A loud cheer went up from the people on the platform.

"The Maid secured the other boat and she's standing by," Tom shouted over the roar of the falls. "In case."

Lyman nodded and turned his attention back to the man on the rock. "Loop it around yourself and clip it," he said, demonstrating the motions himself with a rope. He hoped the rescue raft they were about to deploy would keep everyone out of the water, but he wasn't taking chances. He glanced over at the platform and wondered how the man had gotten over the railing, crossed a series of low rocks right at the water's edge and found a seat on the big rock protruding into the river. Would it be wiser and safer to attempt a rescue from land? The park police from the Canadian side were probably on their way, but Lyman and Tom were in a good position to attempt a water rescue right now.

"Good," he shouted to the stranded man. "Stay where you are."

Lyman and Tom shoved the inflatable rescue raft tethered with a rope over the side of the boat.

He went over the side and got into the rescue raft. With its compact, inflatable design, he could let out rope and get close enough to the stranded man to pull him into the raft without—in theory— either of them falling into the water.

"Ready," Lyman said to Tom.

"I'll hold it steady and reel you in," he said.

As Lyman let the current push him toward the man on the rock, he looked over and saw the Maid standing guard nearby. Having a rescue helicopter on hand would be nice, but he'd taken all the precautions—life preservers, ropes and two boats nearby. He floated close to the man on the rock, glad to see he was wearing the life preserver.

"I'll get close and I'll get you in the boat," Lyman said. He glanced over at Tom, who held the rope so the life raft would stay right next to the rock. Lyman reached up and, without wasting a second, took the man's hand and pulled him toward the life raft. The man made an awkward dive into the orange inflatable and water sloshed over the side, soaking both of them.

"Sit in the bottom. Don't move," Lyman said, using his weight to balance the boat. He gave Tom the signal to reel them toward the larger vessel just feet away. In no time, they were alongside the Maid, and Tom grabbed the life jacket on the rescued man and tugged him over the side.

"Navy experience," Lyman observed to Tom, grinning.

They'd done it. He heard more cheering from the platform, and the Maid sounded its horn.

"Navy and life at Niagara Falls. This isn't the first water rescue I've been involved in, although we're not usually so close to the actual falls. I got lucky and stayed dry this time."

Lyman let Tom help him into the boat and then sat next to the rescued man.

"I feel like a jerk," the man said. "You risked your life to get me off that stupid rock."

"I'm just glad you're okay," Lyman said.

"My girlfriend is never going to talk to me again."

"Maybe it's not so bad," Lyman said. "People get second chances all the time." At least, he hoped so. Did Abigail know why he was late? He hated to think of her standing up there alone. Would she be willing to give a falls wedding another chance after being jilted months ago?

"She was right there watching. I wanted to impress her by showing her I could climb the rocks. I've done a lot of rock climbing and mountain climbing, but when I got close to all that fast-moving, swirling water, I froze. I can climb, but I can't swim."

Lyman didn't know what to say to the guy as he unwrapped a shock blanket for him. He wanted to assure him things would work out, but he also knew the park police would be waiting at the dock to have a conversation. The boat sped back to the maintenance dock, where an ambulance, a rescue truck and two police cars waited, out of sight of tourists and just downriver, where there was easy road access. As the man was taken in hand by the paramedics, Lyman thought about the night he'd taken Abigail to the party and left that dock. He'd tried to tell her he cared about her, but had he been clear?

He knew now what he wanted to say. He was in love with her. Whether she felt the same way or not, he owed it to himself and her to be brave enough to say the words.

Grant Hampton, one of the park rangers, strode up to Lyman. "I've been asked to give you a ride— something about getting to the wedding on time."

"Am I on time?" Lyman asked.

Grant laughed and shook his head. "You're late, but I'm told they're going to wait. We can do the paperwork on this fiasco later, although Tom can probably handle it since he was there."

"Let's get to the wedding," Lyman said. He stripped off his life preserver. His white dress shirt was wet, but he couldn't be picky if he wanted to get there in time to show Abigail he loved her.

"He'll be here," Minnie said. "I just heard from Grant, and he's on his way. I told him to use the siren."

"Do you think he will?" Abigail asked.

"No, but it was fun saying it."

Abigail wore a white dress, to stay consistent with the campaign's theme, but she wasn't a bride today, waiting for a groom to show up. She'd handed out bouquets to brides and helped line everyone up. Macey and Sam stood by. Her mother was there, reveling in the fact that her father was the surprise guest of the day. He'd flown in from his jobsite early that morning to be there for the wedding to support his two favorite women, and he and her mother had taken the spot of the one hundredth couple.

"Who knew there was going to be a dramatic rescue on the day of the big wedding?" Abigail said. Instead of a pretend marriage to Lyman, her parents would have the honor of saving the day and be part of a ceremony like her grandparents had been. The picture in the history display would be a true one. She should be happy.

"I do my best," her dad said.

Abigail laughed. "Says the man who flew in just in time and got roped into getting married."

"I'm the luckiest man here," he said, putting an arm around Ginny. "I already know my bride is a keeper."

Abigail stood, waiting, watching the path that led toward her, her family, her best friend and the people assembled for a Niagara Falls wedding. One hundred couples mingled at Terrapin Point. The wedding officiants waited on a grandstand erected for the occasion. Everyone was waiting for Abigail's cohost.

What would she say to Lyman when he did show up? As she and the hundreds of other people gathered at Terrapin Point had watched the rescue unfold below them, she'd only been able to think one thing.

She loved him. She wanted him back safely. Wanted him to stay in Niagara Falls so she could ride the trolley and walk in the rain with him. Wanted him to be there at Christmas and for her birthday, and maybe someday she'd wear a white dress just for him.

If he wasn't ready to love her back right now, she had finally realized that was okay. She was going to take the leap anyway and tell him she'd wait, no matter how long it took. Happy endings were a matter of when, not if.

"There he is," Minerva said, pointing to the two men hurrying down the tiered pathways toward the wide platform at the top of the falls. Ranger Grant Hampton, who'd delivered the chairs just hours ago, was now delivering Lyman Roberts, in an untucked, wet white dress shirt, just in time for the wedding.

She didn't care what he was wearing or that his shirt was wet. Abigail opened her arms and Lyman rushed into them and held her close, as if he was clinging to a boat in rough water.

"I'll get your dress wet," he said, his words muffled against her hair.

"I don't care."

"You waited for me," he said.

"I would've waited all day."

She felt him chuckle as he continued to hold her close against him.

"But I don't think our brides and grooms want to wait much longer, even though you gave them a show they're never going to forget."

"I was doing my job," he said.

"Is that what Maid of the Mist captains do?"

He pulled back and looked at her face. "Today it was, and it was a team effort."

"We saw it all," Abigail said. "Is the person you rescued okay?"

"He will be, I hope."

"Are *you* okay?"

Lyman smiled. "Just a little damp, and not at all the photogenic partner you need for this occasion."

"I disagree. You're exactly what I need." Abigail drew a deep breath. "We only have a minute before we need to get on that grandstand, but I have to tell you something."

"I have to tell you something, too," he said. "It's what I should have said this morning. The most important reason I want to be here."

"Does it involve the pros and cons list on your phone?" she asked, pulse racing.

Lyman laughed and kissed her temple. "It involves you."

Abigail felt her heart dance.

Lyman put both hands on her cheeks gently. "I love you."

Her smile was so broad Lyman had to move his hands to her hair.

"That's what I was going to tell you."

"Finally," he said. "This has been a long time coming."

"Um, Abigail?" Minerva's voice interrupted her. "I'm sorry to interrupt what is apparently a very crucial turning point for you two lovebirds, but you have a huge audience right now. Maybe you could give them a kiss—something fabulous for the end of your publicity campaign."

Lyman leaned close and whispered, "This kiss is for you, not for them."

Abigail giggled. "They don't need to know that."

They kissed, and loud clapping and cheering erupted. Lyman's boss, Tom, pulled up on a Gator and got out. He held out the dress coat to Lyman's captain's uniform. "You're representing the Maid of the Mist," he said. "Tuck in your shirt, put this on and let's do this wedding. My wife's here, and somehow she's decided I'm worth marrying all over again."

"One hundred and one couples," Abigail said. "We didn't need that license after all."

Lyman buttoned his dress coat, slowly and deliberately, never taking his eyes off Abigail. He reached for her hand and twisted the borrowed ring around her finger. "We don't need to get married for the ad campaign or a picture or for anyone else."

"I know," Abigail said, her words catching in her throat.

"We should only get married if we want to," he said. "If it's the only thing that will make our hearts complete and happy."

Someone in the audience whistled. They were standing on the pathway above the other couples and guests, in full view of everyone. Abigail heard the thunder of the falls and felt the mist and the breeze. She shivered in her damp white dress.

Lyman kept her hand in his and dropped to one knee. The crowd noise silenced, and even the continuous rumble of the falls seemed to grow quiet.

Abigail looked down at Lyman, the man she had once loved and had rediscovered over and over again throughout the summer. All their pretending had uncovered the truth. He loved her, and she loved him.

"Will you marry me, Abigail?"

Abigail heard a loud sob and glanced over to her mom and Minnie. It wasn't clear which of them the sob came from, but it didn't matter.

One thing was very clear.

"Yes," she said.

He smiled, and Abigail put both her hands in his, savoring the feeling of belonging with him at last.

"One hundred and two weddings," Macey said, rushing over. "This will go down in history as a great day for Niagara Falls."

Lyman stood and held Abigail close as the crowd turned its attention to Macey, who was ascending the grandstand with a microphone in her hands.

"A great day for us," Abigail said.

He laughed. "In the land of rainbows and honeymoons. Speaking of which, where would my bride like to go for our honeymoon?"

"Anywhere with you," she said as she took his hand and they joined the other couples at the top of the falls in a marriage ceremony history would never forget.

* * * * *

Don't miss the next book in Amie Denman's
Meet Me at Niagara Falls miniseries,
coming March 2025
from Harlequin Heartwarming